THE OUTER LIMITS™

ALWAYS DARKEST

STAN TIMMONS

ibooks
new york
www.ibooks.net

DISTRIBUTED BY SIMON & SCHUSTER, INC.

For Peyton.
Of course.

A Publication of ibooks, inc.

The Outer Limits

An ibooks, inc. Book

Distributed by Simon & Schuster, Inc.
1230 Avenue of the Americas, New York, NY 10020

ibooks, inc.
24 West 25th Street
New York, NY 10010

The ibooks World Wide Web Site Address is:
http://www.ibooks.net

ISBN 0-7434-9307-9

PRINTING HISTORY
First ibooks, inc. trade paperback edition September 2003
First ibooks, inc. mass-market edition August 2004
10 9 8 7 6 5 4 3 2 1

Edited by Steven A. Roman

Cover design by j. vita

Printed in the U.S.A.

Man is a curious creature, always wondering what might lie over the next hill, or across the great oceans and on the next shore, or on the surface of the moon and beyond the glittering sea of stars.

Man shines his light into the darkness . . . but what happens when something in the darkness shines its light back . . . ?

CHAPTER ONE

When I woke to my cold and moonless room, I felt a mild alloy of confusion and frustration because I couldn't remember where I was or how I'd gotten here. The more I struggled to remember, the more things I realized I didn't know—not the least of which was my name, or the fact I was scheduled to die in three days.

The only thing I could remember was some out-of-context bit of doggerel: *Why do we desire the things that will destroy us, and turn this paradise into a perdition?*

The room was dark—too dark to make out any features—but I doubt if I would have recognized anything, even if I could have seen it, because what I could feel made no sense.

The blanket—there was no sheet—was coarse and thin, like horsehair, and the bed was hard and narrow. Even more puzzling, it was bolted to the wall, like a shelf of some sort, and I was little more than a knickknack for display. The wall the bed was bolted to was smooth, featureless steel, and cold; I withdrew my hand with a sharp hiss.

Steel? A bunk? Darkness? At first, I thought I may have been aboard a ship, or even a submarine, shanghaied into service by... Well, that was where the thread of that line of reasoning ran out, and once again made me acutely aware of the fact I didn't know my own name.

I struggled to sit, and felt a liquid pain slosh through my skull and lodge behind my left eye. Then I became aware of the other pains in my body, as if I had taken a terrific beating, and I wondered if the beating had affected my memory. I wrestled with alarm, even as I tried to swing my feet over the edge of the shelf, but they wouldn't obey my mental directives.

Still my body refused to obey me, and now the alarm threatened to skyrocket into full-blown panic: Not only could I not remember how I came to be in this steel room, I couldn't recall anything before this moment. If I had been beaten, and I was more and more inclined to think I was, it had affected not only my memory, but control over my limbs as well.

I tried one more time to sit up, actually *thinking* it into happening, picturing myself doing it, as if I was forcing new connections in my brain and highway of nerves. I could feel my thoughts trickling through the crevices of my brain like molasses, thick and slow and sluggish.

What if the beating caused a stroke?

Anything seemed possible at this point, but I tried not to think along those lines just yet. I could still feel things, so I wasn't totally paralyzed. Just...confused.

I managed to get my legs over the side of the bed and struggled to a standing position on legs that seemed too long to belong to me. I teetered for a moment, like a sideshow freak on stilts.

As I had lain there in the darkness, my eyes had gradually adjusted to the gloom, and I began to make out a few shadowy shapes in my room. It wasn't total darkness, but a light so dim as to be near enough. The floor—also steel—was cold beneath my bare feet. I stretched my arms and felt with my fingertips, touching one wall to my right, another to my left. The room wasn't much larger than a walk-in closet, just big enough to accommodate my bunk.

I moved toward the source of the pearly light, an oblong opening that appeared to be as wide and tall as the room itself, and I was brought up short by the bars.

At last I knew where I was, but that only deepened the mystery more than it illuminated: What was I doing in jail? Whatever I might have done the night before, it must have been good and wild to wake up feeling like this and not able to remember a thing about it.

"Hello?" I croaked, my voice dry as baked tiles. I swallowed, but it was a dusty, sticky swallow that only made my parched throat ache more. "Someone there? Hello?" I couldn't recognize the deep voice as my own, but then, I couldn't really say what my voice was supposed to sound like. Still...I had a sneaking suspicion it didn't sound like this. Not normally...whatever passed for normal these days.

I gripped the latticework of bars with my hands and called again, managing to add some volume this time, and was told by a harsh, unseen voice to do something to myself that only Narcissus would find any kind of satisfaction in. At least I knew now, wherever I was, I wasn't totally alone, but I didn't seem to be rubbing shoulders with the jet set, either.

"Where am I?"

"Where does it look like?" that gruff voice answered.

"How did I get here?"

"They carried you in, same way they'll carry you out."

There was an insistent, floating sense of déjà vu about all this, as if I had taken the road not taken.

"Who did?"

Now others answered, each successive voice harsher than the one before it. Within moments, the chorus of angry, brutal tones degenerated into animal hoots and cries, and I started to wonder if I had been caged in some eerie zoo. My own voice was lost, drowned out in the shouting.

I watched as a fitful glow of light appeared just beyond my line of sight, growing closer. It wasn't much, but it was enough illumination for me to see the corridor beyond my cell, and I saw I wasn't too far off the mark with my thoughts of being in a zoo.

I was in a wing with the hardcore badasses, and I knew immediately however much trouble I first supposed I was in was nowhere near the rising level of shit in which I actually found myself standing. And me without my waders.

"Shut your hole, you scum!" a voice that spoke of brutal, unquestioned authority demanded. "Shut your cry-hole!"

The light flickered now, just out of my reach, but I heard the harsh ringing sound of ashwood on steel, and the subtler but no less pronounced sound of wood on flesh and bone. It was followed by shrieks, cries, and foul curses, but one by one, the voices quieted, like someone was walking down a line and shutting off pieces of noisy machinery.

Instinctively, I withdrew my own fingers from the bars a moment before the billy club-wielding guard swaggered in front of my cell.

He seemed surprised to see me, but recovered his composure quickly. In a place like this, I suppose you had to, but I had seen something in his face...something...but I couldn't quite place it.

"Up 'n' about, are we?" he growled, his voice phlegmy and raspy. "Why do I think all this started with you? Hmm?" He pressed his face between the bars, inches from my own, near enough to smell the stench of rot on his breath. Teeth that had never heard of the miracle of brushing, perhaps, or some black cancer growing in his lungs or belly. I flinched away from him, but he was fast, and his big fist reached through the bars and grabbed the front of my shirt. He jerked me forward, banging my head against the crossbar. I knew better than to cry out in pain.

The face I found myself gazing into was one of pure, brutal evil, monstrous evil for its own sake. The man was tall, at least six feet; bull-necked and broad-shouldered. His face was misproportioned, more jaw than brow, and his eyes were small and shiny with mad excitement. His lips and ears were little more than raw scar tissue, his cheeks pocked and pitted, as if he had lost an acid fight, gone home, thought about it, went right back for a re-match and lost again. His bulb-shaped nose was red and rutted with countless blackheads, making me think—insanely, given the current circumstances—of fresh strawberries.

"Please," I tried, but my tongue felt spot-welded to the roof of my mouth by the terrible dryness. "Please, I don't know...I'm not...I shouldn't be here."

"You won't be much longer," the guard said, and laughed.

"When? When will I get out?"

"Can't wait for it, huh?" he growled. "Tough guy. Well, we'll see how tough you are when the time comes. I'm bettin' you'll be just like the others, pissin' down both legs and cryin' like a woman."

"What are you talk—" But I had a sudden sense of what

he was saying, even though it made no sense. "Look, this is a mistake," I said, trying to remain calm and reason my way out of this. One look at that high-octane, nightmare-fuel of a face made me aware that reason was the exact thing this guy was looking for, as in, *"Just give me a reason to bust your frikkin' skull."*

"Is there someone I can talk to? Please, I'll make it worth your while." I doubted if I really could, but it was all I could offer.

The guard cleared his throat and spat in my face, but I refused to wipe the hot, offensive wad off; I somehow knew it would only make things worse, if that were possible. I felt the sputum slowly and disgustingly trace the contours of my cheek and chin, where it dangled a moment, then continued its slow, sticky roll down my neck.

"Tough man," he said, a fleck of the projectile hocker still standing on his gray lip. "It finally got to ya, made ya crack. Well, go ahead, tough man, tell me again how you're gonna rip my throat out with your teeth, how you're gonna walk outta here 'n' kill my fam'ly."

I looked at him in genuine surprise. "When did—"

"You ain't gonna do shit," he informed me.

"I want to talk to the warden," I said. "I want to know where I am, and why I'm here."

His fist, which still clutched the front of my shirt, tightened its grip and he pulled me menacingly closer. He started to say something else, when another guard, this one carrying the burning torch which I had seen earlier, strolled up next to him. The new guard looked at me, then Strawberry-Nose, and asked, "Anything wrong here?"

"I want to see the warden," I blurted, not giving 'berry-

Nose the chance to dismiss me. "I want to know why I'm here...*please*."

Strawberry-Nose released my shirt, and I took that moment to step back a safe and respectful distance from the bars. I blinked a bead of blood from my eye, and gingerly touched my fingertips to the rising lump above my right eye, where I had made the intimate acquaintance of the steel crossbar. I could feel a loose flap of flesh dangling there. My left eye, I realized, was swollen almost shut, and crusted with dried blood.

The second guard looked at his partner. "Is he sick?"

"Sick of livin'," Strawberry-Nose answered, then elaborated, "Nah, he's just cracked. Seen it happen b'fore. The tough ones ain't ever as tough as they think they are."

The second guard, the torchbearer, studied me for a long, long moment, and said, "What kind of game are you playing?"

I shook my head, and another bead of blood rolled into my eye. "It's not a game!" I snapped. "Damn it, why won't anyone believe me? Why won't you listen?" Suddenly, I thought of a question even these two could answer. "Who am I?" I asked. "Tell me my name."

"What's goin' on?" the harsh, disembodied voice from earlier asked. "Big boy wet himself? You guys gonna change him?"

That brought another round of laughter from the others; more laughter, more jeers, more threats from the guards, but no answers. Not a one. Strawberry-Nose went off to quell the riot, or as much of a riot as men locked away in cages the size of refrigerator boxes can manage, with his own particular brand of understanding. Almost at once, I heard the sickening thud of ashwood on fingers...and possibly faces and skulls. I wanted to vomit, even though my stomach was empty.

This was a nightmare from which there was no waking, no alarm clock with a snooze button that let you have five more minutes in your own warm, comfortable bed, curled up next to... My mouth worked to form a name. I knew, if I could remember her name, I would remember mine.

The second guard had been studying me all this time, and he still hadn't been able to come to any conclusion. At last he shook his head and said, "Tomorrow, I'll see what I can do."

The name was on the tip of my tongue, like a buccaneer about to walk a pirate's plank, but it was gone now. Irretrievably gone. I turned to the guard with a pained expression on my battered face, a look he mistook as insolence.

"But if you cause any more trouble, if you even say one more word tonight, it's off, you understand?"

I nodded weakly, fighting the urge to ask all the questions I still needed to have answered. His offer to see what he could do was hardly the grand solution I was hoping for, but it was probably the best offer I was going to get in this place.

I nodded again and shambled back to my bunk, laid down and tried to sleep, still no nearer to knowing what was going on, not even knowing so much as my name.

Sometime during the night, I woke to the sound of crying, but I won't tell you whose it was.

CHAPTER TWO

People tell you six A.M. comes early, but it doesn't come a moment too soon when you're waiting for some broken, disjointed nightmare to end. I don't recall sleeping, but spent the night instead in that no-man's territory between waking and sleeping, grasping at snatches of dream-memories the way a drowning man will grasp at straws floating on the surface.

If I could just recall my dream-memories, I felt I might understand who I was and how I'd come to be here. But every time I was within reach, when I actually brushed them with my fingertips, they burst on my face like soap bubbles, melted on my tongue like cotton candy.

I rolled over onto my back—again, only with great concentration and equal effort—and thumped my fist weakly against my bunk, also steel. Even that took some little amount of focus. I sighed, feeling something rattle in my side, as if a rib had been loosened, and folded my forearm across my eyes.

"Oh, Sara," I muttered, and felt my heart break into a cardiac ragtime. Why had I said that? Who was Sara? I felt as if I were on the verge of understanding something about myself—the first thing since I'd woke to find myself here—when I heard the sound of keys, and the sound of a tray being slid through the slot at the foot of the cell door.

They didn't bring breakfast to you if you were in for something simple, like littering or jaywalking. Breakfast in bed in a place like this only happened if they didn't want you mixing with the general population.

"Breakfast," the guard announced unnecessarily, and started away, rattling the keys he wore on a big key ring. There weren't many keys because he was a man with few doors to open in this life.

"Wait," I said, sitting up with a snap. "What about the warden?" But I saw this wasn't either of the guards from a few hours earlier, although the attitude was not that far removed. He stopped, snorted, spat into my breakfast, and stood there, hands on his hips, daring me to say something about his garnishing of my morning meal.

I knew in that moment the warden wasn't going to see me; not unless I made him come to me. I grabbed the tray and bowl of slop from the floor and flung it in the guard's face. He cursed and sputtered, his face the color of a ripe plum.

"Get the warden, you fat bastard!" I shouted, not giving the guard the chance to react, because I knew if I didn't press my miniscule advantage and ride the momentum, he'd open the door to my cell and beat me half to death, and tell the warden I slipped in the shower.

"Get. The. Warden!" I shouted again, almost standing nose to nose with him. I heard my unseen Greek chorus join the drama, just a couple voices at first, but growing in number almost exponentially, until they were all chanting and mocking, "Get the warden! Get the warden!"

The guard said something—I couldn't make out just what over the ruckus—but I thought I could read his lips well enough. He seemed to say, "I'm gonna love to watch you hang!" Even if the content wasn't clear, the intent was quite plain.

I sat down on the edge of my bunk, legs too wobbly now to support me, and waited.

"Would you like to confess?"

I looked up, saw the guard I had assaulted standing with a man I took at once to be the chaplain.

"No offense, Padre, but you're not the man I need to talk to right now. I want to see—"

"The warden, yes, I've been informed," he said, and licked his lips nervously. "He sent me in his place." The chaplain was a gaunt man in shabby clothing that even a third-world native might think twice about and, now that I actually looked a little closer, the guard was hardly wearing regulation issue, either. His uniform was the drab and dingy gray of the prison guard, but it was old and threadbare. It had been patched rather crudely in several places, with fabric that whoever had sewn on hadn't even tried to match with the uniform. Some swatches were actually cut squares of plaid; another was off-white.

There was something wrong here, beyond just my inexplicable imprisonment, and if the warden couldn't be bothered with seeing me, as he obviously couldn't, I'd have to make do with the chaplain and hope he might carry my message back to El Jefe. I nodded calmly and the guard unlocked the door. The hinges squeaked, exactly as I'd expected them to.

The guard stepped—actually, more like a shuffle—aside, and let the chaplain step into the cage. "Keep an eye on him, Father," the guard warned. "He's a vicious one, not to be trusted."

"I think I'll be all right," the chaplain said with certainty.

The guard was less sold, but closed the door and locked it. "I'll be right out here," he both assured the father and warned me.

The chaplain nodded and waved him on, and stood smiling bemusedly at me. From his expression, I had a feeling he'd had some experience in dealing with me, whoever I was.

"Well," he said with forced joviality, and clapped his hands. "Shall we sit, Max?" He indicated the bunk for me, and claimed the small wooden stool next to the wall for himself.

"Max?" I parroted. "Is that my name? Max?"

The chaplain raised his bushy, mad-scientist eyebrows in mild surprise, but said nothing.

I didn't see any way to begin but to begin, so I just plunged in, hoping I'd make more sense than my situation did. "I don't know who I am or why I'm here," I told him. "I can't remember anything about my life before waking up here last night."

"What game are we playing here, Max?" he asked, his thin lips compressed in a tight line. "It's a little late in the day for pleading madness, and we both know it isn't true."

I sat on the edge of my bunk, hands dangling below and between my knees, wrestling with each other. "It's not a game," I said, miserably. "Please, I didn't *do* anything! Whatever you think I did...it's all some terrible mistake!"

"It's no mistake, Max," he said, not bothering to disguise his contempt. And there was a pleasant thought: Did this man really give absolution to the condemned, or did he just send you packing on your way to hell with that look of contempt and a coupon for SPF? "You were so brave when you were sentenced, so smug, so defiant. At least try to act like a man for these last couple of days."

I felt my bowels turn to ice water. "What's going to happen to me?" I asked, my voice barely audible. My throat was fear-constricted to the size of a pinhole.

"This is a waste of time," he said with disgust, and started to rise. "If—or when—you want to make a real confession—"

"No!" I cried, a sob tearing loose in my chest and working its way out in a pathetic gaspy hiccup. I grabbed his ratty frock in my hands, and felt it start to tear from my touch. "No, please, you have to help me!"

He looked at my hands, clutching his frock as if they were two huge, obscene flesh-colored spiders that were crawling up his vestments. But it was more than that—he was afraid of me. Oh, he hated me for whatever it was I had supposedly done, but he was afraid of me. More than that, he was *terrified*.

I removed my hands from him and muttered an apology. I didn't mean it, but then I doubt if he meant he'd pray for my forgiveness. We were just a couple of liars.

The guard stood at the door, watching, key fitted in the lock. The chaplain heard the rasp of teeth on tumbler and raised his hand. "It's all right," he told the guard, who wasn't entirely convinced of that. He seemed to be certain it was *not* all right, until I sat down once again on the bunk, hands once more clasped between my legs.

I could see it in his face as well, that strange mix of hatred and fear. What had I done to earn that hatred? What kind of monster was I? Did I really want to know?

It was then I realized I didn't even know what I looked like.

"I want a mirror," I announced, suddenly. The chaplain looked puzzled. "I want to see my face," I explained. "Surely I can have a mirror...?"

"Do you mean a looking glass, Max?" he asked with exaggerated patience. "Is that what you want? A looking glass?" He sounded like a parent trying to teach his unruly child to say the right name.

I nodded, eagerly. "A looking glass, yes."

"Oh, lah-de-dah, your highness," the guard said with a curl of his lip. "Anything else you'll be wantin' with that? New clothes, maybe? New sandals?"

"Please," I added. Not that it really made much difference. He hated me, yes, feared me, certainly, but I was on this side of the bars and he was on that; his side held all the cards, while mine...well, I had been dealt a bad hand, comprised of nothing but Old Maids, apparently.

"I don't think there's any harm in bringing him a looking glass," the padre said.

Looking glass, I thought. Yes, we were definitely through the looking glass here, all right, and I had a bad feeling somewhere out there was a Red Queen waiting impatiently to command, "Orf wif 'is 'ead! Orf wif 'is 'ead!"

The guard glared at me, then moved off down the corridor. I could hear his footfalls echoing back to us from down the passageway. After a few moments, I heard him shout something, and the sound of a heavy door being opened, then slamming shut with the finality of a coffin lid.

"How can I help you, Max, if you won't accept responsibility and ask forgiveness for the acts you've committed?" the chaplain asked, as if I were simply playing obdurate. He refused to entertain the possibility of a mistake, that I might not be the right man.

I wanted to grab him again, shake him until his head flopped limply, like a balloon tied to the end of a stick, shake some answers out of him and some sense into him. I felt like a character in a free-style Kafka play, *Evening at the Existential Improv.* Any moment now, someone from the audience would call out an occupation; we already had the location, and I wasn't too wild about it. But, that's improv; you have to work with what they throw you.

"How can I repent if I don't know what it is I'm supposed to have done?" I asked, but it sounded like a Zen koan, and the answer was no less Zen.

"Perhaps, if you've truly forgotten your crimes, it's your mind's way of dealing with the horrors you've visited upon others," he answered.

For just a moment, I wondered if that might actually be true. After all, nothing I had come up with—not that I had come up with a lot—explained what I was doing here, and this made as much sense as anything else I'd heard, so far. I felt myself beginning to waver, allowing the possibility to enter like winter wind around a badly fitted window.

It seemed possible. It seemed...*right,* somehow, but it was also a lie. Whatever crime I'd been accused of, I knew I hadn't committed it.

Still...had I been drugged, or hypnotized into committing whatever atrocity...? The moment I allowed that thought, vivid, horrific images flashed stroboscopically through my mind. Oily beads of sweat stippled my forehead, and my stomach did a slow, greasy, forward roll.

"Oh, my God," I whispered. "Oh, my God, oh, my God..."

Body parts, blood, the dead and the dying...

The guard returned with the mirror, but I was too shaken to accept it, so the father took it, and held it in his bony fingers for me to see. I looked in the cracked oblong of silver-backed glass, dimly noting it wasn't a handheld mirror, but a broken-off rearview mirror from someone's car. I was too disoriented at the time to wonder why he had gone to so much illogical trouble, although my wide eyes nevertheless took in the legend printed in gold type across the bottom of the mirror: WARNING! OBJECTS IN MIRROR ARE CLOSER THAN THEY APPEAR!

That was a frightening thought. I sure as hell didn't want the wild-eyed face that was looking back at me from the mirror any closer than he already was. But I didn't know the face in the mirror: brown hair, brown eyes, square hero's jaw, covered with an untidy growth of beard stubble. And the face, whoever's face it was, had taken a beating. The nose had been broken, the left eye puffy and the color of a southern sunset.

But there was another face looking back at me, as well, appearing as if this were a lenticular card, with a second image printed just below the surface of the first, revealed by a slight shifting of the planes. It was another face, also my own, and not my own, and on the heels of that revelation came a flood of memories, two divergent streams coming together in one raging torrent.

Here I was, the second son of Bill and Rena Stein, sickly and spindly as a child, nose in a book and head in the clouds. And here I was, the third child of Mary and Leo, all muscle and sinew. I was the boy who never made a fist or struck another human being in his life, and I was the brawler who killed his first N'lani before he reached puberty. I lived a life of privilege, and I lived a life without rest or roots. Here was my only love, Sara, and here was a procession of nameless women from whom I'd simply taken what I wanted. I was the father of one girl, and I was the father of many boys. I was a pillar of a respectable community, and I was a fearsome legend. I was loved by a few, I was hated by many.

Faster and faster, the images raced at me, too many to catalogue, too contradictory to reconcile, and still they came, on and on. It was like a computer with too little memory, trying to download two monstrous programs at the same time, and, like the computer, there was only one thing I could do: I suffered a massive system error and crashed, pitching forward to the floor, my head coming to rest on the chaplain's sandaled foot.

CHAPTER THREE

No one ever starts out to be the villain of the piece, but someone always has to be. That's just the way it is, and who knows how the roles are assigned?

Maybe the only difference between a hero and a villain is saying "Yes" to the wrong impulse. The problem is in recognizing the wrong impulse, because every moment of every day is filled with them. But I'm just making excuses. Not many days in the history of mankind ever held such a wrong impulse as the one I greenlighted and fast-tracked into production.

In the hills of Mountain View, California, there is a giant radio telescope named Project Phoenix, which listens for broadcasts from other planets and distant civilizations. If it helps, think of it as the world's most sophisticated CB radio setup.

By the late 1970s, NASA had established its SETI project—an acronym for Search for Extraterrestrial Intelligence—in Mountain View, a Norman Rockwell kind of town in the San Francisco Bay area. The satellite swept the sky, quadrant by quadrant, targeting the thousands of sun-like stars and the worlds that circled them, eavesdropping for weak or sporadic radio signals, those that are either being deliberately broadcast in our direction, or those inadvertent transmissions we somehow scoop up, like some intergalactic Big Brother wiretap.

Of course, other dishes are in place, elsewhere, like Green Bank, West Virginia, and Parkes, Australia, but I was the one on duty that night. I was the one who accepted the call.

There were times we thought we picked up chatter, either another civilization wondering about its place in the universe, or just the alien equivalent of Rush Limbaugh, but more often than not, it was nothing more than the pulse of a quasar, the beat of the universe's ancient heart. Tantalizing, but at the end of the day, it didn't prove a thing.

Congress cut funding to the SETI project, but the private sector, with a million dollars in seed money from Hewlitt-Packard, took over. But because of this, there were budget cuts and layoffs, or downsizing, or—and let's be honest here—firings. The Mountain View site didn't really need that many people to run it, anyway. Phoenix pretty much ran itself; we were just there in case that long-long-distance call came.

My shift at Phoenix was the skeleton shift, the graveyard shift, that luckless time of night between 11 P.M. and 7 A.M., the same hours and similar pay to what I could have had if I'd worked in an all-night convenience store. As such, I was my own man. I would have been, anyway. I had seniority over just about everyone connected to the project, except Frank Drake, who founded the whole SETI operation back in the 1960s.

But those hours...they seemed to *do* something to a man. They weren't hours the human psychology embraced to its bosom. I ended up with this shift because the astronomer who kept the chair warm had...well, let's just say he had some very *unusual* ideas. Gary Yokum had the peculiar conviction that he was receiving messages from space, which, after all, was what we wanted. But Gary heard the voices in his head. Gary's thoughts got a little too dark one night and he took the top of his head off with a .38 crowbar to let a little light in.

But it's strange, because some nights, I thought I heard voices, too. Was it possible Gary let out all those bad thoughts when he blew his head off, left them lying around for anyone to pick up like fresh cold germs? I wouldn't have thought so, but there were times when I couldn't recall a single thing I'd done that night. If it hadn't been for my scrupulously kept journals, I would have thought I'd fallen asleep on my shift. It was my handwriting, but I couldn't remember making the entries, as if I'd been in a complete fugue state.

I didn't say anything to Sara, or my coworkers about it, because when I was in college, I had a little bit of an...*episode*. Or nervous breakdown, if you prefer, but all the politically correct words you could glue to the event still couldn't change the fact that reality and I had had a bit of a falling out and refused to associate with one another for a while. Eventually, we patched things up, and my psychiatrist said I probably had a lot of buried childhood traumas I needed to address. I didn't have the heart to tell him childhood *is* a trauma.

The episode never repeated itself, but there were times I thought reality might have gotten a little frayed around the edges. It was the one secret I kept from Sara. I told myself it was because I didn't want to worry her, but the truth was, I didn't want her to look at me with *those eyes* when she thought I wasn't looking. The eyes that asked, perhaps quite reasonably, *Who are you...* really? *And what else don't I know about you?*

We broadcast our message toward Alpha Centauri, or Rigel Kentaurus if you want to be technically accurate, in the Centaurus constellation, the nearest galaxy that was a likely candidate to hold intelligent life, at 1420 megahertz. We encoded our messages in a string of musical notes; simple messages, but hopefully enough to demonstrate to any race receiving our signal that we were a reasonably intelligent planet. We embedded a sketch of human DNA, a sketch of man, a sketch of a telescope, all hidden in those 1679 characters. Stefano and I thought it to be the cosmic equivalent of a "Where's Waldo?" drawing.

There were mathematical equations, too, a series of prime numbers, the square root of Pi, but I never thought math was the way to go, unless we were offering our services as their tax accountants. Math presupposed we all followed a base 10 system. How arrogant of us. How utterly, typically, *humanly* arrogant. I felt that music was the true universal language, as it combines art with a mathematical precision, a tonal architecture. And, it has a beat you can dance to.

We were, in effect, a pirate radio station, beaming our little musical program out into the darkness, hoping the listeners responded favorably to us and phoned in a pledge of support. Call now, and we'll throw in this free, limited edition tote bag.

And so I sat back in my swivel chair, hands on top of my head, waiting and listening. Waiting...waiting... But that's science for you: a little flurry of activity, followed by a widely scattered shower of doldrums. I thought how I'd have given my theoretical soul to discover hypothetical alien life.

The nights blew by in this fashion with all the bland uniformity of sand; night after night, week after week, year into year. But the days...well, they were another matter.

There are some people that, when we meet them, we simply know are going to do great things. There's a certain aura about them, a grace, the way they carry themselves, some indefinable something that sets them apart from everyone else, as if they're in Technicolor and the rest of the world is, at best, the product of bad colorization.

Sara is like that, and she has changed the world, even if that world is only my own. Sara is five-feet-one, 110 pounds, soft, shoulder-length brown hair, gray eyes, and a nice, tight round behind that sticks out like a brownstone air conditioner. We met in an online science-fiction chat room, realized we didn't live that far from each other, and, after a lot of late-night, sun-coming-up already private messenger chats, decided to risk a meeting in person. Let's face it: we're all beautiful on the Internet. It's just when reality intrudes that things don't look quite as rosy. Except in this case.

It's the same old story: nerd meets insanely hot chick, nerd marries insanely hot chick, nerd lives happier-ever-after than he thought he had a right to.

The day the world—not mine, but the whole planet—changed was stiflingly hot. Our little house sat at the end of a shaded cul-de-sac, but it provided little shelter from the heat. California was in the middle of another power cut, sponsored by the fine felons at Enron, so there were no air conditioners, and fans just pushed torpid air from one place to another. Everything in our little house felt as if it were right on the edge of spontaneously combusting.

"Stay home," Sara said as we picked listlessly over a meal of cold cuts, slices of Swiss cheese, and sweating glasses of iced tea on our backyard patio. "Call in sick and stay home with us tonight."

I saw a mischievous twinkle in her eyes, a look before which any nerd is helpless, and she smiled crookedly, a curious little blend of innocence and carnality. It was a smile that said this mouth, these full lips, can do a lot more than kiss. A *lot* more.

"Oh, yuck!" Maryvonne pronounced her judgment upon her decidedly uncool mother and father.

"You say that now," I told her, pouring a little more tea for each of us. The ice in the glasses seemed to wither, and I could hear it crack. Sara took her sweating glass and, rather than sipping it, pressed the cool surface of the glass to her forehead. "But you just wait until Langdon Donahue gets tired of *Yu-Gi-Oh!* and starts taking an interest in you."

I felt a little chill at that thought: Although nice enough in an undistinguished way, Langdon Donahue was the boy who lived next door and harbored a huge crush on Maryvonne. He was too shy to act upon it, but he was a boy, and smitten, and was, therefore, a potential threat to our peaceful family way of life. Time to put the Chevy Wagons in a circle.

"Langdon Donahue?" Vonnie repeated, crinkling her nose and stretching out each syllable. "He's a *nerd!*"

Well, what could I say? When she put it like that, I felt an instant kinship for the poor, nerdly Donahue boy. But I knew my daughter had eyes only for Curt "Buster" Ellis, the neighborhood bad boy. Although it couldn't be proved, I suspected Buster of writing four-letter words in Maryvonne's sandbox.

I looked imploringly at Sara, who actually seemed to

be enjoying watching me squirm. "I don't think I want to live in a world that has so little regard for nerds, dorks, dweebs, and yuppies," I informed my family.

Sara paused with a fat green olive pressed to her lips; I knew what was about to happen to the pimento, foul temptress that she was. "I don't remember anyone saying anything about the yuppies."

"I have my own prejudices," I confessed shamefully. "I'm not proud of it, but there you are. And telemarketers? That's a thread you really don't want me pulling at."

Vonnie giggled, a sweet, clear sound, and asked if she could have a bowl of ice cream. I said she could, just to prove not all nerds were bad, and she bussed her own plate and glass to the sink, and rinsed them.

"She gets that nerd-bashing from your side of the family," I accused Sara. She smiled and reached a hand across the little patio table to mine. The pimento did, indeed, suffer the fate I had predicted for it. If you can call that suffering.

"My side of the family *adores* nerds," she reminded me, her voice dropping to that husky whisper I couldn't resist. "Skip work tonight and I'll show you just how much."

"Tempting," I conceded. And it was, but I had already taken several days off of work recently when first Sara, then Vonnie, was down with a nasty case of the flu.

From her room down the hall, I heard Vonnie's CD player start throwing out the jangling, discordant atonal clatter of some new boy band, a cacophony that even St. Vitus himself couldn't have danced to.

"Listen," Sara said, slipping closer and covering my face with flitting butterfly kisses. "They're playing our song."

That was an untruth, as she well knew. "Baby Beluga" was our song, but I let it slide and pulled her onto my lap, facing me, my hands rolling down her hair, cascading to the ivory shoals of her shoulders, like a chestnut waterfall. She leaned in close, kissed each eyelid and my nose and my mouth, and nibbled my lower lip and chin. And before I knew it, we were one more shadow on the evening-purpled lawn, one more secret kept by the privet hedge.

You'll have to forgive me if I've gone into much detail about my wife and daughter, spent too much time with them, but I'd like to keep them both alive a little longer, all right?

We went 'round again and split the difference; I didn't take the night off, but I arrived late. When I got to my workstation, I saw Stefano had left another of his little calling cards. It was good. Very good. He was cunning.

MEMO

WHILE YOU WERE OUT
Marvin the Martian CALLED
COMMENTS: "You make me so very angry!"
WILL CALL AGAIN

"Touché," I muttered, and crumpled the note. This was going to take some planning. A simple retort of "Klaatu Barada Nikto" would not be worthy of such a pithy opponent. I would have to dredge my pop culture memory bin for a fitting comeback, and I had plenty. You don't end up sitting on your ass eight-plus hours a day, listening for signs of intelligent life in the universe without a wasted childhood spent devouring and memorizing every good—and bad—SF TV show and movie ever produced.

I had managed to waste exactly three and one-half minutes. Not bad. Just seven hours and fifty-six and one-half minutes to go on my shift. The night was flying by. I sat down at my post and put on my cans and listened to the universe, not really expecting anything, but hoping.

There's always hope.

I wish I could tell you that I was at my post, listening intently and knew in a moment that this was the exact second the universe changed, or even that I was lightly dozing and the transmission woke me into a whole new world, but the truth of the matter is, I was in the restroom, pants down around my ankles. Typical. As soon as we're "indisposed," the phone rings.

Nor were my thoughts particularly lofty. I was having a rather protracted debate with myself about what to zing Stefano with, and also trying to decide whether I wanted to eat the baloney sandwich Sara had packed for my lunch, or whether I wanted to splurge, live like a Kennedy and buy a can of microwaveable chili from the vending machine in Phoenix's kitchenette.

I finished my business, washed, and stopped by the kitchenette, studied the choices, and came down on the side of baloney, after all. I retrieved my brown paper lunch bag from the communal refrigerator and ambled back to my workstation.

I put my headphones back on and my heart staggered in its beat, then kicked like a wild stallion at the stable of my ribs. It was vague, almost not there...but it was a definite, recurring message.

I checked to make sure tape was rolling, and just sat

there listening. I made a backup tape, and as I did, the transmission abruptly ceased.

It could have been anything: solar flares interrupting the radio signals, earth's rotation taking Phoenix out of the narrow receiving band, or maybe they'd just said all they had to say. Or maybe Stefano's Post-it note really wasn't that far off the mark. Maybe the encrypted message they sent us would amount to nothing more than "Please, don't call us, we'll call you."

I listened for a long, long while after that, to simple, dumb white noise, but the universe had nothing more to say for itself. I felt oddly abandoned, more alone in the void than I had before we made contact.

CHAPTER FOUR

When I was a kid, my stable, sensible daily world was split open right down to the roots, like a lightning-blasted tree, when I learned I had a stepbrother from my father's previous marriage. It was so stunning to think that my father had ever had a wife and a son whom he had loved, and a life long before my mother and I came into the picture. He'd had a similar life to the one we all lived, presumably just as happy, for the most part. It was like ours...but it wasn't ours.

And I suppose that's how the people of Earth must have felt when they learned man was not the only life-form in the universe, like finding out God had been married before.

SETI protocol was this: First, confirm that the signal is of extraterrestrial origin. Second, release this information immediately to the whole world.

We did, but I always wondered if it was a mistake. The number of reported abductions following our announcement spiked dramatically, until it seemed as if every other person on the planet had been for a joyride aboard the mothership. I mentioned to Stefano they might want to think about carpooling.

I was sought out by all the world media for some kind of pithy insight, only because I was the man in the chair that night and accepted the charges when ET finally decided to phone home. My entire life was put under a neutron microscope and vivisected, looking for the slightest sign that I had simply fabricated the entire incident, message and all, for the fame and notoriety it brought me.

It was a bit of an intoxicant, at first, for the guy who lost by six votes out of ten for the post of President of Mathemagicians back in high school, and who'd been a sterling member of the AV Club and knew all of the words to every Monty Python routine. But that same sudden fame also made me a lightning rod for every nutcase on the West Coast—hell, the whole western hemisphere. People called my home at all hours of the day or night—not just the media, but the general public as well—wanting to know all about the message, which had not yet been deciphered, accusing me of withholding information for my own evil ends when I patiently told them I didn't have any idea what the message said.

The calls became threatening, hostile, ominous, finally morphing seamlessly into death threats for me and my family if I didn't reveal what was encrypted on that tape. I had our telephone number changed several times, and made private, but it made no difference, for the calls resumed almost without interruption. I thought I recognized one of the threatening voices as belonging to the customer service representative who helped me change my number in the first place. "This call may be monitored or recorded for quality control," I told her, and she hung up.

I unplugged the phones, but caravans of believers and nonbelievers camped outside our home. They followed my family everywhere: to work, to the store, to school. As if we were about to make some interstellar drop and pick up a few more alien secrets that we, for our own twisted reasons, refused to let the rest of the world in on.

"Put like that," I told Sara, "I don't trust us very much, either."

"This isn't some joke!" she snapped, pulling the living room curtains closed against the Woodstock-like scene on our front lawn. I watched them, standing there or sitting on their cheap, plastic folding lawn furniture, faces turned toward our house, our window, *us,* and I thought of the zombies in *Night of the Living Dead,* descending on the isolated Pennsylvania farmhouse.

"These people are—"

"Lost," I finished for her. "It's a big universe, and they've lost their way in it."

"Then let them call frikkin' Triple-A," she almost shouted.

Standing in the darkened living room, I pulled back the thick drape with my index finger. They were still out there, still staring at the curtained window like expectant theatergoers, waiting for the show to begin. "Right now...I'm afraid that's *me.*"

The next morning, I sent Sara and Vonnie to stay with her mother, but it did no good. The believers and non-believers followed them there, and by the next day, my wife and daughter returned to me.

It was on the third morning of the eleventh week that I cracked the code, and I felt like a fool that it had taken me that long. It wasn't a language at all, but a schematic buried within the radio wave. A schematic of a portal, and the rough equivalent of a man—or something man-shaped—in the center of it. It was painfully obvious when I put the graphics on my monitor as a 3-D layer, instead of trying to read the many codes individually.

Once-indecipherable symbols resolved themselves as circuitry, equations, Mu, and amplitude. It had all been carefully calibrated to earthly specifications. Our friends in the far corner of Alpha Centauri—our stepbrothers—were taking no chances.

I should have remembered what happened the first time I met my real stepbrother; he gave me an atomic wedgie, broke my Aurora Glow-in-the-Dark Godzilla model kit, and kicked the crap out of me. It was no easier on the firstborn, I realized, to know there was another family out there that had your father when you no longer did. But at least he was family.

"What is it?" Stefano asked, peering over my shoulder at the computer screen. I clicked the mouse and rotated the image.

"Doorway," I offered. "Matter transporter, maybe?"

Stefano studied the diagram so long without speaking that I thought he must have left my workstation without a sound, and when he finally did speak, it startled me. "I don't think so," he muttered.

"Why do you say that?"

He tapped his finger on the screen. "This is designed for receiving, not sending. It's a one-way jump, whatever it is."

"Again, meaning...what?"

He tugged thoughtfully on his lower lip. "It's the other end of a tunnel," he said. "Think of this as an interstellar 'Chunnel,' the French and English underground tube connecting one country with another."

I studied the diagrams, seeing now what Stefano had

already spotted as a potential design flaw. "What's the power source?"

"Right here," he said, pointing. "Uranium. But that's not the real source of power. It's just meant to turn on this end of the tunnel. Whatever powers this thing is on the other side. *Their* side."

That gave me an uneasy feeling, and I didn't know why, exactly. But the curious kid in me, the one who had thrilled to every new issue of *Scientific American* and *Popular Mechanics,* was more excited than alarmed.

Dumbass.

"Their technology obviously has a power-source we haven't discovered yet—"

"Then why not include it in their schematics?" Stefano pointed out. "Why not share it with us?"

"Maybe it's some source of energy we don't even have on the planet."

"What, Dilithium crystals?"

I ignored the alarm bells that were going off in my head, and continued. "Whatever opens the gate on their end must be incredibly powerful, probably dangerous...black hole technology...they've found a way to harness wormholes."

"That's what bothers me about this whole thing," Stefano said. I looked up at him, and saw genuine worry on his face. On Stefano, it was jarringly out of place, as if someone had decided to belch the National Anthem at the start of a baseball game. "We don't have that same advantage."

I looked at him, but said nothing.

"Meaning," he said, but he was only stating what we

both knew, "that whatever comes through that gate is here to stay."

Of course Stefano was right, and I suppose the aliens had been shrewd enough to imagine a Stefano, and find a way around him. Greed, of course. It was simple greed, in the end. It wasn't quite that old catechism, "For the want of a nail, the kingdom was lost," but more like, "For the want of a nail that the rest of the world might get instead of us" that doomed us.

The aliens had likewise beamed the same portal schematics to anyone willing to lend a sympathetic ear; Japan, Germany, China, Russia, England, even Time Warner/AOL claimed to have the same information, but so far, only we had actually cracked the code. But what one man can learn, another man can also learn, and the thought of another country receiving the benefits of making first contact was enough to overcome any reservations voiced by the Stefanos of the world.

The edict to proceed came down straight from the White House.

Stefano suggested we build the portal away from the civilian sector in case whatever was waiting to step across the four-plus light-year threshold lived in an atmosphere of deadly microbes and viruses. I thought that unlikely, because our ET pen pals obviously knew something about humankind, knew we didn't have the kind of power it would take to create a portal to their planet, which should have made us wonder *how* they knew these things. But we were being pressed to finish the gate before the other world players finished theirs, and we had no time to wonder.

Once we committed to building the gate, it didn't take

long for the curious to find out where we were. The site, in the middle of Fort Bragg's proving grounds, was fenced and guarded, but the immediate territory surrounding the project was anybody's game. The circus set up its tents on the perimeter, far enough away to render the NO TRESPASSING! signs impotent, near enough to be looking over our shoulders.

It was a seller's market just outside the gates: Winnebagoes with bright awnings unfurled, shading the occupants and the wares they unself-consciously hawked. Self-published books with several typos and misspellings, with covers made of a material somewhere between cardboard and flashpaper. The content of said books being invariably one man's—or woman's; only the gender changed, the story itself was predictably the same—encounter with extraterrestrial visitors, and the message of peace (or doom; this was about the only point on which the books varied, all depending on the author's worldview) to their guest. What message? Well, you'll just have to buy the book if you want to find that out.

Another cottage industry was like a bad mix of sci-fi and tchotchke, oil paintings of aliens on black velvet. All that was missing was the bad sideburns and petulant sneer and Hey! Presto! ET Elvis! And now that I think about it, one of the books did mention something about Elvis being an alien visitor sent to Earth to spread love and peace through his music, but we weren't ready yet, so he was taken back to the stars, to wait patiently until we were.

I grudgingly had to admire that inspired cross-pollination of conspiracies, and the man who could sell the book for $24.95 (for just $2 more, the author would sign and personalize it for you) with a totally straight face.

Another starving artist was selling signed lithographs

of otherworldly landscapes to which his abductors had taken him. The talent behind the paintings was meager, and the landscapes looked to be mostly of the Grand Canyon, with a couple of moons thrown into a red sky, and I really think some of the cityscapes were lifted right out of *The Jetsons*.

T-shirts and caps abounded, the simplest of them bearing the date 7/4/47, the date of the supposed Roswell crash, to the more obvious message shirts: MY PARENTS WERE ABDUCTED BY ALIENS AND TAKEN TO ALPHA CENTAURI AND ALL I GOT WAS THIS LOUSY ANAL PROBE, or STAR-CHILD ON BOARD, to iron-on transfers of aliens. I thought I detected the work of my ETs on black velvet artist here, but I couldn't prove it.

Rows of videotapes sat in long boxes, the tapes all shot on home video, usually the subject being yet another abductee droning flatly on about the experience, the tedium broken up occasionally by a couple of location shots in the woods or at the lake or on a city rooftop, the site where the purported contact/abduction occurred. Sometimes the interviewee would focus the camera on some physical abnormality—a lump or a scar—allegedly the place of a subdural implant. Often, the camera would linger on parts of the body so long as to verge on pornographic.

Audiotapes, CDs, antennae, pointy ears, Glo-Sticks, even Mom's Famous Out of This World Chocolate Chip Cookies (I asked Mom about this, and she said the aliens were particularly fond of her Tollhouse cookies) were all for sale here.

Too many freaks, not enough circuses.

I had to drive through the thick of this every day, on my way to the portal site, and back through it again on my way out. At first, I laughed at these people and mocked their beliefs, but I slowly came to the realization we were all the walking wounded—lost, alone, just wanting someone to listen. But then I remembered the crystal radio set my brother had helped me build when we were kids, and how I would sit for hours in front of that primitive apparatus, broadcasting messages, waiting for an answer that seldom came. If it did, it was usually so static-garbled it was impossible to tell if the message had been meant for me, or if I had just picked up a CB signal from some trucker passing through our town on the interstate. These people weren't so hard to understand, really; after all, I'd been doing the same thing all my life, until at last I sent a message out into the universe and hoped someone would listen.

It turned out Japan had broken the code at about the same time we did, and were well under way with their own portal. Russia and China had both figured it out the same day.

Work efforts on our own gate redoubled, one crew working all day, another crew working all night under the harsh glare of deep-sea light towers, the equivalent of 35,000 household lights—the same kind of lights Bob Ballard used to study the wreckage of the *Titanic* two-and-a-half miles down in her dark, watery grave at the bottom of the world. We were in a race to prove to the aliens that we were the country most deserving to receive their benediction, like people in the audience trying to be chosen as contestants at a game show.

"Do you ever feel that maybe, just supposing," Stefano said, looking up from his tabletop of circuits, a tangle of microfilaments around his brow like a crown, "that we've bitten off more than we can chew here?"

I nodded, looking out across the campgounds, at the

rising, incomplete skeletal ring of the portal; it described an uneven, massive capital "U." It looked like the ribs of some giant Technosaur jutting out of the ground, or two vast and trunkless legs.

"Yeah," I admitted. "I'm sure we did."

"So...what do we do?"

I shrugged. "Learn to chew bigger."

The stock market couldn't decide what to make of the impending contact with an alien culture, so it fluctuated drunkenly, opening high, closing low, then reversing the trend the next day. Finally, everyone decided to shift their fortunes to technology-based industries, gambling our visitors would share some of their good science with us. Others, not quite so sure of the aliens' intentions, invested heavily in gold.

Churches, synagogues and mosques all over the world either flourished or went bust. People sought guidance, or forgiveness, and many thought the aliens were secretly angels and these were the end times, ushered in by man's own hubris.

Got that in one.

New religions sprung up, of course, dedicated to the gate; their symbol was the vaguely man-like form standing in the portal, just as I'd first seen it when I overlaid the graphics. "Does that make you John the Baptist?" Stefano asked me.

I hoped not. That gig didn't end too well for John, as I recalled.

Camera crews followed us everywhere, recording everything we did, and why not? It wasn't as if we were the only nation given the portal technology. It was almost as common as eyelashes at this point. CNN, PBS and the BBC filmed our every moment, the good and the bad, and I thought I finally had a pretty fair idea of how the Beatles must have felt during the filming of *Let It Be*.

I wish our little group had had a Yoko to break us up. Several times I looked at the portal as it approached completion, like a circle about to close, the jaws of a trap about to snap shut, and I wondered what the hell we were doing. But even if I could halt the project somehow, there was no turning back. The N'lani had seen to that.

Whatever else they did or didn't know about us, they had unerringly zeroed in on the one thing that is a global constant: the heart of man is easily corrupted. By sending us all the same schematics, through Mutually Assured Construction, they had guaranteed we'd leave the light on and the door unlocked for them.

My own little Fellini movie, the road show of *Amarcord*, still cluttered my end of the cul-de-sac outside our home. They were loyal, I had to give them that; they didn't just pull up stakes (if you could even do that to a house with hubcaps), and migrate with the rest of the sideshow out to the desert. No, by God. These were my freaks, and so they remained faithful to me, although I suspected I had probably lost a few here, gained a few others there.

Sara's car was in the carport when I arrived home for my two days off, so I had to park in the driveway. As soon as I stepped out, briefcase in hand, I automatically locked the door. The moment I turned away from the car, the man was there.

He might have been standing in the shadows among the tall bushes flanking the house, just waiting for me to return home, or perhaps he had been standing in that same spot all along and I simply hadn't noticed. My mind may have been focused on any number of things, but the fact is, I had gotten used to seeing people I didn't know standing about, and I had paid this one too little attention. Whatever the reason, as soon as he stepped close to me and spoke, I knew this was the one man I should have been looking out for, even if I hadn't known who it might be.

"Devil," he said, softly. "Judas."

My mouth went dry as a ball of dirt. For a moment, I couldn't speak, because even in this dim, purple evening light, I could see the high, whirling, twirling light of madness in his eyes, burning as brightly as a gas flame.

I swallowed—twice—my throat making a dry, clicking sound, like dice rattling in a gambler's hand, or the sound of a hammer being cocked on a pistol. I knew just what that sounded like, because I'd heard it the moment the man with the gas-flame eyes stepped up to me and called me a devil. He had a .38 leveled at my stomach. I wish I could tell you I was brave at that moment, but I felt tears welling up, threatening to spill down my cheeks; tears of helplessness, of anger, and fear. That, most of all. My wife and daughter were just on the other side of the wall, not knowing I was home, or aware I was about to be shot dead not ten feet away from where they sat, watching television.

I became acutely aware of everything in that moment: a bead of sweat as it trickled its way down the mastoid behind my left ear; how my entire body was covered with an oily fear-sweat; the sound of Langdon Donahue, poor nerd that he was, calling for his dog, Axel; the sound of a bird somewhere twittering something that sounded vaguely like "Che-bur-gah," and I remembered my dad telling me once that this was the cry of the rare Cheeseburger Bird. I could smell fresh-cut grass, and the aroma of red beans and rice simmering on the stove of one of the little nearby campers. And I could see the unnaturally huge barrel of the gun leveled at me, as wide around as a bear cave.

"Whatever you want—" I tried to speak, my tongue as thick as shoe-leather. Inside, from the television, a burst of laughter floated out, lending this whole surreal scene even more of a sense of unreality. I was about to take a gutshot that would blow my intestines and most of my left kidney out a hole in my back, all over the driver's side of my car. "Do you want me to beg?" I asked. "Fine. I want to live. I want more than anything to see my daughter grow up and have kids of her—"

"Shut up!" he snapped, gun barrel weaving and wavering. There wasn't much doubt I was going to get shot, it just didn't seem such a sure thing anymore that it would kill me outright. "Just...shut up!"

I thought it was a bigger risk not to talk to the man with the gas-flame eyes, because in that quiet, I knew—I didn't just suspect, I *knew*—he'd listen to his own inner voices and find the resolve to jerk back on the trigger, just the way Gary Yokum had listened to his own set of voices years earlier. As long as I could keep him focused on me, I thought I could talk my way out of this, or at least keep him occupied until someone in the circus saw what was happening and dialed 911. But I also thought of all those old, wild animal documentaries, where the lion brought down a gazelle or an alligator snapped up a heron while the cameraman just kept filming.

I let a slow, trickling breath out of my chest, like a balloonist releasing hot air to keep from rising too high, and asked, "What's this about? What have I done to you? What can I do to make it right?"

"You're in league with the demons!" he gibbered, and I thought his eyes burned even brighter. "I can smell the evil on you! The stink of the fire pits! You're one of them!"

How long had we been standing here? It felt like ages, but I suppose it couldn't have been more than five minutes, and probably closer to three.

"They're not demons," I corrected, gently. "They're aliens. A very scientifically advanced race, but just aliens..."

"You cost me my job," he told me. "This economy that your demon friends brought about caused my church to close—"

"Church?" This just got more and more abstract.

"—and now I'm living in my car!" He glanced toward my house, and I felt oddly violated, thinking of those eyes of madness even looking at the one place on Earth where my family was supposed to be safe.

And then I thought, what if he shoots me? What if he actually does it, and what happens to Maryvonne if she discovers my body? Worse, what happens if she hears the shot and comes running? Would this madman turn his gun on an innocent child?

Yes, I was sure he would. He'd take down everyone he could before turning the last bullet toward himself.

I had nothing to lose and I knew it, but neither did he, and he outweighed me by a good sixty pounds and a .38 caliber. "All right," I bargained crazily. "I can halt the project, change a couple of equations, sabotage the gate..."

"See how easily betrayal comes to you?" he said, his voice deceptively calm, and squeezed the trigger.

Click.

I gasped and swore I felt the bullet rip into me, but it was only because I was expecting it. Had this all been a joke? A cautionary tale? *This time you get to live, but next time...*

No. The look on his face told me he was as surprised as I was that I was still alive. Misfire, that's all, or maybe he'd forgotten to flip the safety. I wasn't going to squander this moment and allow him the chance to correct whatever rookie mistake he'd made.

Sure enough, he *had* forgotten the safety, and as his sausage-casing fingers fumbled to release it, I brought my briefcase up—a little surprised to see I was still holding it—hard as I could, banging the steel-reinforced corner into the man's left temple, raking it across his cheek as the force of the blow snapped his head to the right. I watched a red seam appear in his cheek, exposing the dental work beneath. His teeth were yellow, from too much coffee, or perhaps smoking, and he showed early signs of periodontal disease.

He cursed something unintelligible and went down, but he was a long way from out. He still had the gun, and still worked to throw the safety. I swung my briefcase once more, slamming the steel corner into his teeth, pulping that pouty, almost fey, mouth.

He lost his grip on his gun but fought to grab it back, even as I delivered a solid kick to his ribs, cushioned by layers of fat. I snatched the gun from the drive, even as his fingers, smeared with his own blood, felt blindly for the weapon. Whatever madness empowered him seemed inexhaustible, like some fissionable material.

He looked up at me, his flensed cheek pressed to the gravel of the driveway, the pilot light of his gas-flame eyes dimming, sputtering, but I knew it would take only the tiniest spark to reignite that madness, hotter and brighter than ever.

I felt my finger tighten on the trigger. I wanted to

shoot this man. I was going to kill him—and I might have, if my hand hadn't been shaking so badly. The bullet whanged off the driveway and went whining away into the evening shadows like some pissed-off mosquito in search of blood. I started to tell the man to beg, but the words were breathless, choking sounds, and I sicked everything up. My stomach cramped up from all the adrenaline that had been dumped into my system, and my knees got that rubbery wobble that comes with averted disaster. I had to steady myself against the hood of my car.

I reached into my coat pocket and got my cell phone and started to thumb in 911, but stopped. I was going to have to subject myself to a lot of questions, not the least of which would be why I had powder residue on my hands and a bullet missing from the drum if I was the one assaulted. A lot depended on the cop who answered the call, presenting me an equation with too many variables and imponderables.

I closed the cell hood and slipped it back into my pocket. "Go," I told him. "But if you ever come back, or come anywhere near my family, I won't hesitate to shoot...I won't hesitate to give you to my demon masters."

That night, without explanation, I moved my family to a small motel near the portal construction site. In a few days, I told them, everything would be back to normal.

Most of the nearby motels were full-up, of course, because of the news crews and interested observers, but a technician on our team agreed to let us have his motel room after I explained what had happened.

"Didn't you ever think that might be the response?"

he asked, point-blankly, in the motel parking lot as I was transferring luggage. Heat snakes slithered and squirmed up from the baking blacktop, rippling and distorting my view of the world beyond.

"No," I admitted. "I mean, I guess I knew this information would change a lot of lives, but I always thought—" *I always thought I'd be a hero,* I heard my inner voice say, whining like a petulant child. "What are you saying?"

He shrugged. "They're scared, a lot of them. Most of them are just simple folks who go through life day to day, happy with the sameness, and feel like they've won the lottery if the local A&P has triple-coupon week. They have simple needs and even simpler beliefs."

"And I shook that up."

He put his hand on my shoulder, drew me close, and gave me a friendly, brotherly hug. "Let me give you a bit of advice my father gave me," he said. "If you keep this in mind, I think it'll make your own day-to-day life a lot easier." He paused a moment, letting the nearby whine of interstate traffic die down so he wouldn't have to dilute his philosophy by shouting it in my ear. When the air was still, he said clearly and simply, and with the gravest of gravity, "People are cretins."

We finished the jumpgate a few days earlier, and the day we declared it officially open was a Saturday. The afternoon was hot and clear; it was not a day packed with omens. It was just a day.

The testing grounds lay flat in all directions for miles, but the grounds were packed shoulder-to-shoulder with the apostles who had come to hear the sermon on the military proving grounds, and those who had come to protest, and those who had just come to see us fail spectacularly.

Stefano told me he had heard on the news that pregnant women had been demanding doctors induce labor. When I asked him why, he told me it was because they didn't want their children born during an alien invasion.

The hurricane fencing was still up, and only a select few hundred had been allowed inside the compound, near the portal. There was a high-school band standing by, ready to play the themes from *2001* and *Close Encounters* for our visitors, like this was all just some big half-time extravaganza. Also standing by were a few military sharpshooters, just in case the N'lani were suddenly filled with the idea of eminent domain, or in case the crowd harbored a suicide bomber with a bad dose of xenophobia.

A shining gold ribbon was strung across the portal opening, which was wide enough to allow two double-decker buses to drive through, side by side, and at the end of the ceremony, the governor, the head of SETI, and I would all cut the ribbon, and Miss California would flip the switch, opening the gate. In fact, the switch did nothing. It was all for show, for the dozen upon dozens of TV stations filming the event. The gate was already "on." It would take a while to power up, and the ceremony was timed to conclude at the same moment the gate came online. Something like this didn't work with a simple on/off button.

Sara sat near me on the makeshift dais, and Vonnie next to her. I scanned the crowd restlessly; my encounter with the man with the gas-flame eyes had left me jumpy and skittish, expecting him or one of his equally insane brethren to step serenely out of the shadows and finish the job.

"...man looked to the stars from the mouth of his cave..." the governor was droning on; I only picked up a few words here and there. I could feel the small hairs on the back of my neck and arms bristle as the gate powered up nearby. I blinked; the fluid behind my eyes began to swim, affected by the ambient energies stirring just a few yards away.

I looked at Maryvonne, who rubbed her eyes repeatedly, and looked as if she were about to cry from the discomfort. We were several years on by this point, since that night I received the message, but Vonnie still looked young and helpless. I reached across Sara and gave Vonnie's little hand a squeeze. "It's okay," I told her. "It's just the portal. I feel it, too."

"Is it safe to be sitting so close to it?" Sara asked.

"Oh, sure," I said, trying to sound as if I did this sort of thing all the time—but the truth was, I didn't have any idea. No one had expected this kind of reaction on organic matter positioned near the portal. If it grew worse, I would pick Vonnie up and walk with her and Sara away from the platform.

The governor was feeling the effects, too, like a welling nausea that keeps rising, but relief never comes. He lost his place in his speech, shuffled his notes, wiped at his streaming eyes, and tried to resume the thread of his ceremony.

The gate stood nearly two stories tall, and its center was a perfect circle, save at the bottom, where a gently sloping ramp had been added. I wanted to add a handicap sign to the platform, but Stefano told me that was not politically correct, even after I pointed out to him, if you really look at that universal symbol for handicapped parking, it looks suspiciously like an alien with a big ass. He laughed, but held firm. It was probably just as well.

I didn't need that kind of notoriety, on top of the disdain that would soon follow.

The gate was perhaps two feet deep, composed of several layers, each layer made of spent uranium, because the gate would need such durable material to contain all the massive energies it would be required to summon. Every few yards, within the center circle, were placed energy ports. The outer rim of the gate was an onyx colored metal, and a few amber lights were set into the surface at irregular intervals. Great, snaking steel cables wound their way from the command center, through the audience, to the jumpgate.

But the look of it—the *design*—was all wrong. It made me think of the gates of hell, all cold and sterile efficiency, sharp edges and jagged bits of steel with no other purpose than to spill your blood if you got too careless. I really wondered what we had been thinking—*if* we had been thinking. Because if we had, I don't believe we ever would have built this obscenity.

My bowels began to liquify, and I heard Miss California, who was seated near me, strangle a duck. The governor was perspiring heavily now, blinking almost nonstop to clear the sweat from his eyes. People seated in the front rows of the audience began to fidget uncomfortably.

"...The moon and Mars are just our stepping-stones," the governor continued, gamely, his voice breathless with discomfort. I turned to Vonnie; she had her arms folded around herself, rocking back and forth on her chair, crying freely. Sara tried to comfort her, but could not. My wife looked at me, her eyes wide and pleading, begging me to do something.

One of the military men came running through the crowd, pushing people out of his way as he ran. He was shouting something, but he was too far away to hear clearly over the beating of the blood-drums in my ears.

"Stop...Japan...attack...!"

That didn't make a lot of sense, unless he was the last man on the planet to hear about Pearl Harbor. Either that, or he'd been running since 1941.

His words took on more meaning as he got nearer the dais, but they didn't make any more sense. "Japan is online!" he shouted, bellowing the news like a drill instructor, competing with the shrill whine of the portal as it cycled up. "Their gate is open! They're under attack! You have to shut that thing down—*now!*"

The shriek of the gate fed through the microphones, creating a terrible sound loop of feedback. I felt something heavy burst in my nose, and a spray of blood coated my shirt. I turned to the portal, eyes squinted as if gazing into a blinding light, and watched a shimmering curtain of energy fill the gate like a kaleidoscope. A greenish mist began to creep out of the portal like some luminescent ground fog.

Maryvonne was running around in tight little circles, hands cupping her eyes, shrieking like a bat. The portal was glowing brightly now, as webs of energy crossed and recrossed from side to side, like a blazing hi-tech pentagram. I didn't want to see the demon this was conjuring. This wasn't a gate to another world; we'd built a door to hell.

"Shut it down!" the general commanded.

I was the nearest tech on hand, since I was supposed to take part in the ceremony, but there wasn't much I could do, except grab up the nearest folding chair and start banging it against the gate circuitry. The problem was, this thing would take as long to power down as it did to build up. There was just too much raw power contained in the conjuring circle (and I saw now with all the clarity of hindsight that that's just what this thing was; the man with the gas-flame eyes was crazy, but he was also right) to simply pull the plug, and I suspected, once it was activated, the gate couldn't be closed, anyway. I think the N'lani had seen to that.

One of the soldiers had found an axe and was trying to chop through the main power cable, as thick as a sewage pipe, wrapped in titanium steel.

In the blazing brilliance at the heart of the portal, I could see a misty figure, big as an Asgardian Storm Giant, begin to form, and another, and another. Beyond those figures, the light of an alien world, a different galaxy. I was momentarily mesmerized by the sight, until I heard Sara scream.

I kept smashing at the exposed circuits of the gate, and thought I might be able to do enough damage to stop the advancing Storm Giants, given a few more moments, but they proved to be moments I didn't have.

"Get Vonnie out of here!" I shouted to Sara, giving her a hard push toward the edge of the platform.

The crowd was screaming now, and all I could think of was, *Don't worry, ladies and gentlemen, those chains are made of chrome steel,* but obscure bits of dialogue from *King Kong* weren't going to help me now.

A widget of some sort darted from the gate, moving at incredible speeds. It looked like a techno-organic dragonfly, with wings like stained-glass windows. The beating of its wings made a whining sound, but if you tried to follow it by sound alone, it was already somewhere else before you even heard it.

The general unholstered his sidearm and tried to draw a bead on it, but it was hellishly fast, and it impaled him on its long, spiked tail. The last thing the general saw in this life was his own shocked features, reflected and reflected in his insectile killer's compound eyes.

I heard the crack of gunfire, flat and hollow, as the military sharpshooters tried to take the dragonfly down. The steel-jacketed slugs cracked the techno-insect's carapace, exposing meat and circuitry. A second fusilade failed to find its mark, because now the creature was aware of the danger and had pinpointed its attackers' location. It hovered in the air, inches above that crowd that, incredibly, remained seated, too stunned by fright to move. The dragonfly's wings beat faster and faster, until they were a blur, then invisible, and I saw the air around the creature ripple. A wave of sound, too high-pitched to hear and as solid as a wall, rolled forward and struck the two nearest sharpshooters, shattering their guns, bones, organs, shredding their bodies into bloody rags and filaments. Gobbets of soldier rained down on the crowd and pavement.

I forced myself to look away, and found Sara and Vonnie, halfway through the crowd, caught in the rush toward the exit.

Sparks erupted from some of the circuitry I was smashing. For a moment, I thought the figures in the portal flickered, but it might have been the spatial distortion/interface, or, more likely, my eyes adjusting to the glow.

There was a strange, disjointed moment, as if time had somehow *slipped*, lending this out-of-body experience feeling, like waking from a dream of falling, jolting suddenly awake in your own body. The gate was probably mucking up time around its accretion area, like a black hole freezing light. I had to stop it—now. While I still could.

I pounded again, bare-fisted, at the exposed circuitry

beneath the cowling I had broken open, reaching in, ripping and tearing relays and microchips out by the handful, like a jewel thief in some mad crash and dash.

"Daddy!" I heard Vonnie scream. I found her in the crowd, pointing at something behind me, her mouth describing the perfect letter "O" like the gate.

I turned to see what she was pointing at, and felt the air leave my lungs in a rush.

"Paul!" Sara screamed.

Paul.

That's my name.

Paul....

CHAPTER FIVE

Paul...not Max...Paul..."

I woke slowly, then remembered the creatures in the portal, and that brought me back to sudden, full awareness. I expected to find myself lying, possibly dying, on the platform in front of the portal, impaled on the tip of the dragonfly's tail, or my bones crushed, organs a mucky stew, scrambled by the gate's power surge.

Instead, I found myself in an infirmary, but I was alone. I couldn't have been the only one injured...I couldn't have been the only survivor. "Sara?" I asked, my voice rising in panicky steps. "Vonnie!"

I lifted my head, inspected my body for wounds, but found none. I levered myself up on one elbow and looked around the room. It was like no infirmary I'd ever seen: the walls were filthy and dreary, and the cots, lined in five neat grids of four to a row, were stained and mildewed. Wooden cabinets, bare except for a few jars and jugs, stood about the dim and dingy room. Civil War operating tents were more cutting edge than this sick-bay, and that only confused me more. Where was I this time?

I had that sick feeling of double-exposure memories again, expecting to find myself in the military infirmary after the alien attack, equally certain I'd wake to find myself in my cell. I looked toward the window, and saw there were bars covering it. I was half right, anyway.

"Sara?" I called again. I knew I wasn't completely alone in the darkened room.

I sat up with a start, driving a spike of pain through my skull. My hand went to my forehead and found a crude bandage there, crusted with dried blood. I supposed I'd probably—

"Struck your head when you collapsed," a voice finished my thought for me.

I turned, slowly this time, because I could feel the pain sloshing around inside my head like a carbonated liquid, and I feared if I shook it too much, my head would explode like a can of shaken pop. I located the source of the voice. "H'lo, Padre," I said. I don't know why, but I was happy to see him.

He was trying to be cool, but I could see, even in the darkness, that something had flapped the unflappable, stone-faced death row chaplain, that giver of comfort, if such a thing could be given in such a place, at such a time.

"What happened?" I asked. "Where are Sara and Maryvonne?"

The chaplain heard my croaky voice and offered me a metal cup half-filled with stale, brackish water. It reeked of algae, but I gulped it down in two grateful swallows, and wished I could have more. He took the cup, set it aside, and checked the bandage on my head. I somehow knew that the chaplain doubled as the prison sawbones. That struck me as a bizarre conflict of interests.

"Suppose you tell me what happened, Max...or Paul, if that's what you call yourself." He was trying hard, working overtime, to sound cool and in control, but the thready breathing and quaver in his voice were anything but cool. He had been afraid of me before, but this was something different.

I took a deep breath, swung my legs over the side of the bunk, and sat there, waiting for the pain that little movement generated to subside. When it did, I said, "My name is Paul Stein," and I knew that was right. "I'm not this Max person you all seem to think I am."

Here, the chaplain seemed a little bolder. He said, "You look enough like him." But he didn't sound quite so convinced.

"Look, you have the wrong man. Check my fingerprints, check my DNA, let me take a polygraph. I'll do whatever you want me to do, but let me prove I'm not the man you think I am."

The chaplain's hands gripped each other, his dirty nails digging crescents in the soft flesh of his palms. "God protect Your servant," he muttered, as if I'd just invoked the names of several minor demons. I don't know why that should have surprised me; after all, a look around my surroundings should have already made it clear they probably hadn't heard of DNA or lie detectors here.

I suddenly wondered if I was even still in America, let alone New Mexico, anymore. Had I been injured and left for dead at the portal and ended up here? My mind raced at escape velocity. There were no answers, and nothing but more questions. The padre was slow at answering, and I knew I'd have to back my way into this one if I wanted to get any useful information out of him. At first, I wondered if he might have been reluctant to even speak with me because of what I had been accused of doing, as if I were beneath his holy contempt. But even though I was confused, I was still clear-headed enough to recognize the padre was...well...a bit *dim*.

"My name is Paul Stein," I said patiently, as if addressing a child. "Please, just hear me out before you say anything."

"All right," he agreed. But I noticed his eyes fidgeting nervously, glancing furtively toward the closed door, outside of which, I was quite sure, a guard stood, ready to rush to his aid. It made me cold to think there was seemingly no one in this place who might similarly come to my rescue.

"Max—"

"You promised," I reminded him. "If a man of the cloth's word isn't to be trusted..." I let the thought trail off. He smiled, tightly, and motioned for me to continue. He didn't like me, and I was pretty sure he'd be happy to watch me do the air-dance at the end of the hangman's rope. "My name is Paul Stein," I began again. "I'm a scientist—well, an astronomer, really."

"Do you read the future in the stars, Max?" he asked. "That's the devil's work, you know. No wonder you don't know your own name. If I ask you your name, will you answer your name is Legion?" He was back on superior, if badly misinformed, ground here.

"What's the use?" I groaned, and instinctively followed his gaze toward the door once more. Everything changed for me in that moment.

Nailed to the wall beside the door was an old, yellowed calendar. It was frozen, like a broken clock, on June 2004. I felt as if I had just stepped into the deep end of a frozen lake.

I stood, pushed past the father, who cried out in alarm. He probably thought I was going to try to escape, but I wanted only to see the calendar. I picked it from the wall. The paper was dry and brittle in my palsied hands.

2004? That couldn't be right, that couldn't even *begin* to be right. It was September 2003, when we completed the gate, not 2004, not almost a whole year later. I had almost convinced myself I had done a *Connecticut Yankee* and traveled back in time, despite the evidence I had seen to the contrary.

I turned to the chaplain, who was watching me as if I were some exotic form of life...and a potentially crazy, dangerous one, as far as he was concerned.

"It's a joke, right?" I asked, fanning the calendar weakly, my voice shrill and skirting crazy. The paper leaves were fat with years of water dripping and drying, and a powdery chalk of dust and mildew coated the pages. "What are you trying to pull?"

But the look on his face said it all. No one was trying to pull anything here. I just refused to grasp the evidence everything kept rubbing my nose in, although it was getting patently harder to ignore. "What year is it? What's the date?"

"Date?" He acted as if he'd never heard the word before.

"Yes! Year! What *year* is it?"

"No one keeps track of such things anymore," he said, simply.

"Anymore?" Now it was my turn to grapple with the English language. Somewhere, when I wasn't looking, we'd taken a sharp turn off the main road, and the houses in this part of the landscape were unlike any I'd ever seen before.

I supposed it wasn't that hard to guess when they stopped keeping track of such things—somebody had forgotten to wind the calendar in July 2004, after all—it was just the *why* that still eluded me. Why...and how long ago.

"May I speak now, Max? Paul?"

"Sure, why not?" I answered. I was feeling generous.

I tried to put the calendar back on the wall, because I really didn't know quite what else to do. I felt as if I were holding tainted time in my hands, and wanted to be shut of it as quickly as possible. But my hands were shaking, and I let if fall. It fluttered to the floor like a stricken bird, wings flapping uselessly.

"Who are you? What are you?" His voice was weak.

"I already told you..." I sighed, massaging my temples with my fingertips. I closed my eyes to lessen the flopping, bumping pain just behind them, but the sight of the thing in the portal kept trying to burn itself into my brain. That, and the look of pure terror on Vonnie's face. It was a look no parent should ever see on a child.

"Yes, yes, Paul Stein, an astronomer," he said dismissively. I gazed at him, and I was looking into gas-flame blue eyes; they were just set into a different face, that's all. "When you looked into the looking glass," he said, edging closer, "I saw something I can't explain..."

"What did you see?" I asked, feeling a knot forming in the pit of my stomach. I thought I already knew.

He licked his lips, said, "For a moment...it looked as if you wore another man's visage...like you had a...a demon fighting to possess you."

I broke out laughing, but I think I was crying, too. "A demon?" I said, and laughed again. "I wish! Oh, shit, that's funny!"

I wanted to tell him that, somehow, I thought I had been blown through time and space, out of my world and into this one, but the man was talking demon possession with a straight face, and didn't know what an astronomer was. He didn't even know what *year* it was, for God's sake, so my odds of getting him to suddenly grasp the notion of quantum physics and parallel worlds were too small to measure with a neutron microscope.

In fact, even *I* was having a great deal of difficulty believing it. It was unfair of me to expect this man to throw away a lifetime's belief and accept what I was telling him as anything other than what it sounded like: the desperate ravings of a death row inmate who would say or do anything to avoid his blind date with the hangman.

"I'm...sorry, Father," I said.

Even as I said it, I heard a commotion of voices from outside the window, which faced onto the prison courtyard. I started for the window to see what all the excitement was about.

"Don't," the padre said, although it wasn't really expressed as an order. "No good will come of looking."

I regarded him for a moment, then moved to the window and looked through the rusted, pitted bars, out into the common area, which was boxed in by the four walls. The light was beginning to fail, but there was still enough daylight left in the sky to see the sight the padre had tried to spare me.

There was a rough, wooden gallows and gibbet standing in the compound, a weighted straw effigy standing on the platform, the hangman's noose looped around its neck. The steps—thirteen, of course—up to the gallows were well worn, making it clear there weren't many last-minute reprieves from the governor in this place. One of the guards—I recognized him as Strawberry-Nose—stood next to the effigy, supporting it upright as his partner pulled back on the lever, drawing the bolt that opened the trap. The effigy dropped hard and stopped harder, the taut rope around its neck thrumming like a plucked bass string.

The body swung and twisted a bit in the wind that circled the courtyard, and the guards laughed and joked. It didn't take a stretch of the imagination to guess what they were rehearsing, and who that effigy was meant to represent. Strawberry-Nose looked up, saw me standing in the window. He squinted, narrowing his little pig eyes, like black marbles sunk into spongy dough, and smiled when he recognized me. He thumped his partner on the back and pointed me out. They both looked at me and laughed, pretending to be hanged men, jerking on an invisible rope, twisting their heads to the side as if their necks were broken. Their eyes bugged comically, and they stuck their tongues out in a tasteless parody of strangulation.

"Wait your turn, sunshine," Strawberry-Nose advised me. "It'll come, soon enough."

I'm not sure what I expected. This place didn't seem likely to offer a Chinese restaurant menu of execution options, like the chair, or gas chamber, or lethal injection, but I hadn't expected anything as crude as hanging, either.

Strawberry-Nose grabbed the taut rope in his right hand and swung out onto it, like Quasimodo ringing his beloved bells. "Don't worry! It's plenty strong! See?"

"Why torture yourself?" the chaplain asked, and I had to agree. There was any number of people willing to do that for me. I turned away from the window, slowly. It was like watching a car crash you were about to be involved in—terrible to contemplate, impossible not to watch.

The guards continued to call after me, taunting me to look, telling me how long it would take to die by strangulation if the knot didn't break my neck cleanly when I dropped through the trap. I suspected they would somehow see to it that the noose wouldn't do its primary job, guaranteeing I stuck around long enough for its backup function.

"Oh, God," I heard my voice rising in a whine; I didn't like how it sounded, and I certainly wasn't proud of it, but neither could I help it. I was facing my own death, as impossible and abstract as it seemed. It was only that abstraction that kept it from becoming paralyzing. "What horrible world is this?"

The chaplain placed a hand on my shoulder—the first human contact I'd known since I woke in my cell, and I nearly wept. He had offered scant comfort up to this moment, and, meager as this was, I found I was desperate for it.

"How long?" I asked.

"Max..."

"How long?" I asked again, with a little more control over my voice this time.

"Dawn."

"As soon as that..." I muttered.

"Max, the warden has said he might commute your death sentence if you just give us the names and locations of your co-conspirators," the padre said. "Now, that's reasonable, isn't it?"

I shook my head. It was totally unreasonable. I wasn't being brave; I just didn't have any names to give them. If I'd known any names, I would have spewed them out like a rapper on speed.

I glanced out the window, avoiding the sight of the courtyard this time, focusing instead on the chiaroscuro sky. In the west, the sun was sinking, dragging the cover of night along behind it like a blanket.

Dawn was less than twelve hours away. If a miracle was going to happen, it was going to have to happen fast.

CHAPTER SIX

The chaplain, more human than I might have guessed, let me spend the night in the infirmary. He thought it best not to return me to the general populace of the prison, and I nodded my agreement. Of course, I would have agreed to just about anything at that point, even if he'd suddenly proclaimed shit was more valuable than gold.

There was no hope of escape from my cell—the walls were steel plate—but the infirmary was another matter. I tried the door and found it locked, just as I'd expected, and I thought there might be a guard posted in the corridor on the other side of the door. Even if it hadn't been locked, I didn't think I'd get far before I got cut down.

I looked out between the bars, studying the stars in their cold courses, and the bulimic moon. The moonlight lay like a silver dusting of snow on the prison walls, the courtyard and its grisly lone occupant. A slight breeze, caught in the confines of the common area, stirred the noose and its effigy, making the rope creak like a sailing ship's rigging.

But I was stalling. I had allowed myself to be frozen into inaction, as if part of me still believed there could be some last-minute realization that I was innocent, that this had all been some Kafka-esque case of mistaken identity. Or, even less likely, that the gateway back to my own world would open for me as I climbed those thirteen rugged gallows steps and whisk me out of this nightmare and back into my own life.

It was all fanciful thinking, a seductive, velvet-lined trap in which I had nearly allowed myself to get comfortable. But now the opposite was true, and shrill alarms and whistles were going off in my head, telling me time was running out. I couldn't allow myself to get caught up in that, lest I miss something that might allow me to escape.

I searched the shelves and cabinets methodically, but all of the instruments that might serve as weapons had been locked away in another room, if there ever were such instruments here. For all I could tell, the only surgical equipment available on this world was a bowl of fat, slimy leeches.

I made another circuit of the room; I couldn't afford to be so submissive. I had to look at everything with a critical eye. Anything that might be useful, either by itself or in conjunction with something else, I would set in a pile on one of the cots. Behind a loose, wire-weave screen on the cabinet shelves were a couple of bottles of ether. I set them on the cot. There were a few other jars, mostly filled with herbs, salves, unguents, lotions, or tinctures. I found a crude mortar and a rough steel pestle that looked as if it had been something else before being pressed into medical conscription. In the drawer I found old gauze bandages and a bit of surgical tape.

A half-hour's search had resulted in nothing more than a few items stacked on the mattress of the nearest cot. I stood, hands on hips, looking at the pile of junk, knowing on a subconscious level there was something here that could help me. I just had to hope my conscious mind would listen to the jailbreak whispers from down below, that wee, small voice that sounded as if it had done all of this before.

After a few moments, I had an idea of what I had to do. I used the pestle to tap the small, rusted nail loose from the wall, where it had been holding the calendar. As I was working in the darkness, my only light that of the rind of moon, I noticed what I hadn't noticed before: there was an old, unused light switch set into a metal plate beside the door. I pressed the recessed button, half expecting a bank of cold fluorescents to stutter into life overhead, but there was nothing. Still, it was something of a revelation: At one time, there was technology here, but something happened to change all that, and I suppose I already knew what that was. I just chose not to think about it yet.

The nail wriggled free, and I inspected the tip. It was still pointy, not much oxidization here, but I scraped the tip of it against the stone wall a few times, flaking off any bits of rust that I might have missed in the darkness, honing it to a sharper point. I saw it strike sparks a few times as I scraped it, and I thought for the first time this plan might just work.

I listened at the door, afraid my slight motion might have alerted the guard, but the corridor seemed quiet. Apparently, they thought I was a broken man. Fine by me.

The surgical tape was still sealed in sani-wrap, and still sticky, and I used this to affix the nail, tip-down, to the bottom of the door, so the point would scrape the concrete floor. There were a couple more things I had to do before I was ready, and I set about them as quickly and quietly as I could. There were no clocks, so I had no way of knowing how much time had passed, only that it *was* passing. But I couldn't rush. I couldn't afford a mistake now.

I gathered up all the mildewed, urine-sodden mattresses from the cots and piled them in a corner of the far wall, then overturned a cot frame, around which I stacked the mattresses, sandbagging them together in a sniper's nest.

I tested it for integrity; it was about as solid as you could expect from moldy mattresses, and I just had to hope that would be solid enough. As I worked, I was distantly aware the room had gotten darker. The moon had gotten tired of keeping an eye on this forsaken world, and had clocked out for the night. Dawn couldn't be far off.

I returned to the door, where I had stood the bottles of ether. I gauged the arc of the opening door, and placed the big, crude mortar just outside the door's apogee. I opened the first bottle of ether, instantly filling the room with that antiseptic medicinal stench. I moved quickly, holding my breath as much as possible, and poured the contents of the first bottle into the bowl. I felt nauseous and lightheaded from the fumes. I grabbed the second bottle and the surgical gauze and hurried across the room on legs that felt like stilts, and slipped into my sniper's nest.

I had planned on creating a commotion to lure the guard into opening the door, but, as it turned out, that wasn't necessary. With perhaps no more than an hour 'til dawn and my scheduled appointment with the ol' hemp chiropractor, the guards had come to fetch me. No surprise there: they'd want to make sure my last hour on this side of the curtain was as filled with pain and torment as possible. *Oh, those bruises? He resisted us, warden, you know how it is...*

Except, I didn't really think the warden would question any bruises.

The door opened, and the guard with the strawberry nose stepped in. I could see two other figures framed in the doorway behind him.

My escape plan turned out to be something of a cross between Rube Goldberg and the Marquis de Sade. The nail I had taped to the bottom of the door scraped across the rough concrete, striking a comet tail of sparks as it went. The air nearest the door was thick as a London fog with ether fumes, and ether, mixed with flame or static electricity, or even a spark from metal on stone, is highly volatile. That unpredictability was one of the reasons ether was eventually replaced by safer forms of anesthetic; patients had been known to catch fire on the operating table in the old days.

The fumes ignited, ripping the room with a brilliant, blinding flash and a deafening crack like thunder. Armageddon itself couldn't have been bolder.

The room filled with a concussive pressure, rippling out, slamming into the empty cots nearest the eye of the blast and throwing me and my pile of mattresses back against the wall, dazing me. I managed to hold fast to the second bottle of ether, trying to keep it from being shaken too much or broken.

The force of the blast was chased immediately by a wall of flame. I hugged the ether closer to my chest, wondering if I had made a fatal miscalculation by keeping a jar for backup, and then the wall of flame receded, and I could hear, through my blast-damaged eardrums, the sounds of screams. At first, I mistook them to be some primitive form of fire alarm, rising and falling like a glissando along the piano keys.

Dazed and groggy from the blast and the ether fumes, I pushed the burning tumble of mattresses away and saw a sight that chilled me, despite the heat from the inferno. The blast had funneled out in the narrow confines of the corridor beyond the door, flattening the figures I had seen standing there. But Strawberry-Nose had been at the heart of the explosion, and he was swathed in a sheet of flames, running back and forth in a panicked, narrowing gyre.

I grabbed one of the mattresses and, holding it before me, ran across the burning room. Pools of ether had splashed out of the mortar, and these puddles burned and blazed on the floor, on the walls, on the ceiling and cabinets. I tackled the guard, knocking him down, trying to smother the flames with the mattress and the weight of my body.

I could feel the terrible heat from his body, baking through the thin mattress that separated us, and his fear and agony gave him an insane strength. I fought to hold him down, trying to save the life of this man who wouldn't think twice about taking mine. His eyes were wide and showed nothing but white, like the eyes of a terrified horse in a thunderstorm. I thought they were wide with fear, shock, and pain, but I saw his eyelids had incinerated in the first flash. His flesh had sloughed away from the rough geometry of his face like wet clay. The flesh that remained bubbled and hissed and ran like hot tallow, the smell of burning fat clogging my nose and throat. Great, oily clouds of smoke rose from his body. Boils formed, erupted, and sizzled as their thick oozing contents struck super-heated flesh. His hair was nothing more than a few smoking wisps, like recently snuffed candle wicks.

I was staring into his wild, unblinking eyes when I felt a searing band circle my throat. He was trying to strangle me with his last, dying strength, and I thought he might actually be able to do the job before his brain got the message his body was just so much overcooked meat.

He was making insane, glottal sounds in the back of his throat. His tongue had burned and swollen, fused to the roof of his mouth and occluding his airways. The strength of his deathgrip seemed to double, and I felt his fiery hands burning fingerprints into my neck.

The heat from the fire was intense, burning the oxygen from the room, filling my eyes with smoke. If I could have drawn a breath, my lungs would have filled with the poisonous fumes instantly. I had to worry about my own safety. My attempt to help the guard, while perhaps noble, was misguided. I hadn't gone through all this to escape the hangman's noose, only to perish in flames, locked in a madman's embrace.

I quit trying to beat out the flames that lapped hungrily at Strawberry-Nose's flesh, and grabbed his fingers dimpling my throat. I grunted and pried, and heard his bones, charred and brittle, break and crumble like ashen briquettes.

His nerves were clipped. He felt nothing, even as his broken and missing fingers jutted at crazy angles. I felt for his keys, which he wore on his belt, but they were all melted and fused into a white-hot lump, seared to his hip. As I did, he tried to grab me, to enfold me in his arms and hold me close, perhaps to crush the life from me, or perhaps just to hold me there long enough for the smoke and flames to finish me. Maybe he just didn't want to make the trip into the afterlife alone.

I wrenched free, clutching a length of gauze over my nose and mouth as I crawled along the floor. I retrieved the bottle of ether and, half-blind from tears, eyes baked and covered with soot, I could only hope I was making my way for the exit and not farther into the room. I heard something massive crack overhead, followed by the crash of ceiling and supports collapsing. The infirmary was falling in upon itself.

I crawled over one of the bodies in the corridor, feeling my way along the floor and wall. The air out here was a little friendlier, and I managed to gulp down some. I coughed and ratcheted up black bile, tasting smoke and the pungent aftertaste of ether. I wiped my mouth with the surgical dressing and smeared some of the burning tears out of my eyes.

I removed a set of keys from the guard's belt. I felt his carotid with my fingertips and felt a pulse, slow and steady. He was out, but at least he was alive. I didn't have time to drag him, or the padre—who had apparently come along with the guards to hear any last minute confessions and perform the last rites—to safety, but I felt sure help would arrive at any moment. Even without a fire alarm, the rest of the prison staff had to be aware of what was going on.

I reached the end of the corridor, where it branched off in a T. The smoke followed me, but it wasn't quite as thick, so I was able to stand and make my way toward the steps...when I heard the sound of running feet and excited voices. My ears were still ringing from the explosion, and I couldn't tell at first from which way they were approaching. At last I decided they were coming from the way I was going, and reversed direction. It didn't matter; my original choice had been arbitrary.

I rounded the corner, and came up against a bank of

elevators. The doors had all been removed, to turn the shafts into wells by which to hoist heavy objects from the basement to whatever floor the supplies were needed on.

I swung out onto the rope hanging from the pulley system mounted somewhere on one of the floors overhead, and slid down, feeling the air growing cooler and more breathable by the moment. The shaft was pitch-dark, and I had no idea how far I'd descended. The friction from the rope was burning my hands and thighs as I slid farther and faster. My palms felt raw and bloody as fresh hamburger, and I had to bite down on my lip to keep from crying out in pain. I passed another open elevator door and leaped for it as I slid past. I hit the floor in a crouch, my numb hands beginning to wake up. In fact, they were wide awake and screaming.

I studied my palms in the dim light of the corridor—there were candles mounted on stanchions at irregular intervals along the wall—and saw they were not as bad as they felt. I looked from my hands to the shaft: painted on the inside of the open door was a faded number 3. I groaned. Still a long way from home free. Well, most of the action would be upstairs, fighting the fire, but I couldn't count on that being enough of a distraction for me to just walk on out of here unnoticed. But I had the keys—I just had to stay alive long enough to use them.

I hurried into the T juncture of the corridor, rightly assuming all floors were laid out as the ones above and below, and listened for voices. Nothing.

I moved deeper, coming to a locked door. I tried the keys I'd removed from the guard and found the right one on the third try. I eased the door open, expected to encounter a guard posted inside, but there was another door beyond this. I slotted the key and uncorked the bottle of ether. I shook a little of the anesthetic into the gauze I had used as a breathing mask and replaced the stopper. I was certain there would be a guard beyond this door, and I was right.

He was half-dozing already, his chair tipped back on its hind legs, feet up off the floor, and the ether mask I pressed tightly over his mouth and nose finished the job. He fought, trying to sit up, his flailing only making the rear legs of his chair buck like a mustang, and he went down hard.

I held the ether mask to his face a few moments more, just to be safe, then tossed it aside. I still had one more pad of gauze, and that was all I would need.

The corridor he was guarding was lined with identical, featureless cell doors. I looked in the first one, and spotted a man sleeping on his side with his back to the door. I used the guard's key to open the door, making enough noise as I did to wake the prisoner, but he pretended to slumber on.

"Wake up, buddy," I announced, my voice still thick with inhaled smoke. "The parole fairy's here."

He rolled over on his bunk, cat-quick, to study me with a wary eye.

I slid his door open and stepped back. I had no idea what he was in for, but then, I really had no clear picture what I was in for, either. "We're leaving," I told him, and moved to the adjoining cell before he could argue or question me.

By now, the noise had awakened the other prisoners, and they clamored to be set free, like animals at the pound. I tossed the second set of keys to the first prisoner I had freed, and told him to get busy on the other side of the corridor. I could see him bristle at the brusqueness of my command, but he did as he was told.

"Who died and made you boss?" he asked as he set about his task.

"Couple of guards," I told him. "If you were boss material, you wouldn't have needed me to unlock your cell."

That didn't set well, but I didn't have time to campaign on the popular ballot. Anyway, the straw poll taken at the exit of each cell seemed to mark me as the clear favorite. The people had spoken.

On the upper floor, I heard another crash as something collapsed. The entire building shook, and puffs of plaster and dust rained down from the ceiling. We all stood still, and waited for the building to collapse in fiery ruin around us. It didn't...this time. Without water to fight the fire, it would only be a matter of time before the upper structure collapsed, pancaking the floors below. I didn't want to be here when that happened, and for whatever crimes these men may have committed, I didn't think they should perish like rats trapped in their cages.

"What's the plan...*boss?*" the first prisoner asked as he finished unlocking the last door.

Another rumble, this one louder, deeper, like a giant trying to clear a bone caught in his throat. The structure was weakening, twisting, shifting. Another shower of plaster and dust rattled down on us, and a steel I-beam punched through the ceiling, falling into one of the vacated cells. Cracks appeared in the floor like bolts of black lightning.

"Get out of here as fast as we can," I answered.

"I guess that's a good enough plan," one of the others agreed. "Good enough for my taste, anyway."

It was only half true that I had freed the others to spare them a cruel end. Mostly, I had made the effort because

I thought they would provide whatever secondary distraction was necessary to give me the chance to escape. Between the fire that threatened to consume the prison and the riot that was about to erupt, I felt somewhat confident in my chances. Besides, for all the guards knew, I had perished in the infirmary blast.

I really thought we were going to make it...until we exploded out of the stairwell onto the ground floor just as the morning shift of guards was arriving. They had probably seen the fire, which was visible for several blocks around, and hurried to lend their aid.

There was a momentary, absolute comic stillness, when each side stood like statues, facing the opposition. And then the prisoner I had freed first—I had come to think of him as my second-in-command—let loose a bloodcurdling war-whoop, and I thought I had an idea what the legendary rebel yell must have sounded like.

"Smash the bastards to hell!" he cried, and that broke the frozen moment and gave time the forward shove it needed to get moving again.

There were perhaps nine of us, and easily double that number of guards, and they were armed with weapons the like of which I'd never seen. They had no guns, but their sidearms were no less deadly for that. They carried homemade weapons, clubs wrapped with rusted coils of barbed wire, or studded with nails, or gardening shears, blades slightly parted like the beak of a hungry bird. One guard carried something akin to a cestus, but it was a pair of brass knuckles with short, wedge-like blades protruding from each knuckle. For every guard, there was a different type of weapon, the only limit being that particular guard's imagination or capacity for violence. So far as I could see, the only difference between the guards and the prisoners was on which side of the bars you stood.

Violence always looks so smooth and choreographed in the movies, and that's because it's been rehearsed over and over, until any potential for mishap has been sanded down, like a rough plank. In reality, violence is loud, and sloppy, and clumsy. The guards were armed, but we were desperate.

As the barbed-wire mace descended, laying open one prisoner's face, another prisoner clambered over his back and wrenched the club away from the guard. He flipped it around, caught the handle, and swung it like a baseball bat, ripping open the guard's jugular.

The cestus blade dug deep between the ribs of my second-in-command, but it brought his tormentor close enough for the prisoner to wrap his muscled arms around the guard's neck and twist. There was a loud, wet snapping sound, and the guard was suddenly looking back over his own shoulder. He was dead, but my lieutenant was caught up in a red haze, and he kept twisting and ratcheting the dead man's lolling head.

I watched in sick horror as the shears buried themselves in the base of his neck. The guard pulled back, releasing the blades with a muddy sucking sound, and swung again. The blades buried themselves to the hilt between the prisoner's shoulder blades, and still my second-in-command refused to die. He lurched forward, pulling the handle from the guard's grip. He staggered about the room, cestus blades still embedded between his ribs, shears buried between his shoulders. It was like watching Rasputin take everything Yusupov and Purishkevich threw at him and come back for more.

By now, the prisoners had broken the legs from chairs in the entry hall, and were using them as bludgeons. The sound was chilling as bones broke, then splintered, under the continued beating. The walls dripped with bright, gaudy splashes of blood, and sanguine pools gathered on the floor. Where the combatants had struggled through the bloody puddles, red footprints marked the floor like a grisly parody of an Arthur Murray dance lesson.

I held back from the battle, telling myself I wasn't a fighter, but the truth is, I was afraid. I had freed these men to create a diversion so I could escape, and now they were paying the price for my callowness. And still, knowing all that, I couldn't bring myself to fight, whether I might have made a difference or not. I prayed, but even that was selfish. I prayed for my own safety, my own escape. If I could have reached the doors without passing through the heart of the bloody rioting, I would have been gone.

Nearby, in the open elevator shaft, something like a comet went blazing past; that something looked like a burning man, and his screams were terrible but brief, as he struck the basement floor one flight down. A jerking, fitful light illuminated the walls of the shaft. The burning man, of course. A few sparks billowed and skirled upward, riding the air currents, chasing after one another like playful summer fireflies.

I was too intent on what had just happened in the elevator shaft to notice the guard who had managed to get near me, and it was only the grunt of breath as he raised the club over his head that alerted me to his presence in time to dodge the skull-cleaving blow. Nevertheless, I wasn't fast enough, because his cudgel struck my shoulder and I felt my arm go numb. I sank to one knee, gagging in pain. I looked up, and saw he was streaked with blood. How much of it was his own, I didn't know.

He smiled, a jagged, jack-o'-lantern grin, and raised the club.

Sara. I thought, and waited for the deathblow, head lowered, eyes closed. I heard the sound I was coming to know quite well already, the sound metal scraping against bone makes, and a hot, sticky rain pattered down on my cheek and the back of my neck. I jerked my head up and saw the guard standing there, a look of stunned disbelief on his face. He let the club clatter out of his hands and his head seemed too heavy for his neck to support. His throat had been slit from ear to ear, down to his spine. He fell like a bundle of loose rags, and I saw the face of my savior: Rasputin.

He swayed unsteadily on his feet, a sailor in a sudden squall, but his eyes were clear. "That part of your plan, boss?" he asked. "T'get 'cherself killed?"

I had to admit it wasn't.

He nodded at the jar of ether I still had tucked into my waistband. "What's so important you couldn't've dropped that t'defend yourself?" he asked, and blinked. I suppose the world was starting to lose its sharp focus for him.

"It's an explosive," I told him, standing, holding the bottle as I did.

Rasputin shook his head. Clearly, explosives were not common in this place.

Even as the battle was winding down around us, the inner doors opened and the guards who had been fighting the losing battle with the fire above burst into the lobby. It was an odd folding back of time. Just a few minutes earlier, we had been the ones to emerge from the stairwell to face superior numbers, and now, the roles were reversed, although their numbers were still greater.

Several of the prisoners had fled the building as soon

as they had fought their way clear. The rest lay tangled with their killers on the floor. That just left Rasputin, myself, and a volatile bottle of ether. Rasputin waded into the mix, not allowing the guards the chance to exit the narrow doorway. They'd have to fight him one at a time.

"Whatever you're gonna do, you'd better hurry up!" he shouted as he impaled the first man on the cestus he had dug from his own rib cage.

He was right. I uncorked the jar of ether and jammed the last of the surgical gauze into the open neck, leaving a few inches dangling. I grabbed one of the candles from the wall and held it near the makeshift fuse.

"Get clear!"

"Just do it!"

"You'll die, too!"

"I'm already dead!" he shouted back, and vanished under the crush of guards. They stumbled over him, still fighting, and began to advance on me.

I hesitated, but there was nothing else I could do. He was as good as dead, and I was, too, if they got their hands on me. I touched the guttering candle flame to the strip of gauze and began backing toward the door as the fuse burned down. I suppose I was still hoping Rasputin would miraculously emerge from the swarm of guards and race with me for freedom, but he was down. I cursed the loss as much as my own indecision and weakness and threw the Molotov cocktail at the guards, watching it tumble end over end as it flew.

I bolted down the last few steps to the outer doors, the force of the blast pushing me along, shoving me out into the early morning streets of downtown Los Angeles.

CHAPTER SEVEN

Science begins with observation and moves on to hypothesis. Science is also fluid and ever changing to incorporate new data, but it usually doesn't happen as quickly as stepping outside a burning building and into a semi-familiar city street.

I had deluded myself into believing the portal had transported me to a parallel world, similar to the one I left but technologically retarded. The evidence in front of me made me discard that theory and just accept what I'd been trying very hard to deny. This was my planet, but not my world.

There were cars parked at curbside, or abandoned, or crashed into one another in the broad middle of Venice Boulevard. They'd been stripped and cannibalized for parts, though not for engine parts, I saw. They were untouched because...well, because they were too technologically advanced for these people, I supposed. The hulks of automobile metal had been left to rust. Pools of oil and coolant and gasoline painted murky rainbows on the pavement where the radiators or fuel tanks had simply rusted through. I stood open-mouthed and shaking my head. How long would something like that take?

I moved closer to the nearest car—a police cruiser, of

course—half-fearing I'd find a decomposing corpse seated behind the wheel, one hand clutching a mocha-latte, the other locked around a cell phone, as if whatever had caused this had been sudden and caught everyone by surprise as they went about their daily business. But the car, although reeking of mildew, was long since empty. I leaned in through the open window: the radio was untouched, and the keys still dangled from the ignition stalk.

I looked up and caught my own reflection in the askew rearview mirror, and again I was looking at a face I knew not to be mine—and yet a face I knew well. I noticed the upper part of my body in the mirror as well, and blinked in surprise at how broad my shoulders were, and how thick and corded my neck. I would have allowed I might have been in a coma for a few days, perhaps even a few weeks, but muscles tend to atrophy in such cases, not pump up like some bodybuilder on a steroid crash-diet.

Whatever the truth was—and I was starting to think *this* was it and the life I thought I remembered from before was nothing but a fever-dream or a hallucination caused by the obvious beating I'd taken—I wouldn't find it by standing here. I had to get as far away from this place as I could, before the authorities came looking for me.

I glanced back at the jailhouse, and watched a thick plume of smoke billow out of the shattered windows and collapsed walls of the top stories. It would only be a matter of minutes before the top floors burned through.

I turned onto La Cienega Boulevard, feeling the long city blocks devoured by my easy stride. I felt invincible in this body.

As I ran, I passed countless parked or crashed cars, SUVs, even semis, their doors broken open, their cargo emptied and made off with, if it was something useable; if it was a shipment of electronics, the cartons were simply thrown to the streets. Hundreds of thousands of dollars worth of wide-screen plasma televisions lay strewn down the length of La Cienega.

The shop fronts had also been broken into, looted of valuables, or, I should say, looted of *essentials*, like food, clothes, knives, but not TVs, stereos, or, oddly, guns. From Wilshire I made my way to Rodeo Drive, the swank shopping place where all the name brands had once gathered. Although there was damage to these shops, they didn't appear to have been looted. Of course, tastefully designed bars protected the doors and windows, but I didn't think that was what kept the looters out. There just wasn't anything here that mattered anymore. I passed unbroken windows, where glittering, jewel-encrusted watches, diamond necklaces, and rings sat, where they had sat for many years, so long that spiders had worked them into several generations of webs. It was oddly beautiful.

Most of the buildings I saw were undamaged, but a few of them had been burned down, perhaps by looters, but more likely when people fled their homes, leaving the gas burner on, or an outlet had overloaded, or a cigarette had been left unattended. No fire departments responded to the emergencies, no sprinkler systems slowed the flames.

I wandered on, glancing back over my shoulder periodically, with the unnerving feeling of being followed. Whenever I looked, I was quite alone. Even the prisoners I had freed were nowhere to be seen, clambered back into whatever bolthole they had been rousted from by the authorities; I no longer thought of it as the law, or the police.

I stopped to study my reflection in the intact, grimy shop windows as I passed them, feeling like Narcissus on a particularly vain day, but I couldn't help it. My upper body was solidly muscled, with a tapered waist and long, powerful looking arms. A couple of times, I was sure it wasn't my reflection, but some stranger standing inside one of the shops, looking out at this curious little man who was so clearly out of place.

In that regard, nothing had changed. Sara and I had come here once to see where they filmed parts of *Pretty Woman,* and we felt as if the hoi polloi were looking at us like we'd just torched a busload of nuns, war orphans, and fuzzy blind puppies.

I turned along Santa Monica, unable to shake the feeling of being followed, but unable to find empirical evidence to support my theory. I stopped, ostensibly to study my reflection once more, and thought this time I caught a flurry of movement behind me, but it was difficult to tell in the sooty glass.

I kept moving, coming at last to the place I suppose I always knew I was headed: the public library. I climbed the low, broad steps and found the double doors open, hanging aslant on their hinges. I stepped cautiously across the threshold, into the cool shadows. At once, I became aware of the overwhelming stench of mildew and rot, and the smell of mouse droppings. I imagined domestic animals, turned loose to fend for themselves, had probably formed packs, hunting for prey and shelter, and many deserted buildings such as this were no doubt home to many wild animals...insects...even people. They had to be somewhere, although were it not for my experience at the prison, I might be inclined to think there were no people, based on all the data I'd seen since then.

Row upon dusty row of computers sat, screens broken.

I didn't bother with the microfiche machines—there wouldn't be any electricity, and even if there were, I doubted the library had bothered to transfer newspapers to microfiche when whatever happened...happened.

I moved deeper into the library, my footsteps kicking up chalky clouds of dust; I looked down, and saw some form of fungoid growth, like cancerous mushrooms, had sprung up through the weave of the thin carpeting. Down long, shadow-choked stacks, I saw piles of books lying on the floor between shelves like birds with broken backs. The pages had been torn or chewed, doubtless by rats and insects looking for nest material.

The newspapers in the periodicals room were in even worse shape than the books. Still, I dug into the pile of papers carefully, lest the brittle, yellow pages crumble at my touch. I selected the *L.A. Times*, and flipped through the pile until I came to September 2003.

My rummaging disturbed a horrible sight: A millipede, I suppose, but it was gigantic, two or more feet in length, its segmented body as large as a preschooler's pop-bead blocks. I felt my skin rash out in gooseflesh, and I was certain more of the hideous things were crawling over me, up my back, across my neck and arms. I had to grab the papers and leave the suddenly claustrophobic periodicals room, making certain to shake the pile of papers as I did.

In the main room, lit by a decorative roundel of skylight, I found a carrel that was relatively free of dirt and detritus. As I looked around a bit more, I saw there were many dead and desiccated insect husks, each about the size of a man's fist, many of them from some genus I didn't recognize. I sat down to pore over my past. If I just had a dog and a pair of slippers and a cup of coffee, it would be like any Sunday morning at home.

Almost at once, I found the paper I was looking for. The headlines positively screamed the news at me: **WAR OF THE WORLDS!** I checked the date: September 12, 2003. It was the day after we unhooked the velvet rope and let...well, I still didn't really know what we had let into our little nightclub, but at least this crumbling relic from a past that was near, or distant, proved it was not a fever-dream. The more I read, the more I wished it were.

> THE INVADING FORCES USED MAN'S OWN CURIOSITY TO LAUNCH A WORLDWIDE SNEAK ATTACK, KILLING DOZENS OF MILITARY PERSONNEL AND ONLOOKERS. IN A SYNCHRONIZED ASSAULT, THE ALIENS SENT TERRIBLE WEAPONS OF MASS DESTRUCTION THROUGH THE ACTIVATED TELEPORTALS IN BOTH JAPAN AND THE U.S. THE INVADERS QUICKLY MOVED TO ESTABLISH A STRONGHOLD AROUND THE TELEPORTALS, AND REPORTS THAT OTHER GATES IN THE U.K. AND CHINA HAVE SOMEHOW BEEN BROUGHT ONLINE HAVE NOT BEEN CONFIRMED.
>
> AMONG THE MISSING IS PAUL STEIN, 36, THE ASTRONOMER WHO FIRST RECEIVED THE FATEFUL MESSAGE FROM SPACE...

There was a photo of the gate, a blurry image of something huge in the bright light that filled the portal. Below that, a small black-and-white photo of me, and I recognized when it had been taken. It was when we held the press conference, way back in the sensible days of late 2000, to announce we had made contact with a sentient life form in the Alpha Centauri system.

There was a list of known fatalities and the names of those missing in action, but there was no mention of

Sara or Maryvonne. They had managed to get away, presumably.

U.S. FIGHTING BACK

–September 13, 2003

ARMY AIRBORNE TROOPS PARACHUTED INTO THE ALIEN-HELD, FORMER MILITARY BASE UNDER COVER OF DARKNESS.

JUMPING FROM LOW-FLYING PLANES INTO THE NORTHERN CALIFORNIA NIGHT, AN ESTIMATED 1,000 PARATROOPERS LANDED NEAR FORT BRAGG, NOW UNDER ALIEN OCCUPATION. FIGHTING IS REPORTED TO BE FIERCE AND HEAVY, BUT FURTHER CONTACT WITH THE PARATROOPERS HAD NOT BEEN ESTABLISHED. IT IS FEARED THE MEN HAVE EITHER BEEN KILLED OR CAPTURED.

JAPAN REPORTED SIMILAR HEAVY FIREFIGHTS, AS DO THE U.K. AND CHINA. THE PRESIDENT OF THE UNITED STATES SAID, "VICTORY OVER THE FORCES OF EVIL IS ONLY A MATTER OF TIME," AND ADDED, "THERE WILL BE A DAY OF RECKONING FOR THE ALIEN INVADERS, AND THAT DAY IS DRAWING NEAR."

There was a gap of several days' worth of papers, and I couldn't guess whether I had left them back in the periodicals room, of if the papers had even been published those days. I don't suppose it really mattered, because the next paper pretty much summed it up.

ALIEN INVADERS USE EMP

–October 6, 2003

COMMUNICATIONS AND DEFENSIVE WEAPONRY WERE KNOCKED OUT WITHIN A 50-MILE RADIUS WHEN THE INVADERS DETONATED AN ELECTROMAGNETIC PULSE

WEAPON, WHICH KNOCKS OUT ALL MECHANICAL DEVICES. THE LAST REPORT FROM U.S. FORCES STATIONED NEAR THE ALIEN BEACHHEAD WAS THAT THE INVADERS WERE ERECTING SEVERAL MORE OF THE TELEPORTALS NEAR THE ORIGINAL. IT IS SUSPECTED THE ALIENS WILL USE THESE ADDITIONAL GATES TO BRING THROUGH LARGER ASSAULT FORCES, OR POSSIBLY WEAPONS OF MASS DESTRUCTION.

CIVIL AUTHORITIES ARE URGING ALL CITIZENS TO STOCK UP ON ESSENTIAL SUPPLIES AND MOVE TO A PLACE OF SAFETY...

The story continued along those lines, and stated that top scientists and military strategists had seemingly been targeted by forces unknown, but it was easy to speculate the alien invaders, who still had not made their demands known to their earthling hosts, were behind the disappearances and deaths.

I spent the next hour or two sifting though the papers, reading about Earth's futile attempts to retaliate, then negotiate, all to no avail. There was another gap in the sequence of publications, but the last paper in the pile, not much more than a Christmas newsletter, was the ol' one-two punch, the O. Henry ending I suppose I had known was coming. Even so, I had to look at the headline again to make sure I was reading it right, or, indeed, if it was even an English paper, because in massive, uneven block letters, the headline proclaimed:

SURNDER!!!!

Below that, in the sidebar reserved for these things, it said: LUCKY NUMBERS: NONE. LUCKY STARS: COUNT EM IF YA GOT EM. WEATHER: CHYEAH! The date was nothing more than a series of ???????????? and the rest of the story made no more sense than the headline, full of incoherent sentences and misspellings. It was as if animals had suddenly mastered the skill of typing, but hadn't quite grasped the finer points of spelling or punctuation. It read:

ERTH GIVVS IN TOO ALLEN INVADS WE LOSE GOD HAV MURCY ON ARE SOLS...

It was like reading the unhinged ramblings of a madman. What had happened? It degenerated from there to a string of vowels and consonants slammed together like particles in a super-collider:

JJJKKMOOS KAA RAHA FEH HEPBA. (STRY CONTINYOOS PAYGE TOO)

Below that, there was a childish drawing, presumably of the alien invaders, and a smaller, terror-stricken figure labeled "me" next to it. Huge cartoon tears, the size of coy fish, leaped from the stickman's eyes.

I felt as if the millipedes were crawling all over me again, but it was nothing more than a chill radiating from the core of my being. I continued staring at the paper, as if I was the one out of whack; I looked at the earlier paper, just to make sure I hadn't suffered a cerebral blowout: WAR OF THE WORLDS!

And I looked again at the thin tract that I held. SURNDER!!!!

No, nothing wrong with me. I wasn't insane, just incredibly confused. I laid the thin sheaf of paper carefully aside, partly to preserve this last, however tenuous, connection to my past and my old world, but mostly because I could almost feel the insanity and panic squirming in those gibberish words...as if contact with them for too long would infect me with their madness.

I slapped my hands on my thighs and pushed away from the carrel. I had to get moving again, find someplace safe to hole up while I figured out what to do. No; I had to find Sara and Maryvonne, *that's* what I had to do. I wondered why I kept doing that, as if some part of me had already accepted they were gone.

I crossed the great room and descended the steps to the street, trying to make sense of everything I had read. No one knew what had happened to me. Paul Stein was just...gone. It seemed that whatever had happened had slapped me out of my time and into this one. It just remained to be seen how far into the future I had been bumped, and if it was possible to reverse this. The paper said top scientists and military strategists were being targeted, disappearing...could they have been sent ahead in time, as I was? But one look around the ruined city put the lie to that idea. Whatever had happened to them was in no way connected to what had happened to me.

There was a sound to my left and I turned to look, expecting to see the authorities, but I was surprised to see a woman of breathtaking beauty and perfection, her hair long and golden in the early morning sunlight; her legs were long and well-turned. Our eyes met and before I could speak, she turned on her heel and started to run from me.

"Wait!" I called after her. "I'm not going to hurt you! I want to talk to you!"

I started running after her, chasing her down the broad avenue, darting in and out between the abandoned cars. But as fast as I was, she was faster still, and I never seemed to lessen the distance between us. If I would have had any sense...well, I'm getting ahead of myself.

"Stop!" I called again, knowing I should just use that breath for running instead.

She reached the four-way intersection, racing down the wide-open middle lanes, when the lid flew off the manhole she had just run over, and a spider the size of a German shepherd sprang out, its hideous, long, jointed legs scrabbling crazily after the woman.

Trap-door spider, I heard my inner reference librarian inform me. *They hide underground and wait for vibrations on their hiding place to tell them prey is near, and then it drags its prey down into its nest and...*

I thought of the techno-dragonfly, and thought, *It isn't real, is it?* And then I thought, *What difference does it make? She'll still be just as dead.*

I had stood by and done nothing at the prison and several men died because of that. They were criminals, yes, killers, probably, but men all the same. Whatever place this was, I was no longer the man I had been in my time. I had been reborn into a powerful new body, and it was no longer acceptable to do nothing. I was sprinting for the spider before I knew it, letting my body take over, doing what had to be done before my brain could question the wisdom of this course of action.

The spider was half-in and out of its hiding place, the manhole cover resting on its bulbous back. It would grab the girl, drag her down into its hiding place, the trap door banging shut, trapping her in the pit with it, where it would inject her with paralyzing venom, and then...Oh, and then...I didn't want to think about that, because her fate could too easily become mine if I miscalculated.

I launched myself, coming down flat-footed on the manhole cover. My weight drove the spider back down into the pit, the closing lid scissoring off its two foremost legs in a sickening gout of thick, snot-green liquid. The legs, big around as a fence post, twitched and jittered and tried to drag themselves along the asphalt. The coarse, spikelike hairs glittered in the sunlight.

"Are you all r–"

That was all I managed before the spider, bitter as an ex-wife whose spouse hit the Irish Lottery the day after their divorce became final, burst once more out of its pit, mandible clacking like furious castanets, stinger dripping numbing poison, its eight eyes burning with a mindless, insectile hatred.

Trap door spiders are fast, relying on their speed and the element of surprise to snare their prey. Fortunately, they weren't built for running races, and amputation of its two forelegs made it clumsy. It was angry, however, and determined, and came thundering down the street after me. It ran with its head low, its thorax in the air, quivering like a black egg yolk on a sextant's tower of legs.

The girl was screaming something, but I couldn't tell what over the bucking of my own heart. I glanced back and saw the spider was much closer than I would have liked, and that slowed me enough for the tip of its taloned leg to rake down my back. I was almost helpless with terror, because there it was, the Miss Universe of arachnophobia, every horrible, unspeakable fear the darkness holds, all of man's deepest, darkest nightmares all rolled up and tucked into one egg-shaped body and a set of chittering legs. Whatever else man may evolve away from, this deep-rooted, almost supernatural fear, would forever be embedded in his genes.

I dodged left and ran right, throwing myself into the open driver's door of a parked SUV. I fought to slam the door shut; its hinges had rusted, and I just knew I wouldn't make it, when the spider accidentally helped me. Its monstrous body thudded into the outside of the door, pushing it closed. Its grotesque face was pressed to the window in a moment, smearing its poison on the glass. I could hear its hairy legs scrabble and scrape over the door and roof, like nails scraping metal. The spider tried to shake the car, and if it ever realized it could break the glass, it would all be over for me.

I had trapped myself, and the spider, far from losing interest, grew frenzied and furious. Its claw-tipped legs raked the steel, gouging long grooves and troughs in the side of the SUV. Sooner or later, it would simply shred the metal and force its way in. I climbed into the back, looking for a weapon, and found a heavy black tire iron tucked away in the spare wheel well. It would have to do.

I looked out the window of the cargo hold and didn't see the spider on either side of the car. I had lost sight of it while I was searching for a weapon, and sat as paralyzed with indecision as if I'd been doped-up with the spider's toxin. Had it gotten tired and gone away, in search of other food? It didn't seem likely, and yet...

I slipped to the rear and quietly opened the hatch. I had to put a little shoulder into it, but it opened easier than the driver's door closed, because these hinges, at least, hadn't been exposed directly to the elements. I crouched there in the rear hatch, the iron gripped so tight in my sweaty palm that my forearm shook. Nothing. I eased one leg out of the SUV, and the moment my toes touched the ground, I knew I had made a terrible mistake.

The spider had been waiting for me under the SUV, and snared my leg with its own. It pulled me out of the hatch and onto the pavement, trying to drag me under the car with it, near enough to inject me with its venom-tipped stinger. I dropped the tire iron and grabbed the bumper and held fast, resisting its strength, its bristly, angled leg hairs embedding themselves in the meat of my calf and thigh. The pain was excruciating, like hundreds of needles burrowing under my flesh, but I ignored it as it pulled me again, dragging me a little farther under the SUV, banging my head on the bumper. My vision filled with purple splashes like skyrockets, and I felt my scab-crusted injury begin to spill fresh blood into my eyes.

I gripped the tire iron where I had dropped it, and the spider whisked me closer. I could feel broken glass and gravel cut into my back. Before I lost the courage, and before I became trapped in that enclosed space under the SUV, I rammed the wedge end of the jack into the spider's open, ravenous maw... Deep...deeper...until I felt its mandibles brush against my knuckles.

It let go of me, and I hauled myself out from underneath the car with the aid of the bumper. I was hoping the spider would forget about me, but spiders have simple nervous systems, making it difficult to land a blow in a fatal spot. It would simply keep coming and coming until it wore me out. I pushed to my feet and ran, leg on fire from the hundreds of hairs still piercing my flesh, stumbling and larruping. Behind me, the spider scrambled out from beneath the SUV and resumed its single-minded pursuit.

I dodged and weaved between the parked and deserted cars littering the street, but the spider simply skated along over the roofs and hoods, leaping from car to car like a man jumping from stone to stone in a running stream. It was only its amputated forelegs that slowed it down enough for me to have survived this long, but it was adapting, learning the new rhythm of six instead of eight.

I stumbled up the steps of the library, the spider close

behind, like a panhandler that just won't take "no" for an answer. I had a plan, a desperate one, but no doubt better than hoping for a giant shoe to fall out of the sky and crush my nemesis.

I disappeared among the stacks while the spider hesitated in the doorway, sensing the room for danger and, finding none, entered.

The spider moved between the stacks, its probing legs sweeping books from the shelves. My other plan, no more likely, was for this spider's natural nemesis, such as a wasp, to have likewise mutated to gigantic proportions and fortuitously have its nest hidden away in the library, but that would leave me with a giant wasp to contend with.

It spotted me in the cross-aisle, and rather than following me, it scampered up the side of the bookshelf and began racing across the top of the stacks, leaping from Dewey decimal to Dewey decimal, from fiction to science-fiction to western to romance. I ran down the center aisle at the ends of the bookshelves, the spider keeping pace with me on its own little path over my head. Books, bloated with water-swollen pages, exploded under the spider's weight, raining choking clouds of confetti down in its wake. And then the spider did what I had been hoping it would do: It raced ahead of me, reaching the last standing bookshelf, where it would follow nature's genetic program and lay in wait.

I ducked into the path parallel with the shelves, and threw my full weight against the freestanding units. The stack shuddered, and books shook off the shelf, but that was it. I threw myself against the unit once more, and this time it started to go over. I kept pushing, feeling my muscles shake from the strain, until the bookcase passed its point of balance and toppled with a loud crash into the next unit, and the next, like a string of giant dominoes.

The spider was perched atop the last bookcase, waiting to pounce down upon me as I ran down the end aisle, but now it sensed the danger and reacted as I'd hoped. It leaped down to the floor, just as the falling line of heavy wooden shelves knocked over the last unit, pinning the spider beneath the crushing weight of books and bookcases.

A tremendous chalky cloud of dust and mildew filled the air, making it impossible to see if my plan had worked, but at last the smoke parted, and I could see the spider's legs flailing in their death-throes, the frenzied thrashing growing weak, then weaker, then stopping altogether.

I doubled over, hands on my knees, trying to catch a breath and slow my hummingbird heart. When I was finally able to lift my head, I saw the girl standing in the doorway, watching me.

"You all right?" I asked.

She nodded. "Yes. Are you?" She smiled, and there was something magical about it, something soothing.

"Yeah," I said, and returned her smile. It was the first time I smiled since finding myself here. "Yeah, I think I will be."

CHAPTER EIGHT

She said her name was Jasmine, but the rest of my questions would just have to wait. I was starting to get used to that, but she was right—we had to get out of here before the authorities organized themselves enough to launch a search detail for the escaped prisoners, and the city had already proven itself an unsafe place to be.

Jasmine lifted a sidewalk grating and dropped lightly down into the tunnel. She looked up at me. "Well?" she said. "Are you coming, or not?"

I hesitated, then climbed down after her into the warren of access tunnels that ran just below the surface of the sidewalks. I fought down a shudder, as unbidden images of the trap-door spider and its underground nest came to my mind. She saw the look on my face and smiled.

"It's safe here," she said. "We have patrols that check all the time."

I wrestled the grating back into place, lest something unfriendly decided to try to make these tunnels a home before the patrols checked again. Then I followed her through the narrow, winding passages, the underground utility access that connected the city's now useless electrical and steam pipes.

The tunnels were cramped, the pipes on all sides of us, even above, and I had to walk in a crouch to avoid banging my head on an exposed pipe as big around as a suspension bridge cable. The passages were dark, broken only by the intermittent light that entered through the sidewalk gratings just over our heads, and I had the uneasy feeling of being in a submarine prowling beneath the streets of Los Angeles.

I have no idea how long I followed her in silence; whenever I tried to ask her anything, she would simply raise a hand, tell me to wait, and lead me onward. She moved with a catlike grace, obviously having traversed this route many countless times before. I had a feeling she could have run this labyrinth blindfolded, certainly faster than we were walking now. I realized she was walking deliberately slow, so I could follow.

We came at last to a featureless gray steel door sunk into the brick wall, no more prominent than any of the other countless steel doors we'd passed along our route. She opened it without hesitation or uttering a word to me, as if it was a given I would follow her...which, it was.

I knew she could have been the two-legged equivalent of the trap-door spider, taking me deeper underground for her own dinner party, but I trusted her as I'd trusted no one since waking in this who-knows-how-distant future. As I'd trusted Sara implicitly the moment I saw her face and shy smile.

"Steps," she warned me as we entered the darkened room. I couldn't see anything, but I sensed her nearby, and I felt a slight breeze. Wherever she was taking me, there was another opening somewhere ahead. I pressed my right palm to the wall and slowly, carefully descended the steps. The last thing I needed was a broken leg...or neck.

We reached the bottom and I overstepped, stumbling into Jasmine. I could feel her wonderful, firm body against mine, and she laughed, her lips next to my ear. I held her a moment longer than I had to, but she didn't seem to mind.

She took my hand and led me on. I smelled raw earth. We paused again, and she opened another door and stepped through, pulling me along behind her. The room into which she led me was darker than the tunnel, and I could tell from the sound that this chamber, whatever it was, was vast. As my eyes grew accustomed to the darkness, I became aware of flickering points of light, like stars in the night sky, bristling with secrets best left untold.

I heard voices nearby, but the chamber was so huge it swallowed the sound, leaving the words unintelligible noises. One of the voices was Jasmine's; the others sounded like men.

"Where am I?" I asked, forcing my bravado. "Who are you? Show yourselves, now."

"You don't give the orders," a man's voice informed me. I saw now the half-illuminated shapes of men, women, children, standing in a loose semicircle, turned to study me.

"Who does?" I asked, making it sound like a challenge. I suppose it was.

"I do," the same voice told me in a tone that said that was the end of it. I knew better. I knew it was really only the beginning.

My eyes took that last step toward adjusting to the darkness and I saw the room we were standing in was as huge as a cathedral, the walls made of glazed brick that curved gradually as they rose, forming an arched vault overhead. The room itself—the north and the south of it—stretched away and away, either end shrouded in shadow, and I knew where we were.

My father had told me about this place: Once, in the 1940s, Los Angeles had its own subway system. Although most of the line was actually above ground, the first few miles of track, below Union Station, were underground. When the subway closed a few years after opening, the tunnels were sealed up and forgotten. Even after they were rediscovered by a curious security guard in the 1990s, they were still largely unknown.

I recognized some of the faces now as the light seemed to grow brighter. I had freed two or three of these men from prison earlier today.

"All right," I said, dropping the issue of leadership for the moment. "What do I call you?"

"Jude," he said, and offered a warrior's handshake, our hands clasping high up the forearm of the other man, his on the outside of mine.

"I'm—" I started, then hesitated. I wasn't really sure who I was.

"I know who you are," Jude said, and released my arm. Still, I noticed he had to give it a testing squeeze first, as if taking my measure, the first step in the inevitable macho pissing contest. "You're all I've heard about today."

He nodded, and the faces I recognized from prison stepped forward. "That him?"

"I guess," one of the prisoners said. "Seemed bigger at the time."

"It's him," the other prisoner said, decisively. "Look at those eyes. Crazy. You don't forget eyes like that."

The first man studied me again, and said that was for sure. Crazy.

Jude nodded, and that settled the matter of my identity, even though I'd never seen him before a few moments ago. "You're welcome to stay with us," he told me, this time really seeing me. If the stories the prisoners had told about me were true, I was a potential threat to his position.

"Thanks," I said. "I'd like to stay for a while."

Jasmine stepped forward, her palm lightly touching my arm, her blue eyes dancing lively as they sought—and found—mine. "Thank you," she said, and kissed my cheek. The warmth of her breath on my skin, the gentle touch of her lips, sending an electric tingle through my body, jangling my nerve endings, all made me know in that instant she was going to be mine.

"Do they all get that big?" I asked her, not sure quite what to talk about. "Insects? I saw a millipede at the library that must have been two feet long."

She gave me the look I was coming to know pretty well, since I'd seen it on the faces of just about everyone I met in the past few days: It was the look that combined the question, "Are you kidding?" with "Are you speaking Moon-Man?"

"Many are bigger," she told me, studying my head. She placed a tender hand there, brushing my fallen locks away. I winced slightly, aware of the lump growing above my eye and the tautness of the skin over it. "Don't you know that? You must have seen them."

"I'm still a little shaken," I answered. I had to be careful; my presence here was allowed, not guaranteed. I didn't want to say or do anything to make them think I was anything other than what I seemed to be.

"Told you," the second prisoner said. "Crazy."

"It's a bad bump," she agreed, shifting to her nurturing mode. "Does it hurt?"

"Nothing a handful of Tylenol couldn't fix," I replied, glibly, knowing as I said it Tylenol hadn't been on anybody's store shelves anytime in the recent past.

"Handful of what?" she asked with a curious laugh.

"He'll live," Jude proclaimed. "Nothing a man can't handle." He interjected himself between Jasmine and me, like a dog defending its bone. There was no great love lost between him and me. I remember reading once, in a book about karma and reincarnation, that the people we feel instant animosity toward when we first meet them are those people from past lives with whom we have had bad dealings. I never really believed that...until now.

I'd always scoffed at the thought of reincarnation; for one thing, the numbers don't work, but as I got older–say, about the time I learned conclusively there was life on other planets–I suppose I started questioning my mortality and my place in the universe. Life is only energy, after all, and the law of conservation says energy can neither be created nor destroyed, only converted. Although that didn't go terribly far toward proving the existence of an afterlife, much less reincarnation, waking up to find myself in a body not my own, in a time not my own, certainly did make me begin to eschew the analytical for the supernatural...or at least the paranormal.

But I also knew Jude's instant dislike for me had nothing to do with any unresolved past-life business. He knew Jasmine was mine already.

One of the men I'd freed showed me to a place farther back in the tunnel where I could throw a blanket and have some privacy. He hesitated a moment, then nodded to himself, as if in agreement with some voice only he could hear. "You'd best watch yourself," he said.

"What do you mean?"

"She's a pretty one, all right, but she's Jude's, and no doubt about it," he told me, trying to hide his annoyance at my coyness. "You done me a kindness today and now I'm doin' you one by tellin' you to stay away from her. You don't want Jude to take a dislike to you."

"Jude a badass, is he?" I asked, feeling myself prickle at the warning, however good intentioned. "Doesn't like people playing around in his toybox?"

I knew word of this indirect challenge would reach Jude, but that was fine. I'd sooner face him on my terms, on my time, than wonder when the hammer was going to drop.

He shook his head and walked away. "Crazy," he muttered to himself. "Crazy."

A couple of the Tunnel Tots, as I called them, perhaps eight and ten years old, grub-faced and whip-thin, had followed us, hanging back enough so as not to be obtrusive, near enough so as not to be invisible or miss any of the conversation.

"You don't look so tough," the older boy ventured at last, when it was clear I was not going to speak first. Even the kids around here had their own version of the pissing contest. You still had to prove how tough you were, it was just a little better disguised, that's all.

"How tough?" I asked, sitting back on my coarse blanket. The train tracks had all been dug up long ago, the trains sold to foreign markets or burned. The floor was little more than hard-packed earth. It was home to these people. It was now home to me.

"Tough enough to do all them things what they say

you did," the older boy answered. He seemed emboldened enough by my question that he and his friend—or brother, I couldn't tell—felt they could move closer.

"What do they say I did?" I wasn't being coy this time—not completely. I thought this might be my chance to actually find out something about Max.

The boy looked around the tunnel, to make sure no one was close enough to overhear, "They say you killed some of the Masters," my unofficial biographer responded, his voice growing soft and conspiratorial. He sat cross-legged on the far edge of my blanket.

"The Masters?" I asked, casually. "You mean those poopheads?"

The boys looked at one another, noses crinkled, and burped out laughter. Some words are classics, no matter what era you might find yourself in.

"Yeah, the poopheads," the boys agreed, breaking out in freshets of laughter once more.

"I killed them," I said, and I knew it was true, just as I knew that was why I had been in prison, awaiting execution. I had answered their questions, and now it was time for them to answer some of mine. "How long have the Masters been here? How long have they been in charge?"

The younger boy shrugged. "Always," he said. "Long as anyone can 'member."

I didn't trust that anyone in this grated community had perfect recall, but I thought the boys were probably right in that regard, based on what I'd seen topside. The Masters had been here quite a while, as long as a generation, perhaps as much as two, certainly long enough for this generation to drift back into a second Dark Ages, one without lights, or cars, or even guns, but how could that knowledge have simply vanished so totally? Something like that could only happen if the oldest generation, the one that birthed this set of lives, had either all died at once, or had lost the knowledge before they could pass it down.

"Doesn't anybody fight the Masters?"

"The poopheads?" The boys looked solemn-faced at one another. "Fight them? No."

"No one but you," the young one said, his eyes wide with open admiration.

"No one? Why not? They can be killed. Didn't I prove that?"

"No one fights them," the older boy repeated, a little more stridently this time, as if someone might overhear.

"Am I no one?" I asked. "I fought them."

I could see the muscles just below the surface of skin covering the boy's jaw twitch as he struggled helplessly with these two contradictory truths. "No one—"

"—fights the Masters, I know," I finished. It seemed as if, with each successive generation, the will to fight, the urge to freedom, was being bred out of their genes. This boy was not much older than Vonnie, perhaps not even that old. Perhaps his hardscrabble life had simply made him look older than his actual years, and yet he had already accepted defeat, had embraced this non-life as his way. And if he were to look into his future, assuming he could imagine one, is that how he saw himself? Squatting in a dark, cold tunnel, hidden away from the light of the sun, until the end of his days? Would his children suffer a similar existence? Repeating that same frightened mantra: *No one fights the Masters.*

Thousands of years after leaving the caves, man had ended up right back where he started, and Paul Stein, if only peripherally, was responsible for that big red letter day. We talked a bit longer, the boys and I, but I was careful to avoid mentioning anything too politically incorrect that might upset them. Before long, their mother came to fetch them, telling them to leave me alone. But the look she gave me said she wasn't concerned about my "me-time" so much as she didn't want her children fraternizing with Mad Max. They said they'd see me later, and I said Sure.

I laid back on my horsehair blanket, and folded my arms behind my head and closed my eyes. The world spun dizzy-drunk around me as the fatigue of the day overtook me, and I could have sworn I heard someone whisper, "Crazy."

"Just give us a name, Max, and all this can stop."

"They wouldn't do this for you, you know, so why suffer for them?"

And when he said that, I *was* suffering. I opened my heavy eyes, puffed and sticky with my own blood, and looked at the faces of my tormentors, but I already knew who I'd see. I was back in prison, strung up in a featureless room—the interrogation room, I knew. I could just see my own reflection in the two-way glass off to my right. I was suspended by my arms, my toes just touching the linoleum floor. I looked down, saw a patina of blood—mine, mingled with countless others'—beneath my feet. My shoulders felt as if they were dislocating, the big muscles in my thighs trembling with the strain. Terrible cramps seized my calves, and when I tried to shift my weight from my protesting legs to my arms (my arms being twisted wrong-way around and pulled stiff and straight over my head and behind me, shackled at the wrists and suspended from the ceiling by chains), the agony in my shoulders would flare into hot life.

"One name can make all this—" one of my torturers

said, sensibly enough, spreading his arms to take in the interrogation room and, a little more nebulous, my misery "—go away."

The pain was so real, so urgent and insistent, I couldn't tell if it was a dream or actually happening. I blinked the fresh blood from my eyes, and looked at my tormentors. Strawberry-Nose, of course. What was a good old-fashioned, near-to-death beating without the party animal himself? The sensible man, whom I knew to be the commander of this little L.A. gulag, stood by, as well as another guard, his hands hanging in loose fists at his side, my blood dripping in slow, thick rivulets down his massive, hairy knuckles; the chaplain stood next to him. I suppose he was there in case I needed some last-minute last rites.

"Tell us where they're hiding," the commander continued, softly. His hand touched my cheek gently, almost fatherly. "Is that really so hard?"

His palm was still resting on my cheek as I suddenly whipped my head to the side and snapped my teeth shut on the meaty ball of his thumb. I tasted his hot, bitter blood spurt from his nearly severed digit and fill my mouth. I had to swallow it, or choke to death on it. He screamed, his voice starting out low and, well, *sensible,* then arpeggio-ing up through the octaves with a frightening ease.

Strawberry-Nose was on the job, cracking me on the chin with his club, making me bite down hard enough to crunch through the last bit of bone and ligament holding the thumb together.

The warden cursed something unintelligible and jammed his bleeding stump under his opposite armpit. Blood darkened the tunic under his good arm. He looked at me with angry, pain-maddened eyes and before he could make whatever threat he was building up to, I smiled and spit what I had been holding between my teeth at him. His thumb smacked against his cheek and held there a moment, sticky with blood and spit, before dropping to the floor.

The padre was at his side, trying to staunch the bleeding, looking at me with undisguised horror and contempt. "Max..." he muttered, as if he took this lapse in my etiquette personally. It wasn't as if I *swallowed* it.

"Give as many names and locations as you want," the commander said; even in that dim light, I could see his face was ashen with shock. "Your torture hasn't even begun."

The chaplain turned and led the commander from the room to, presumably, the infirmary. The commander paused at the door, long enough to give an unspoken order to the guards. Strawberry-Nose nodded gravely, and stepped out of the room with the commander and the padre.

The remaining guard tapped his nightstick against the callused palm of his left hand, casually, absently.

"Pretty good, Max," he said in the voice of a man paying a genuine compliment. "You truly are an animal—aren't you?"

I said nothing, but continued to stare at him.

"Like a mad dog," he continued, still tapping that baton against his palm. "Know what happens to mad dogs? Do you?"

I smiled, my teeth and lips still dark with the commander's sour blood. "They keep killing," I informed him.

That unnerved him for a moment. I knew he had been trying to lure me into relaxing, and then he would strike me in the ribs or kidneys with his baton, and I would be coughing up blood, but now he was rattled. I was chained and suspended from the ceiling, incapable of moving, and he was frightened of me.

Strawberry-Nose returned with an odd-looking affair I took to mean bad news for me right away.

"Tough man, huh, Max?" Strawberry-Nose asked, unrolling the bundle he was carrying. Unfurled now, I could see what it was, but still couldn't quite make sense of: it was a hood of some sort, perhaps sewn leather, or a bladder. "That help make the mate more attractive?" I asked, but I was starting to worry.

"Always a joke with you, isn't it, Max?" he asked, stepping forward with the hood. I could smell it, a mix of leather and something mean and onerous clinging to it. It looked like the kind placed over the condemned man's head just before hanging, but I doubted if they were made of leather. "Well, see if you can laugh your way through this," he said, and threw it over my head. He cinched it tightly around my throat with straps and buckles. I thought they meant to suffocate me, but I had badly underestimated the inventive cruelty of my hosts.

A small tube was attached to the crown of the hood, and air, however slight, was able to enter the hood through this. I couldn't see anything through the black cowl, although I could hear, somewhat muffled, and I thought I heard the sound of a filled pail being picked up.

I was right, for a moment later, a foul liquid–most likely urine, or some other wastewater–poured into my airtight cowl through the tubing at the crown. The hood filled around me, and I could only helplessly wait as the water rose past my lips, nose, and burned my puffy eyes. I gasped in pain, swallowing some of the noxious waste, coughed and choked. My lungs ached for a clean breath that wasn't going to come. I shook my head fiercely, trying to dislodge the hood, but it was cinched too tightly. All my struggles accomplished was to strain the muscles in my shoulders even more.

I moved my head about in the hood, trying to find one small, clean pocket of air, but the water was up past my eyes. There was no air.

The guard who had asked me about mad dogs finally got his nerve back and placed a solid blow to my ribs, making me wheeze and inhale more of the liquid. I choked and sputtered and gagged, and felt my head pounding in time with my heart. I was sure my lungs would burst in a red, misty spray inside my aching chest.

I wondered how long I could hold out before I had to take a breath. Thirty seconds, perhaps? Less? It didn't really matter, because I *would* breathe, even if I passed out first.. Involuntary functions would take over and I'd drown in this wretched slop.

Just as I had resolved myself to this miserable fate, I felt the buckles that cinched the hood to my throat being undone, and all the wastewater filling my cowl spilled out down my front and back. I coughed and wheezed and nearly vomited, trying to clear my chest and burning sinuses.

"Buh—bastards..." I cursed weakly.

"What's that, Max?" Strawberry-Nose asked. Although I couldn't see him through the hood, it was easy enough to imagine him cupping one palm to his ear, head tilted as if to hear better. "Still thirsty? Well, why didn't you say so? We have plenty left, and it's all yours!"

His friend started to cinch the buckles at my throat once more.

"Let me down," I said, trying to sound more defiant than I felt.

"What then?"

"Then, I'll kill you. I'll tear your throat out with my teeth... and kill every goddamn one of your family. Both of you."

I tried to provoke them. I had to take this next bit of torture if my plan had any chance of success at all.

"How many men you killed, tough guy?" Strawberry-Nose asked.

"Two less than I should've."

That was it. The other guard cinched the straps hard, tight enough to strangle me. Almost. They were still having too much fun trying to break me to let me out of here that easily. I was able to gulp down a foul lungful of air this time, but I could still only hold it so long, and they had all the time in the world. The bag filled again, and the guards began beating me once more—on the sides, in the kidneys, on the heels and other intimate places. I was determined not to swallow any more of that sewage water, but they were just as determined that I would. They kept beating me until, in the end, I had no choice.

I thrashed and kicked, pain stabbing through my shoulders and arms. And just when I was sure they really would let me drown this time, when I actually contemplated inhaling all that I could and finishing the job for them, I felt hands fumbling to undo the straps. Again the polluted water cascaded out, and I coughed the liquid out of my lungs, snorted it out of my sinuses. I could only grit my teeth as I felt it trickle down into my ears.

"I'll talk," I gasped. "Please."

"What?"

"Said I'll talk," I coughed and gagged. "Names, places...anything...everything you want to know." I made sure my words were muffled by the mask, more than they actually were. But I really could have spared myself the act; they wanted to see the beaten look on my face. The hood was going to come off anyway. The guard stepped close, his chest almost touching mine as he slipped the hood up over my head.

Before he could step back, I brought my legs up, shifting all my weight to my shoulders. The pain was huge, but I couldn't stop now, and they would never give me this chance again. I locked my legs around his neck and squeezed hard, using his body to leverage myself just high enough that I could put some slack in my chains. He clawed and beat at me, weak as any baby. I slipped the chains out of the hook holding me suspended, nearly dislocating my shoulders in the bargain. My arms, if not my hands, were free.

So what? Don't stop now. It's only pain, and pain never killed anyone.

I wrapped the chain around the guard's throat and pulled hard, jerking his head to the right. Even with diminished hearing, I could make out the sweet, satisfying dry snap of his neck breaking.

"Well? Go ahead, pour me another one, asshole."

His body went suddenly lax and dropped straight down to the floor, taking me down with him. The muscles in my legs were still watery and cramped, and before I could get back up, Strawberry-Nose was there to pound me with his club, alternating the beating with solid kicks to my ribs and head.

"You won't live to hang!" he was grunting, fitting his words in around his exertions, like mortar between bricks. "Bastard!"

I tried to raise my hands to defend myself, but the chains manacling me were still looped and tangled around the guard's neck. I felt the baton impact with my forehead, hard enough to actually splinter the club, and that was about the point where consciousness and I parted company for a while

After that... Well, for Max, there was no after that. When he finally opened his eyes again, with the ol' Death-Clock at 72 hours and counting, he was a new man.

CHAPTER NINE

I woke all at once and alert, and saw Jasmine standing at the edge of my blanket, holding an earthenware plate and tin cup.

"I saved you some food," she said, and sat on the blanket with me, folding her long legs beneath her. "I thought you might be hungry."

"Thanks."

She set the plate of some kind of watery stew and a dry, coarse bread down in front of me, and the cup next to that. Until I smelled the aroma rising off the food, I had no idea how hungry I was, and I realized I couldn't remember the last meal I had. I laid into the stew and bread and drained the cup in two deep gulps. I held the plate, still smeared with traces of stew, in front of me and, with my eyes on Jasmine, and hers on me, I licked it clean.

I couldn't remember a time I had ever been so hungry.

"How would you like to go shopping?" I asked.

Jasmine crinkled her nose and tipped her head to the side.

"Never mind," I said softly, my cupping her cheek in my palm. "It's in the genes. You'll pick it up fast."

When I had earlier checked out the state of things in

downtown Los Angeles, I noticed anything above a certain level of technology was left behind. Granted, computers and electrical appliances weren't going to do anyone much good without the Internet or electricity, but guns had been passed over in favor of knives, bows and arrows. Cars had been left to rust. I didn't completely understand the meaning behind this yet, but after a couple days talking with my hosts, I had the idea they were all...functionally illiterate, for want of a better term, almost uniformly emotionally and intellectually arrested at a certain level of development.

Conceptual things eluded them, and while I allowed the day-to-day act of survival took precedence over learning to read and write, I didn't see how it was possible for no one in the whole tribe to know how to do either. And that bizarre newspaper headline: SURNDER!!!! There was still a lot going on here I didn't get, perhaps because I was trying to look at things too linearly, but I would figure it out.

After all, I was now the smartest man in the world, wasn't I?

We emerged not far from where we first entered Jasmine's underground railroad passageway, not far from where I was sure we'd find what I was looking for.

There is a huge seven-story shopping mall called the Trocadero on the corner of Sunset, rising like some neon-lit Tower of Babel. I had shopped there a few times with Sara and Vonnie, so I was acquainted with the lineup of businesses in this mall, with its flaking blue exterior and its cracked-glass cinderblock facade. The outer doors hung half-open, like a dare, and I accepted. Jasmine followed close behind.

The grand foyer had been used as a lair at one time;

sodden mattresses were piled in one corner near the escalators, forming a crude sleeping area. Bowls filled with moldy and rancid food were scattered about the mattresses, as if the owners had been interrupted in midmeal. Looters? Maybe, but I suspected it was probably some kin to the spider I had killed not far from here.

I shivered at that thought: Just what might have taken up residence in this place? I looked up the seemingly endless flights of escalators, half-cluttered with wood and fallen bits of plaster and concrete, and imagined a giant insect lurking just around each successive rise of escalator treads, each more hideous and deadly than the last.

As we moved closer, past the mattress cove, I saw the stains that I had taken to be water spots were actually dark patches of dried blood. Quite a lot of it, actually. It had soaked the mattresses and sprayed halfway up the wall in a mad spackle.

"What?" Jasmine asked. I had only paused a moment at the scene of the crime, and she had instantly picked up my hesitation.

"Blood," I told her, pointing at the pile of mattresses. And for no real reason, it made me think of the couch-cushion forts my stepbrother and I used to build on those long-lost Saturday nights, downstairs in the family room, when we would stay up late to watch *Creature Features*. Apparently, pillow-forts weren't much protection against the monsters that prowled the dark rooms of the real world.

And just how much blood did *a human body hold, anyway? Enough to fill a wading pool, if this was any indication.*

"So?" she asked, without judgment or guile. "You're not afraid of a little blood, are you?"

A little blood? I started, then caught myself. This probably *was* a little blood for her. She had no doubt seen this and much worse several times over in her brief life, and that saddened me. There was still an air of innocence about her I wanted to save.

"It's dry," she said, touching her palm to the crusted surface of the mattress. "Whatever happened here happened a long time ago." She held up her palm for me to judge for myself. "See?"

"I see," I said, and folded her hand in mine. She smiled, and what could I do but kiss the corners of her mouth?

I drew my knife and cautiously climbed the first flight of the escalator. I thought of the spider, and those horrible splashes of blood just below me, and I wondered just how much good my little blade could do against whatever had done that. Probably none, but it was better than hoping there was nothing lying in wait. Jasmine padded lightly along behind me, her own blade still sheathed. I wanted to tell her to be ready, but this was her world. She knew the dangers better than I did.

We climbed around the debris lining the treads. Occasionally, a tree of some indefinite origin grew up through the gaps between the steps. Eventually, the earth would reclaim the cities, grow up around the fleshless bones of the crumbled buildings, and Los Angeles would be as much a myth as sunken Atlantis. I had played my part in this, and now I felt as if I were being punished for my hubris, like some modern-day, time-hopping Flying Dutchman, forever trapped in his perdition.

"What are we shop-ping for?" Jasmine asked, over-enunciating the word.

Light tumbled down from the huge skylight that covered the mall rotunda, but I wasn't so sure about the hallways and shops sitting in shadow. I paused at the escalator top, peering into the gloom of the third floor.

"I think this is our stop," I told her, and stepped off the treads onto the horseshoe-shaped floor plan of shops. I could remember bringing Sara here, to the multiplex of theatres up on the seventh floor for our first movie as a couple, an *Annie Hall* revival. Bold as a pickpocket, I slipped my arm around her shoulders in that theatre and stole my first of what would be many kisses. I felt the burn of tears in my eyes and the thickening of my sinuses, and I turned my back on that memory.

"Max?" Whatever she lacked in book-smarts, Jasmine was acutely attuned to the world, and the emotions of those around her. But more than that, she was kind. In a world of sudden and brutal violence, and bloody pillow forts, she was kind.

I smiled at her. We moved around the walkway, passing an Orange Julius stand, a Sam Goody, a Foot Locker, and Disneyana. As before, only a certain few of the shops had been looted. Down the center of the seven levels of the mall used to run a waterfall, pouring into a wishing pool in the center of the ground floor, but the well and the wishes were all dried up now. I stood at the railing, looking first down, then up, looking for any signs of ambush either by man or...not man.

Jasmine was looking in the display case of a jewelry store, where millions of dollars of precious gems and metal sat untouched, like an ancient pirate's treasure just waiting to be discovered and dug up.

"See anything you like? My treat."

She shrugged indifferently, her fingers laced together behind her back. "They're just shiny rocks," she informed me. "They're not good for anything."

"That's not really true," I said, and stepped behind the

counter. The shop would normally have been protected by a steel gate, but it was still rolled up in the overhead slot. I slid open the case, selected a ruby and diamond necklace. It was on a small and delicate chain, and I slipped it gently around her slender throat, lingering just a moment to feel the soft touch of her hair on my hands, the heat rising off her perfect body. "Once upon a time, jewelry like this was used to express how much a man loved a woman, and a wedding ring—" I tapped the glass counter to call her attention to the gold and silver bands that sat in their display boxes like pearls in velvet-lined oysters "—were used to show that a man and woman were married, that they belonged to each other."

"I belong to Jude," she said, matter-of-factly, and I felt a sharp pang at those words. "Does anyone belong to you?"

"Once."

"Where is she?"

"I don't know."

Jasmine touched the stone resting at her throat, moving it this way and that, watching the firelights sparkle in the stones' facets. "Did you ever give her one of these?"

I nodded. "Something like that, yes."

"And she's still gone?"

"She's still gone."

"Then it's like I said," she concluded. "The shiny rocks aren't good for anything."

I had to laugh, in spite of everything. "You have a way of cutting straight to the heart of the matter."

"Is this what we came for?" she asked, lifting the necklace gently with her fingertip.

"No," I said, and pointed to a sporting goods store

directly opposite where we stood. "That's what we came for."

The motorcycle was in cherry condition, just as I'd hoped it would be. It was indoors, protected from the elements and vandals, free of rust. The tires were a little flabby, as I'd expected them to be, but they were easily repaired. There was no fuel in the tank, but points, plugs, and everything else I could check seemed serviceable, certainly in much better condition than the cars I'd seen out on the streets.

I found the generators, but it would take a couple of Jude's men (*I belong to Jude)* to carry them back to the tunnels, and could I even convince them to help me? The answer, of course, was not while they were Jude's men. Maybe I'd have to do something about that, and very soon, but first, there was one last thing I wanted to check.

I figured I had about as good a chance that the shell would misfire and blow up in my face as fire cleanly, but, unfortunately, there was only one way to find out.

I put on a motorcycle helmet, eliciting a great deal of laughter from Jasmine. I suppose I did look pretty comical, at that.

"Is that like the pretty stones?" she asked, her small hand cupped to her full lips, trying to hide the laughter that was welling up there. I didn't mind if she laughed; it was a sweet, pure sound, and rare. I had a claustrophobic flashback to the water-filled hood, and I had to fight the urge to claw the helmet off my head. I compromised and flipped the visor up.

"No, this actually has a purpose," I told her. We stood outside the sporting goods store, in the rotunda, the deer rifle in the crook of my arm. The gun department looked like some terrorist Santa Claus's workshop. The gun rack was still locked down, the weapons untouched, until I broke into the cabinet and hammered off the lock-bar holding the row of rifles, lined up side by side like soldiers on parade, in place. I selected a .30-.30 deer rifle, a gun I knew because my uncle used to take my brother and me hunting after our dad died, cleaned and oiled it, and found a box of shells.

The casings were still shiny, but that told me nothing. These shells could be...what? Ten? Fifty years old? The powder could have turned long ago. I fitted one bullet into the magazine, flipped the safety off, and pumped the bullet into the chamber.

"Step back," I told Jasmine, and lowered my visor back into place. "Way back," I amended, and raised the rifle to my shoulder. I couldn't sight anything through the 'scope with the helmet on, but I wasn't concerned about my sharpshooting skills right now. I was just hoping the shell didn't explode and leave me blind. I had a feeling there weren't many Seeing Eye dogs running around these parts.

I eased the trigger back, but flinched at the last moment, causing my shot to go wild. The bullet splashed off the stone of the storefront across the rotunda and ricocheted back to where we stood, narrowly missing Jasmine and blowing out the display window of the sporting goods shop behind her.

Jasmine yelped in surprise—I suppose it was good to find out she was still capable of being surprised—and drew her knife.

"It's all right, I meant to do that," I lied. No point in telling her how close she came to being the first shooting victim in who-knew-how-many years. I pulled the helmet off and lowered the gun, ready to comfort her, but she was more curious than alarmed, and why not? She'd never seen a gun before and had no idea how deadly they were. She looked at the broken glass, then at me, her nose scrunched and the corner of her mouth turned up in a crooked smile.

"You did that?"

"Yes," I said, and flipped the safety back on.

"Really?"

"Really."

The smile grew mischievous. "Can you do it again?"

"Probably not," I admitted, and slung the gun over my shoulder. So much for the five-day waiting period.

We wrestled the Soft-Tail bike down the three flights of escalator treads and out onto the streets, which were already explosively hot enough to make small animals burst into flames after just a few moments' contact with the pavement. It was no wonder Jasmine's people chose to live most of their time underground. I shaded my eyes and looked toward the sun. It was huge, red and swollen, like a blood-filled tick.

Jasmine looked dubiously at the motorcycle. "We can't push this all the way through the tunnels."

I smiled and uncoiled a flex-tube with a hand-pump siphon attached. "We don't have to, now that we've gotten it down to the street." I got down on my hands and knees and inspected the nearest automobiles. The first couple had already lost their fuel tanks, but the last one was still in reasonably good shape. I opened the driver's side door to flip the panel covering the gas cap, and a desiccated bundle of bones tumbled out, loose as a pile of rags. Its mummified fingers brushed my cheek, leaving an ashen smudge.

"Shit!" I cried, and jumped back.

The corpse struck the pavement, literally bursting apart on impact. Husks of insects spilled out, like the contents of some gruesome piñata. I spat on my palm and scrubbed at the corpse-kiss on my cheek.

Jasmine laughed and asked, "Blood...bodies... Is there anything else you're afraid of?"

"Clowns," I answered, taking her kidding in the same good nature in which it was delivered. "But that's just common sense."

I looked at the corpse, little more than a vague man-shaped pile of dust and unidentifiable insect husks now. I wondered how long that poor sod had been sitting in his car, windows and doors forming an almost hermetic seal, unreachable by the predators that prowled just beyond the glass, baking in his car to the point of near-mummification. "Sorry," I whispered to the dust-man.

I slipped one end of the tube into the tank, the other into the tank of the bike, and squeezed the bulb until I saw a golden thread of liquid appear in the hose, looping and swirling its way from the forever-parked car to my bike. After the tank was filled, I slung my leg over the seat, turned the key and prayed.

The engine ground and coughed, sputtered, threatened to die. I fed it more gas, the engine beating like an unsteady heart. I'd recharged the battery with a portable generator I'd found in the sporting goods shop, but I doubted if the charge would last too long. I just hoped it would last long enough to get me where I needed to go.

Jasmine hung back, more frightened by the smoking, roaring bike than she had been by the gun. "It's all right," I shouted over the noise of the choppy engine, and opened the throttle. The choppiness smoothed out a little bit. "It's perfectly safe. I give you my word on that."

She wanted to trust me, but that was asking a lot on our first date.

"What is it?" she asked, backing away until she bumped into the fender of a car.

"It's a...horseless carriage," I answered, feeling very much like a turn-of-the-century motorist. "It carries us wherever we want to go."

An idea occurred to me, and I drove the bike in a wide, slow, wobbling circle around her, stopping where I had started. I braced the bike with my right leg, letting the engine rev. It was actually starting to sound pretty good.

"Get on," I told her, and smiled.

She looked at the bike, and at me, and after only a moment's indecision, climbed onto the wide, soft seat behind me.

I revved the engine, told Jasmine to hang on, and turned the bike once more in a slow gyre, weaving in and out between the frozen traffic, making my way north.

Toward home.

Paul's home.

CHAPTER TEN

The view from the Pacific Coast Highway is some of the most beautiful natural scenery I know, but I barely noticed as we barreled along, heading steadily north. Jasmine, at first, was rightly skittish about the motorcycle, and she rode with her arms wrapped tightly around my waist, her breasts pressed into my back, her left cheek resting on my right shoulder. As the miles unspooled beneath us, without incident, and as the monotonous lullaby of the highway soothed one more traveler, the first in who-knew-how-many years, she gradually relaxed.

She sat up now and watched the landscape glide by, the wind on her face and exposed arms and legs, her hair blowing it out long behind her like a comet's tail. Soon, she felt confident enough to let go of my waist and hold onto the roll-bar behind her.

The trees we passed on the inland side looked like spent matchsticks, burned and blackened, and the grass was brown and brittle. The highway, mostly free of abandoned cars, was nevertheless filled with jagged cracks, like some endlessly long gray jigsaw puzzle.

Several times, we had to push the bike to its limits, climbing over dirtslides that had fallen across the Coast road from the baked and crumbling slopes to our right. Heat-blighted trees, canted by the landslides, their roots exposed like a network of veins, hung low at tipped and crazy angles just over our heads, forcing us to duck several times. It was just dumb luck that no trees had fallen yet. A few more years and this road would probably be gone, covered by landslides and deadfall.

I didn't think global warming could account for all this incredible heat and ruin, and began to wonder if low-yield nuclear weapons or some other manner of weaponry had been unleashed by the Masters. I kept checking the fuel gauge nervously, watching as the needle dipped a little closer to the red.

Well, in for a penny, in for a pound.

The miles and the hours ground on.

As we coasted through the empty downtown of Mountain View, I absurdly kept expecting to see my friends and neighbors going about their business, unaffected by the end of the world. Except there weren't going to be any more Saturday night potluck dinners or Junior Achievement call-outs, or Sundae Socials or church raffles. All of those things couldn't be more over. The buildings, although more small-town architecture, were much the same as those in downtown L.A.: dark, abandoned, windows broken, shelves looted.

As the bloated sun began its nightly ritual, slipping down a little lower below the Pacific Rim, it cast shadows out, long and flat, like black crepe cutouts. The bloody light spilled over everything, flashing off rusting metal and broken glass, lending everything an otherworldly feeling, a nightmarish fever quality. I used to love to watch sunsets with Sara, but this was a lonely, enervating light.

"Are we there yet?" Jasmine asked, so unself-consciously and innocently that I had to laugh.

"Yeah, just about." I fed the bike a little more gas and left downtown and a lifetime of memories behind us in that eerie, lonely light.

The streets to my home were the same, but they were also very different. Houses had collapsed to rot or fire, street signs were overgrown with spiked and barbed weeds that had cracked the pavement stones and hove them at tent-like angles. But I couldn't find the street to my home, and I felt a wild, skyrocketing panic, madly convinced I had imagined the whole Paul Stein existence. An anguished cry tried to escape my lips, and I only managed to bite it back because of Jasmine's presence.

I circled back, driving slower this time, unreasonably sure I wouldn't find my street this time, either. I was making small, grunting sounds, and I was just glad the engine was making too much noise for Jasmine to hear me.

One more circuit, and I was about to let loose a mad shriek when I glimpsed the cupola of the Petersons' house, the house behind ours, and I knew where I was. The mouth to the cul-de-sac where my home sat was overgrown with thick, wild and exotic vegetation and brambles, a thorn forest, like the fable of Briar Rose and her enchanted blood. Familiar trees had collapsed, perhaps due to a gas main explosion, changing the once-known geography of my neighborhood.

"Hold tight," I warned Jasmine, and before she could do as instructed, I drove the bike up a rugged peak of concrete, through the thorns that cut and grabbed our flesh and clothes, and then we were through.

I pulled the bike to a stop on the curb in front of my

home and shut the engine down. The silence was staggering, and the vibrations of the great bike still thrummed in our muscles and bones.

The house was many years the worse for it: the paint had chipped and flaked, exposing the rough, warped wood. Shingles had fallen off the roof and lay scattered about the overgrown lawn like oversized playing cards. Part of the roof had taken on a definitely pronounced sway. Windows, their frames warped by the relentless heat, hung askew, and the door stood ajar and crooked, giving the house the appearance of a slack-jawed yokel.

"Home again, home again," I muttered, and stepped off the bike. I walked slowly up the weed-covered path to the house, expecting... I don't know what I was expecting. To reach into the time stream and pluck those missing years out of that fast-moving current the way a young boy reaches into a cold stream and plucks a shiny stone from the rushing water?

No.

No, seeing the house, here, now, slammed home the realization that too many years had passed. Sara was gone. I swallowed and pushed open the door.

The house was dark, but enough of that otherworldly light still remained that I could see everything in the living room was covered with a thick blanket of dust. The bones of small animals littered the floor like an ossuary. The scene, terrible enough on its own, was made all the more heartbreaking by the sickly light of the fading sun.

The furniture had been ransacked, overturned or simply taken. Papers were scattered all about, and the family portrait had fallen off the wall and smashed on the floor. "Oh, babies," I crooned to Sara and Maryvonne, "I'm sorry, so sorry..."

I lifted the photograph, the brittle frame and glass sloughing away at my touch. The picture crumbled like ancient parchment, and I watched as the pieces scaled from my hands and fluttered to the floor like confetti.

"Max?"

I turned. Jasmine was standing in the doorway. In my hurry to get home, I had forgotten her, left her on the bike.

"Where are we?"

"I used to live here."

She looked dubious. "No one's lived here in a long time." Jasmine moved a little farther into the house, not entirely at ease with these surroundings. *City mouse in the country,* I thought distractedly. *Not used to the open yards and sky, instead of streets and tunnels.* Not hard to understand, really. She'd probably grown up in the underground. Being here was like a massive attack of agoraphobia just waiting to happen.

"Is this where she belonged to you?" I knew then that it wasn't just agoraphobia at the root of Jasmine's unease. She was scanning for some sign of Sara. She was jealous.

"Yeah," I said, dusting my hands down, washing my hands of the past. If I wasn't Paul Stein, then these weren't his memories that threatened to crush the breath out of my soul, not his grief coming at me from a hundred different directions at once, like a whirlwind of claw and fang, ripping and tearing and flaying. And all I could do was wait. Ride it out and wait until Paul's memories got tired of hurting me and went away.

I stopped myself entering Vonnie's room. The sight of her dolls and stuffed animals, waiting patiently for her return, her CD player with the last disc she listened to, still in the carousel, was nothing I needed to see. No good, and only bad, could come of it. Instead, I moved into the kitchen, where the linoleum tiles were all curled up at the edges, forming dozens of little troughs.

I told myself not to think about it, not to think about *them,* but what else could I do? How can you live so many years of your life in one place, with two people, and return to that place many years later and not wonder?

The basement door, where I kept a small lab, was locked, and the key was nowhere to be found. Not in the bowl on the counter, nor on the peg beside the door, but it didn't matter. The door was warped and dry, and one good kick dislodged the latch and striker plate. The door swung open, banged on the inside wall, and swung slowly back toward me. I caught it with my palm.

The air was stale, but I didn't detect the smell of rot or mildew. The basement had been thoroughly waterproofed to protect my equipment, and with luck, everything down here would still be in reasonably good condition. I eased onto the first step, just in case the wood didn't hold up any better than the door, and then to the next, and the next. The wood creaked under my feet, but made not a sound as Jasmine descended softly and surely behind me.

She was just full of surprises, that one.

A little light reached the basement through the windows set high in the cinderblock walls near the ceiling. The glass was grimy, covered with old grass and dead leaves and rain-spattered dirt, about as transparent as the bricks surrounding it, but it didn't matter; I could have walked it if there were no light at all.

The furnace and water heater sat huddled silently together in the pie wedge-shaped space under the stairs. The entire north wall was covered with shelf upon shelf, row upon row, of my books. In the center of the room, like an oasis, sat my workspace. The computer, which was dedicated to the SETI network, sat silent. SETI had a program any interested person could download to listen on their home computer for radio signals. When I wasn't listening at work, I listened at home, and kept copious journals. But there was one journal in particular that caught my eye: It was sitting across the keyboard, trying to call attention to itself.

My heart thumped and clattered like an engine running without oil as I picked up the log. I flipped it open, saw the first few pages of my notes had been torn out, so the first thing I saw was Sara's entry.

I looked at the date: September 13, 2003. Two days after my disappearance. I reached to switch on the gooseneck lamp on my desk out of reflex, and was actually surprised when it didn't light up. Jasmine occupied herself looking around the little storage room just off my work area. I felt a moment's peevishness when I wanted to tell her nosiness was not a virtue, and to leave our things alone, but she'd lived her life as a scavenger, finding uses for things from a forgotten age. It was odd to think of items I bought in my present as turning up on another person's *Antiques Roadshow*, but that's what they were now. I realized that, but I didn't accept it yet.

I heard the sound of boxes being moved, opened, rummage through, an occasional puzzled grunt, a laugh, a mutter, "What is this?" Considering the amount of junk we had stuffed back there, I figured Jasmine was good for a few hours. I pulled my old office chair out of its kneehole in the desk, sat down, propped my feet up, and began to read.

9/13/03

It's been two days since the invasion began and you disappeared. One moment you were there, trying to smash the portal, and the next, you were simply gone. The news reports you as dead, but if you were, I would know it in my heart. I know I'll see you again. I'll look up and there you'll be, smiling that slow, sly Nerd-Boy smile of yours.

Just thinking that warms and comforts me. I'm not the journalist in the family, but I know you'll want to know everything that's happened when you return, so I'll do my best to report things. I know it's a matter of time before our forces beat those things back.

Vonnie is crying. I have to go to her. Do you remember how you used to log off when we first started chatting on the 'Net? I'll close that way now.

Later, 'tater

"While, 'dile," I whispered, and gently turned the page. I wanted to read everything, know everything, but this was all I had left of them that was new, and I wanted to parcel it out and spend as much time with them as possible before they were really gone.

"What are these?" Jasmine asked from the alcove. I looked up to see what she was holding, one in each hand, like a hunter showing off his pheasants.

"Lawn darts," I said. "We used to use them in a game."

She touched a fingertip to the point of one. "You could kill someone with these."

"Yeah," I absently agreed. "You know what they say. It's funny until you put someone's eye out, and then it's frikkin' hilarious."

She apparently took that pronouncement to heart, for she tucked the brightly colored darts into her belt and returned to the alcove to rummage for more weapons.

The next few entries, though filtered through Sara's feelings and perceptions, were similar to the newspaper accounts I'd already read. Still, I lingered over them and read each word, because once upon a time, her hand touched this paper; they were her words.

But it was the entry two weeks later that caught my eye.

9/29/03

Dearest Paul,

Terrible day. Terrible. More units have been wiped out by the aliens—they call themselves the N'lani—and their stronghold grows. The Army tried a low-yield nuclear strike against the Fort Bragg portal, but they have some kind of force-field (did you ever think we'd live long enough to see such a sci-fi convention come to pass? Neither did I) that the nukes can't penetrate, but with typical Army mentality, they keep throwing more nukes at them. Most weapons are already useless because of the EMP, and several of the nukes have gone off-course because their guidance systems are fried. I don't want to think about where they come down.

Those poor people.

Everyone is pressing me to have a funeral for you, and I refuse. But today, one of those vultures from the media stopped me and asked if you were a willing alien collaborator, and is that why your body is the only one never to be recovered? "Is he safe back on the N'lani homeworld?" he asked, and stuck his microphone in my face. I struck him, Love, I actually struck him! Hard enough to break his nose, I'm sure. If civilization survives long enough, we can look forward to a costly lawsuit, and endless replays of my pugilistic act on CNN, every half-hour.

I know you're not a collaborator, Paul, but if I refuse to believe you're really dead, then I have to ask, Where are you? Why don't you come back to us?

Sara

It was the first entry that didn't end with a "Later, 'tater," or "Soon, Baboon," and I could almost feel Sara's doubts as a tangible presence, and I was too many years too late to do anything to allay those fears. I dreaded looking any further in the journal, for fear I'd expose more resentment, anger, even hatred, but I had to go on, because I had to know just how many lives were ruined in this train wreck.

"Everything all right in there?" I called to Jasmine. I'd taken her out of her natural habitat and then all but ignored her since we hit the road.

"I'm fine," she called back. "You have to tell me what all these things are."

I nearly asked, *All what things?* but knew how stupid

that would have been. If she could tell me what they were, she wouldn't have needed me to explain them to her. "I will," I promised, aware of the gathering darkness. In a few minutes, I wouldn't be able to read the journal, and I didn't want to wait until tomorrow. I flipped ahead a bit. It wasn't like cheating, like skipping to the end of a mystery novel. I didn't know who had been killed, but I sure knew whodunnit; my wife had named me as a prime suspect. Whether I had intentionally sold out the human race didn't matter; Sara *wondered.*

For the first time since I had known her, she wasn't so sure about me.

10/6/03

Paul,

(I noticed it didn't start with a "Dearest Paul," just...Paul. The kind of salutation you might expect on a bad news telegram, stop)

Eye've notised somthing funny; Mmaryvon can no longer red or rite. She was crying becos she was looking at her book and crying becos the words we're all forein to her. When Eye tried to red it Eye had trouble to. The allens are bulding a city in the dessert at Reeno, Neverland.

Sara

It was a lucky thing she signed the entry, because I wouldn't have associated that childish, uncertain handwriting as belonging to my wife, the misspellings so out of her nature. If I hadn't seen her signature, shaky as it was, I would have doubted Sara's involvement with this entry.

I thought of my daughter, who must have heard the rumors of her father being a N'lani conspirator (I knew Sara would never have shared her concerns with Vonnie, no matter how angry with me she may have been, but people talk, and kids are cruel), and I thought of how much she loved to read, and her fear and pain at not being able to do the thing she loved, and I felt sick. Sick and angry at the monsters who had hurt my baby.

10/10/03

> *The man on TV suddenly couldn red teh nooz an he started too cry*

SURNDER!!!! I thought. My mouth tasted like pennies, and I felt hot and sick, like when I sat at my father's bedside in the hospital and watched him struggle for every breath, wondering when the last one would come as the valleys between them grew longer and wider. Watching Sara struggle for every word was a lot like that.

I flipped the page. There were several cross-outs now, the pen scratched so hard and angrily across the page that the paper was gouged and slashed.

> *It's in the watr they do they are puting something in the watr to make us dumb Eye can fell is sliping away from me. Eye will stop riting befour Eye forget why Eye am doong this and lleave it for you Godbye Love thank you*

for a wunnerful lif!!!! You surched so hard for the meening of lif and it was always right here.

Your Sara

The sheer force of will it must have taken for her to stay focused long enough to write these last words humbled me. But in the end, I reclaimed her love, if I'd ever lost it. I closed the book and held it to my chin, imagining Sara finishing her final entry, and then coming down here to leave the journal where I would one day find it, returning upstairs and locking the door. And then...?

I didn't know, but maybe this:

Possibly the authorities helped the people evacuate, relocate somewhere safe. In my mind, that's how the story ends, with as few tears and as little heartache as possible. The N'lani, whatever they were, seemed to be content keeping a low presence, relying on lickspittle thugs like those back in the prison to keep the freemen repressed.

Sara wrote in passing that the N'lani were building a city in the desert. What was it for? Was it still there? She called it Neverland, but I thought, since she mentioned Reno, she probably meant Nevada.

More questions, but at least a few personal ones had been answered, however cryptically, by Sara's journal.

The basement was almost full-dark now. I pushed away from the desk and went to the alcove to fetch Jasmine. She was curled up on her left side, a jumble of old toys, games, clothes, Christmas tree decorations and lights, strewn about her. The fingers of her right hand rested lightly on the necklace I had given her, her head resting on her shoulder; in her left hand she held a Mr. Potato

Head. She had apparently figured out how to use my old Rock-em, Sock-em Robots, because the blue one had had his block knocked off.

I found an old blanket that Sara and I had decided was no longer good enough to use, but still too good to throw out, and covered Jasmine with it. I stood over her, watching her, until it got too dark to see her anymore.

Something in the water, Sara had said. I wasn't sure what, exactly, but that was the first useful information I'd gotten since arriving here. At least it gave me a place to start.

I laid down behind Jasmine, spooning her back to my front, my lips to the curve of her jaw, my right arm over her waist, my own left arm stretched out to match hers, and reminded myself to find syringes tomorrow.

CHAPTER ELEVEN

We woke, hungry as bears after a long winter's hibernation and no food in the cave. A few rusted, unlabeled cans sat on the pantry shelves, their contents leaking through the ruptured seams and all over the surface, calcifying, all but fusing them to the shelf. It wasn't likely we were going to find a Denny's that had managed to remain open, despite their claim that We Never Close. The apple and orange trees that once filled the backyard of our nearest neighbors were barren and stunted, as if they had been cursed by the Wicked Witch of the West Coast. And the squirrels and rabbits and birds that once lived in the trees and shrubs just beyond where our patio ended were long gone.

"Well," I said, turning to Jasmine. "You know what this means, don't you?"

She thought about it a moment, and her perfect face lit up with a smile that could have coaxed the moon and Mars from their courses. "It means we go shop-ping," she said.

The day was hot and close, the sky overcast with politician clouds, the kind that promised relief but never delivered, leaving the day more humid and sticky, doing more damage than good.

We took the bike into town. I had to find more gas for it, and soon, if we were going to make it back to L.A. or anywhere else. I swear, a tumbleweed actually bounced listlessly down the center of Mercy Street. The air was filled with grit and dust, as bad as the Oklahoma dust bowl. The only thing missing was Woody Guthrie.

Blind traffic lights creaked and swung and swayed on their stalks like hanged men. On the same corner as the traffic lights, an antiques shop stood and, standing guard outside, an old, wooden, cigar-store Indian, dreaming his painted dreams.

I steered wide of the manhole covers and sewer gratings, just in case. I pulled the bike to a stop in front of the Rite-Aid Pharmacy. As with just about every other building in town, this one had been looted, but I felt sure they would have what we needed. Jasmine slipped off the bike, looking first at the building, then me.

"There's food here?" she asked.

"We'll see," I told her, inwardly cursing myself for not being honest with her and for placing my own survival ahead of our more immediate needs, like food and drink. Well, maybe by some incredible stroke of luck, there would be something edible in here, such as powdered milk...except, if there was something in the water that deadened the IQ, anything with a recipe of "Just Add Water!" was probably a good thing to avoid.

But that reminded me of a place where we might find some food, and we would head there next, after our shopping spree was over.

We moved past the checkout lanes, the service desk, and the photo center, where packs of photos waited alphabetically to be claimed. Most of those people whose images were burned into Kodachrome prints were doubtlessly gone by now, their nameless bodies buried in unmarked, shallow graves, hastily dug by relatives in an attempt to give them one last shred of dignity. There would be no headstones, no names or dates, because that simple skill was now gone from this planet. The only elegy the dead had now was in those packs of photos that would never be claimed.

Fuzzy dice and car fresheners and bins of three-for-$10 CDs and cassettes still lined the shelves, as if they had been newly stocked. I found a wind-up travel clock, and dropped it in the back-to-school backpack I had grabbed in the school supplies aisle, along with some pencils, notebooks, and a hand-crank pencil sharpener.

There were hundreds of bottles of vitamins, cold aids, stomach relief medicines, and countless other reliefs and cures, but they were all long past their sell-by dates. At least I was in the right neighborhood for what I wanted. I stepped up behind the prescription counter and looked through the shelves to find a box of insulin needles and syringes. I glanced over my shoulder, feeling guilty, and dropped the box into my backpack.

Jasmine was too busy inspecting the brightly colored pills in their bottles to notice what I was doing—and truth be told, how likely was it she would have known what a syringe was? She twisted the childproof top off a bottle and shook a handful of pills into her palm. She sniffed them, and started to put one in her mouth.

"Don't," I warned her. "They can kill you, at least make you sick."

She dropped them on the floor and wiped her palm on the front of her tunic. "Those little berries?" she sounded doubtful. "Are they poison?"

"Yes."

I moved more boxes under the prescription counter and found a full-size first-aid kit, with cotton, surgical dressing, and wipes. I put the kit in my already loaded bag and told Jasmine we were done here.

She tried to peek into my shopping bag. "Is it food?" she asked with a smile, as if I had found something special and was trying to surprise her with it. It made me wish it were so.

"No, but these are things we'll need."

If she was disappointed—and how could she not be? I had promised her food and shopped instead for myself—she didn't show it. Jasmine was a good woman, in this time or any other.

As we walked toward the exit, I paused a moment in the beauty aids, by one of the overturned display spin-racks. "One more thing," I told her.

There were dozens of sunglasses spread about on the glass countertop—cheap-looking cat's-eye things to Buddy Holly-strength tinted glasses, to chic *Matrix* knockoffs. I selected a pair for Jasmine and slipped them onto the bridge of her nose. Her hands went instantly to them, but I caught her wrist with my free hand. "Leave them on. They'll make the sun seem not so bright."

The sunlight had been bright and hard on my eyes; I could only imagine how painful it was to someone who spent most of her time in a dark, abandoned subway tunnel.

She looked toward the front windows of the store, raised her glasses, then lowered them back onto her nose, raised, lowered, amusing herself while I selected a pair of wraparounds for myself. I lifted the spin rack and studied myself in the little mirror. Just because it's the end of the world, it doesn't mean I can't be stylin'.

Jasmine leaned in closer to see her own reflection. She

froze, surprised by what she saw, raised her glasses and burst out laughing.

"What?"

"Is that me?" She laughed and pointed, then slipped her sunglasses back on. "I look..." She didn't know how to finish that, so I finished it for her.

"You look beautiful, is how you look."

She looked at her reflection a moment longer. "Yes," she agreed. "That's just what I was going to say."

They were waiting for us.

Perhaps a half-dozen of the mutants had watched us from a distance as we entered the pharmacy. They'd waited until we had trapped ourselves in the back aisles, and quietly entered, interjecting themselves between us and the exit.

The first of the creatures showed himself too early, perhaps unable to wait any longer; driven mad and reckless with hunger. He leaped out at us over the top of a shelf full of beauty aids, sending me sprawling and going after Jasmine. Their presence revealed now, another of the creatures attacked me, keeping me from reaching Jasmine.

The first one stood over her, straddling her, his snaggled yellow teeth ringed in his blood-colored lips. It was not really the mouth of a man, but something more akin to the mouth of a sucker eel.

Jasmine fended off his gnashing teeth and slavering jaws, but he was insanely powerful. She kept the mutant's fangs from her neck by levering her arm under his chin and jaw, but she wouldn't be able to keep him at bay like that for long. Any moment now, the adrenaline pump that powered her would simply dry up and those hideous, foaming jaws would snap shut on her throat like a steel trap.

I was grappling with my own creature, who swung two heavy wooden clubs studded with rusted spikes, one in each hand. I blocked the blows with the barrel of my rifle, feeling the impact all the way up to my shoulders, but he wouldn't give me the moment I needed to flip the gun around, pump a shell into the chamber, and fire.

I had to go on the offensive; his blows would surely break the stock of the rifle, given time, and then we'd be weaponless. I dropped to my back, dodging his swinging maces, and pointed the rifle. In one swift movement, I threw the safety and pumped a fresh round into the chamber. Feet flat on the floor, knees bent, I positioned the gun between my legs and squeezed off a shot.

The bullet struck him square in the chest, tearing an exit hole in his back the size of a soup can. The force threw him back into the mountain of beauty aids. Jars of rancid cold cream smashed on the floor, filling the air with their foul stench.

"Get his head up!" I yelled to Jasmine as I tried to steady my aim for a shot at her attacker.

The mutant was close, his fangs just inches from her soft flesh and the warm blood that pulsed just below. His tongue, flat and forked, flicked snake-like, as close and intimate as any lover's kiss.

"Jasmine! Get his head—"

She didn't need my help. She kept his lamprey-mouth away just long enough for her free hand to pull a lawn dart from her belt and drive its heavy bolt into the creature's throat with a wet, smacking sound, like a fist punching through a wet paper bag. Jasmine shifted her grip on the bolt and gave it one more thrust, driving the spike deeper, until only the plastic tail feathers protruded from the mutant's throat.

The dart jigged and jagged in sympathetic time with the mutant's slowing heart. He mewled something long and low and pitiful, and collapsed, his left leg pistoning twice on the cold cream-slicked floor, then fell still.

Before I could reach Jasmine, two more of the mutants attacked us, rushing us from either end of the aisle. I raised my rifle and shot the one nearest to Jasmine—who was still pinned beneath the corpse of the mutant she had killed—hitting him in the shoulder, tearing out a huge divot of green, scaly flesh and muscle, leaving a twisted wreck of nerves and veins exposed. The force of the shot spun him around so he was facing the opposite way, the change in scenery confusing him, as if we had suddenly developed the power to turn invisible. It might even have been funny, if he hadn't been so hell-bent on our death.

He clutched at his suddenly useless arm, blood spurting between his clawed and webbed fingers. I shot again, this time finding my mark, hitting him square in the back, the bullet exploding out his chest, evacuating his heart with it.

"Cleanup in Aisle Two," I muttered, and spun around, slamming the rifle butt against the temple of the creature behind me. His eyes fluttered comically, and he went down.

Jasmine was on her feet, crouched and ready, her eyes restless, scanning the dim interior of the pharmacy.

"Let's get out of here!" I shouted, scooping up my backpack and heading for the exit. Jasmine grabbed her pair of sunglasses, knocked off during the attack, and followed closely. "You all right?" I asked her. She was streaked with blood, but I didn't think any of it was hers.

"I'm fine," she said, and added, "But I don't think I like shop-ping here."

I agreed that they'd never get our business again.

"What are those things?" I asked as we hit the side-walk, emerging in a dead run.

"Throwaways," she answered. "In-betweeners."

"In-betweeners? In-between what?"

"In-between us and the Masters," she said, as if it was obvious.

But I suppose what she was saying *was* obvious: The In-betweeners were some obscene hybridization of man and N'lani, but I couldn't imagine what purpose that might serve.

Just as we reached the bike, the other two creatures that had been stalking us in the pharmacy came bursting out of the store, their flinty eyes full of hatred and hun-ger, threads of saliva actually flying back as if in a slip-stream.

Jasmine was ready to fight to the last.

"Get on the bike!" I shouted. She started to protest, but I repeated my order, making it clear it was not nego-tiable. She didn't like it, but she did as she was told. I tossed her the bag of things I'd gotten in the pharmacy and raised the rifle. The Throwaway ran right into the barrel just as I did.

But the hammer came down on a dead shell. *Click.* The aural equivalent of craps.

I tried to eject the shell and clear the chamber, but it was jammed and the In-betweener was on me now. His weight slammed me back against the side of a car, and only the rifle barrel kept him away from my throat. I jerked the rifle, feinting to the left as I did, hooking the In-betweener's throat with the rifle's carrying strap. I angled behind him, wrapping my legs around his tree-trunk waist and riding him like a wild horse, pulling back with all my might on the reins.

The strap cut a groove in the creature's pebbled flesh, and its claws raked and flailed behind itself, trying to catch me. If it grabbed me, dragged me around in front where it could employ those slavering jaws, it would all be over.

Blind with panic and pain, the Throwaway raced headlong into the street, pinballing from car to parking meter, whatever was in its path, trying to dislodge me. Instead, I cinched my grip on the rifle, left hand on the barrel, right hand on the stock, and redoubled my efforts to throttle the beast. I dug a knee into its spine, scrambling for leverage. I pulled back, and suddenly, with a loud *Pop!* its head lolled loosely on its thick neck. It faltered and stumbled, pitched headfirst, somersaulting me over its shoulders as it went down. I landed hard on my back, unable to get up for a moment.

I looked back to find Jasmine, still on the bike, her attacker sitting against the edifice of the Rite-Aid, a brightly colored lawn dart sticking out of the center of its chest.

Now I saw the others, perhaps a dozen or more Throwaways shambling down Mercy Street. I cursed, forced the jammed shell out and pumped a fresh one in. I crossed the distance separating myself from the bike in a few quick strides, running up over the hood of a car and leaping onto the seat, like one of the best of the Wild West cowboys.

I fired blindly at the nearest In-betweener, missed, and the shell kicked up a puff of dust and stone where it hit the brick face of a building. The noise startled him, made him turn to examine the chipped stone, and I used that moment of uncertainty to start the bike.

I had an idea, and I didn't know whether it would pan out. I cruised slowly, letting the Throwaways close the already narrow gap between us.

"What are you doing?" Jasmine asked.

"Gambling," I answered.

I aimed the bike toward the manhole at the broad intersection of Mercy and Frontier Street, maybe thirty yards away, our pursuers less than half that distance from us. Timing was going to be everything.

Jasmine glanced back over her shoulder, biting her lower lip. If she was frightened, she wouldn't say so. "Is gambling like shop-ping?" she asked.

"No, it's like a game."

Twenty yards.

"Well, can you gamble faster? They're awfully close."

Fifteen yards.

And there it was: so slight that if you weren't looking for it, you wouldn't even notice it. But I was sure I saw the heavy manhole cover rise slightly, and shift, then come to rest slightly askew.

"Get ready to hang on," I warned Jasmine, opening the throttle. The In-betweeners were near enough to us now that one of them managed to scratch Jasmine's back with his claws, but she refused to make a sound. But I couldn't hit the gas just yet—the timing of this was critical, and I had to count on the single-minded determination of the Throwaways to keep them from sensing what I was about to do.

Five yards...

"Hang on!" I opened the throttle and fed the engine a big shot of gas, and we roared over the manhole cover. The Throwaways weren't fast enough to avoid what happened next.

The lid blew off the manhole, and a trap-door spider

flowed out of the pit like a gusher of oil. It was big, much bigger than the city spider I had killed, and I couldn't fight back the chill I felt at the sight of it.

I turned the bike into a half-circle at the other end of Mercy Street and stopped, letting the engine idle as we watched.

The spider grabbed an In-betweener, pulling him close enough to inject with its venom. The other Throwaways tried to pull him free, but the spider was just full of surprises. A moment later, dozens of newly hatched spiders, each perhaps as big as a lap-dog, streamed out of the sewer like a black, chittering wave of nightmare. The babies were quick, eager, and they were all over the Throwaways, climbing up them and stinging them, trying to drag their paralyzed bodies back down into their underground lair. They weren't quite strong enough for that, but it didn't stop them from trying, or from attacking still more of the In-betweeners.

"Max!"

Jasmine was pointing at the hood of a car next to us, and I saw what had alarmed her. One of the babies had crawled onto the car and was ready to leap at us. Its razor-sharp hairs scraped and skittered on the metal, and its maw hung open, stinger ready to strike.

I flipped the gun around, one-handed, aimed, and fired.

The huge, quivering body exploded in a spray of ichor, and one of the forelegs, lying on the hood of the car, coiled and uncoiled, coiled and uncoiled, still trying to twitch its way toward us. I grimaced and flicked it off with the rifle barrel and watched it flip end over end, until it smacked the window glass of a shop. It stuck, then slowly skidded down, leaving a slimy trail on the glass.

"We have to get out of here," I told Jasmine. It was

foolish to stop in the first place. Why had I done it? The truth was, we could have just sped away on the bike without relying on the trap-door spider. But I knew the answer, of course. This used to be my town, and I didn't like the idea of the In-betweeners walking my streets.

I didn't like the idea of the In-betweeners at all.

I glanced in the rearview, and saw the Throwaways fighting back, laying waste to the baby spiders with their nail-studded clubs. The babies burst in a black, jelly-like mist, but it was a losing battle. As one spider fell, one of its brothers would clamber up the Throwaway's back and inject him with the neurotoxin. The Throwaway would reach back over his shoulders, grab the baby and crush it with his bare hands or fling it to the ground, before the toxins, cruising through his system at an accelerated rate because of his exertions, would strike his nervous system and paralyze him.

There were more Throwaways running toward the melee, hell-bent for leather, racing our way. I braked and turned into a skid, slewing the tail of the bike around. I brought the bike up, sighted a Throwaway in the scope, and grimaced. The scope magnified the face of the creature, filling my vision, and I could almost smell its fetid breath. Its eyes were a dull yellow, and strands of Gollum-like hair grew in crazy tufts from its broad, flat head. Its nostrils were flat and flared, and when it breathed, a dew-sack on its throat swelled and deflated, swelled and deflated.

It was monstrous, foreign and alien, and yet, there was something disquietingly humanoid in its appearance. I squeezed the trigger absently and watched the horrible face with which I was transfixed vanish in a red, pulpy spray of bone and fang.

The body stumble-staggered onward, arms ramrod

straight and groping, feeling its way and then tripping over its own faltering feet. It went down, hit the tarmac, rolled, and sat up for a moment before it finally collapsed.

What the hell...?

Because it has a second brain in its body, a primitive brain that controls the body's involuntary functions, like the dinosaurs, my scientist's mind interjected, as if this were all just some hands-on game of *Trivial Pursuit.*

Well, there wasn't much to lose at this point, so I turned the rifle scope to the Ram truck parked sideways in the middle of the street, and put the gas-cap in my crosshairs. I lowered the sites just a little, to where the gas line would be, and squeezed back on the trigger. I watched a hole appear in the metal, and then another.

"What are you doing?"

"Come on..." I muttered through gritted teeth, and fired off one more shot.

The next shot did it. The residual gas fumes in the tank sparked and ignited, and the Ram went up in a spreading flower of black and orange flame, with the dull *Kerwhumpff!* of a mortar shell. The spraying fuel squirted tongues of flame in every direction, catching the nearest of the In-betweeners, setting their ragged clothes ablaze. They shrieked in a high, piercing voice like pigs at the slaughter, and ran in smoky circles, beating at the flames, managing only to fan them into a brighter intensity.

Creepers of flame rolled across the street in all directions, sending their fiery tendrils to other abandoned cars, igniting them in turn. The explosions hopscotched from one vehicle to another, the shockwave spreading out like a ripple in a lake, shaking the earth in a grand mal seizure. Windows exploded inward from the spreading waves of the blast, and cars reared up on two wheels like wild horses, then crashed back down to earth, bouncing on their springs like a souped-up low-rider.

The Throwaways were surrounded by the spreading fire, their only hope for escape lay back the way they had just come, but their mindless anger was greater than their sense of survival. They raced on, as if they could run between the lapping flames the way a child believes he can run between the raindrops. They emerged on the other side of the inferno, little more than fire with legs. Black, greasy smoke billowed off the creatures, and their pitiful death cries echoed off the buildings.

"That was incredible!" Jasmine shouted, sitting close to me on the bike, squeezing her legs around my waist.

"It was terrible," I said. Behind us, the In-betweeners keened in their dying agonies like lost and weary children.

It *was* terrible, but all the same, a part of me had enjoyed it. The Paul Stein part of me believed all life was precious, but the Max part, which seemed to be growing more dominant, gloried in the death of his enemies. It was like a video game, the most violent, interactive game ever created, where there was no objective save slaughter, and the more hideous, the better. There were no consequences for your actions, just rewards, and if that was true, then why shouldn't I take what I want, do what I want?

Who was going to stop me?

We drove for a while, and came to a huge A-frame house. The front of it was mostly glass, with a long, wide deck on the second level, the slope of the roof nearly touching the ground on either side. The mailbox, in the shape of a birdhouse, proudly proclaimed this was the home of the Martins.

I had passed this house every day on my way to work, and had seen something in their sprawling backyard that might come in handy. There was an attached garage, and in the great orchard behind the house, I had spied the roof of a bomb shelter, built during the height of the Cold War.

I coasted the bike past the garage, through the yard, and up to the steps leading down to the shelter. I put down the kickstand and got off, descended the three steps to the steel door. I shrugged the rifle off my shoulder and into my hands, placed the muzzle to the padlock, and fired. The lock fell away in a smoking, twisted lump, and I pushed the door open and stepped in.

I groped blindly in the dark shelter, banging into a table placed in the center of the room, and my hands felt a hurricane lamp sitting on the table, a book of matches next to it. I wasn't counting on either one working, but the dry atmosphere of the shelter had kept the matches well preserved. The lamp was ready for business, filled with kerosene, and I lit the wick and adjusted the flame.

"Come on in," I told Jasmine.

She was already standing at the doorway; again, I hadn't heard her soft footfalls. I turned my attention to our surroundings. There were three folding Army cots, and cans of fruit, vegetables, juices, tins of meat, powdered milk, powdered ice cream, cases of bottled water, peanut butter, dried fruit, jerked meat, stacks of Army-style Meals Ready to Eat, and a little gas camping stove. Hidden behind the kiddie-treats, I found a couple bottles of wine stashed away. I checked the date on the food, afraid it had been sitting here since Joe McCarthy was taking names, but I saw it had been recently re-stocked, or recent by Paul Stein's calendar.

I wondered how we would manage to lug all of this

stuff back to my house without a trailer, then thought, This *is my house now*. The fact this food was still here, untouched, probably didn't speak well of the Martins' fates.

Jasmine tipped her sunglasses up onto the crown of her head, unconsciously echoing the archetypal California girl, and, why not? Blonde, beautiful, well-tanned, and with an IQ lower than the temperature at the South Pole, she screamed Valley Girl.

"What is that?" she asked, nodding at the lantern.

"It's like a candle," I told her.

She studied the cold, blue light, the only sound in the room the hissing of the lantern, and at last she asked, "Where's the candle? Are you a wizard?"

I laughed and shook my head. "Does your tribe hang wizards?"

"No," she answered, offhandedly. "We stone them."

I must have shown my surprise, because she pointed at me and laughed, one hand to her lips, the other pointing at me.

"What?" I was starting to feel a bit self-conscious.

"Your face," she said, and howled laughter. She struggled to regain control of herself, but every time it seemed that she would, she sailed away on seizures of laughter once more, her shoulders shaking, until she was breathless. "Oh, Max," she finally managed to gasp. "There is no magic. Even children know *that.*"

Later, much later, after gorging ourselves on MREs, washed down with a bottle of wine, and with the hissing of the lantern, I made love to her. It was an old, and tired, and creaking bit of magic, but it was about the only magic the world had left.

CHAPTER TWELVE

I doubted Jasmine had ever had much experience with alcoholic beverages, and never had to deal with the morning after, which made what I had to do a little easier.

I drew two vials of her blood, one from each arm. She stirred, somewhat drunkenly, once, looked at me rather unfocused, said something that trailed off into a rattling snore, then slid back into a deep sleep. I swabbed the needle marks with an antibiotic gel from the first-aid kit, then placed a ball of cotton over each pinprick, and taped them into place with a Band-Aid.

I stood watching her sleep, and brushed an errant strand of hair from her face. I kissed her, softly, and left the bunker, pulling the door closed behind me. I didn't like leaving her alone, but I also knew she could take care of herself.

I crossed the field of brittle grass and spiky weeds to the small shed that stood at the edge of the orchard, and opened the door. It was a handyman's workshed, with a long, handsome bench, and tools hung in neat, sensible rows on pegboard. A couple of tools—hammer, axe, awl—were missing from the board, and I could see their outlines drawn on the wall in pink paint, like a flamboyant crime scene outline of murder victims.

Jars of screws, nails, and bolts, hung from the ceiling within easy reach; a garden hose dozed in a coil nearby, like a neon-green snake. There was a LawnBoy, and next to it was a five-gallon container of gasoline. I checked, found it half-full (or half-empty, if I were a pessimist), and took it, along with a funnel, back to my bike.

I fueled up and, within twenty minutes, I was coasting up the driveway to Paul Stein's old house, and the emotions that threatened to crush me yesterday were merely overwhelming today. A time-share in another man's head can heal all wounds. Everything felt distant as I moved through the house this time, as if viewed through the wrong end of the telescope, or filtered through another man's heart. Max was a man who believed in taking what he wanted–hadn't he said as much last night?–and now here he was, taking my intellect, and applying it to his life. I felt as if I had been carjacked.

I went down to my little lab, unhooded the microscope, prepared slides of Jasmine's blood, and adjusted the magnification. I picked up one of the new journals from the pharmacy, and a nice, sharp new pencil. For a moment, I couldn't remember what I was thinking, or even how to form the letters.

I jumped out of my seat and took down a book from the shelves, flipped to a page at random and watched in rising, sick horror as the letters swarmed and squirmed on the sheet like maggots, twisting into unrecognizable shapes, words that weren't words. I closed my eyes, squeezed the bridge of my nose until I saw red, leaping splashes, telling myself to calm down, calm down...

I slowly opened my eyes and looked again. This just in: *It was the best of times, it was the worst of times, it was the age of reason, it was the age of foolishness, it was the spring of hope, it was the winter of despair...*

I flipped farther into the book, reading passages at random, just to make certain I hadn't memorized the opening to *A Tale of Two Cities,* that I had actually read it and my brain wasn't just filling in the blind spots. Just to be safe, I fetched *Othello* and turned automatically to my favorite passage: "Now a sensible man, by and by a fool, presently a beast."

I felt the claustrophobic terror back slowly away, one measured step at a time, like someone who was about to try something stupid and was caught before he could do it.

I supposed it could have been the stress that made me incapable of writing–honest, it's never happened to me before, I just have a lot on my mind–but I didn't really think so. Until my mind piggybacked Max's body and brain, he was probably on even ground with the others: illiterate, a functional IQ. But the same additives in the water were present in his body–and now, my body–and were beginning to overcome the jumpstart my consciousness invading his comatose body gave him.

I became acutely aware how limited my time truly was. I was not only fighting Max to remain the dominant personality, I was racing the inevitable destruction of my IQ by the drugs, which still saturated Max's brain. I rubbed my hands down my face, which had never been a Paul Stein nervous tic, but was, I thought, a Max idiosyncrasy.

Calm...calm...

When I felt I was calm enough to proceed, when I was sure it was Paul in charge and not Max, I sat at the microscope once more, placed my eye to the lens, and looked for anything that didn't belong.

It didn't take long to find.

It was a cunning little chemical cocktail the N'lani had whipped up for us Earth folk. As near as I could tell, using the extremely crude lab I had to work with, the chemical deadened the receptor sites of the brain, causing the electrical thought impulses to misfire. Think of a million tiny lightning rods, and picture thought as lightning bolts. All but the most basic of thoughts—lightning—are prohibited from completing the arc by the rods. That's a cheeky oversimplification of what was actually going on, but the principle was about the same.

Why hadn't anyone else seen this when it was first happening, when there was still a chance to do something about it? And then I remembered the newspaper account, saying scientists and biologists had been among the invaders' early targets, and those they didn't round up probably noticed too late that their faculties were slipping. It was like having Alzheimer's, and that's just about what this chemical was: liquid Alzheimer's. The problem was, you didn't notice your faculties were eroding because it was gradual. Worse, the ones around you who might notice were similarly affected.

I doubted if it would do any good to fast. The biochemical was probably part of their cellular makeup by now, a self-writing program that would simply keep on replicating itself. It was cunning, like some kind of organic nanite, and for all I knew, that's exactly what it was. I simply didn't have the equipment, much less the time, necessary to fully research it. All I could do was try to treat it like the disease it most resembled.

And I wondered if the nanoterrorists of the brain kept

causing mind and automatic body functions to deteriorate, as these things did with true Alzheimer's. Somehow, I didn't think so. It was like a disease that, once it reached a certain plateau, stopped its destructive march. If the children were born with it in their cellular makeup, then old age would be...what? Thirty? Thirty-five?

There was no cure for that one, and I wasn't the guy to find it at this point, but there were drugs that helped restore some little lucidity to the Alzheimer sufferer.

The light was already starting to fail, taking on that lonely, early evening, otherworldly color, and I realized I had left Jasmine alone all this time. Would she think I'd abandoned her? Worse, would she go looking for me? Possibly. I knew she could take care of herself, but even so, it was still a world where crooked trees cast crooked shadows, and a place where pillow forts were no good against monsters, because the monsters were real. It was not a safe world for the best of us.

I looked in my desk drawer for some paper clips, and uncovered the plaque Sara bought me years ago at a yard sale as a joke. An elderly couple was, apparently, trying to unload every bit of crap in one weekend that they'd spent two long lifetimes accumulating. There was a box full of useless things on a table in a place of prominence, such as a key that no longer had the lock it opened, and an extension cord with one prong missing and its plastic casing cracked, several frayed wires exposed. And this plaque...

Or, rather, half a plaque. It was broken straight across the middle, so that only the top half of the sampler—a night sky filled with twinkling, five-pointed stars that spelled out IT'S ALWAYS DARKEST—remained. Sara swore she looked in that box for the bottom half, but it simply wasn't there; presumably, someone else had needed just the BEFORE THE DAWN part of the plaque. But she knew she absolutely had to have it for me.

"Oh, God, Sara," I exhaled the words, turning the plaque over in my hands. I looked again at the sampler, and this time the spray of stars was just that: a random arrangement of a child's interpretation of a gaseous, heavenly body. They spelled out nothing to me, as if this were a color-blindness test and I couldn't discern the green "3" hidden among all the yellow dots.

I pushed the plaque back into the drawer and banged it shut, as if the plaque were somehow causing my inability to read. I sat there with my fingertips on the edge of the desk, fighting down the frightened anger.

"Not yet," I muttered, "not yet, not yet..."

I was in the middle of the longest prayer you've ever heard, afraid to look up, afraid the lettering on the spines of the books across from me would look like the remains of a dead language...which they were. What if the confusion didn't clear this time? Would I still have enough lucidity to work on a treatment?

But, at last, the not knowing became even worse than knowing, and I had to look. I slowly raised my head, and opened my eyes.

I felt a relieved breath trickle from my nostrils and an iron band unclamp itself from around my chest. It was all right again, but had it lasted longer than the first time? I thought maybe it had, but that may be the way it happens: confusion followed by clarity.

I packed the microscope, blood samples, and my *Physicians' Desk Reference* and hopped my bike. Even with my sunglasses, the horrible, unearthly light still stirred in me something indescribably sad. I coasted down the hill to the main boulevard and drove as fast as I could to my home-away-from-home with Jasmine.

Even from a distance, I could see the shelter door was open. I jumped from the rolling bike, letting it wobble and fall. As I ran, I set the backpack down and shrugged the rifle off my shoulder and into my hands. I leaped down the steps to the shelter, ready for anything.

Anything but what I found.

Jasmine was gone.

CHAPTER THIRTEEN

I was frantic with worry, searching the grounds around the shelter, the empty house, the toolshed, anywhere I could think to look for Jasmine, but she was nowhere to be found.

There had been no blood or signs of a struggle, as would surely have been the case if the Throwaways had captured her, but the lack of blood meant nothing. She may have gone looking for me and then run afoul of...well, God alone knows.

I biked around the area, one eye out for her, the other open to potential dangers, but I could find no trace of her anywhere. It was as if she had vanished as completely from her time as Paul Stein had from his.

The sun followed its well-worn path across the sky, sliding down behind the edge of the world like a coin dropping into a slot. The stars appeared in the darkness, scattered like buckshot, as if the sun-coin had paid for their presence, but they didn't spell out an aphorism reminding me *It's Always Darkest.* I already knew that. The moon rose, dogging the sun's path.

A thick pillar of smoke spiked the burning earth to the dark, cloud-filled sky, the small town of Mountain View still burning. The fire would continue to feed on the buildings and homes, leaving only blackened skeletal remains. I didn't stop to wonder what would happen to the Throwaways with their own environment reduced to ruin, and I should have. They would have to go *somewhere*, and the only place left to go was into the hills.

I heard movement in the scabrous weeds that lined the sides of the road, and for the first time I began to truly wonder what things moved and lurched through the nighttime of this place I no longer belonged to. I'd seen the monstrosities the day produced; I had no desire to make the acquaintance of anything the night had to offer.

But I hadn't found Jasmine, and she could be just around the next bend in the road, or the next, or... And that was the problem. She could be anywhere. She could even be back at the shelter, waiting for me.

I sat on my bike for a long while, trying to decide, engine throttled down to conserve gas, when I heard movement again, closer this time.

"Who's there?" I asked, my voice calmer than I felt. No answer. I knew whoever was in the deadfall was lying still, watching me. I fetched a softball-sized rock from the road and whipped it, sidearm, into the scrub. I heard a solid thud as it thumped off something, but whatever it was remained where they were.

I turned the bike in a slow, half-circle and began to pick up speed, headed back to the shelter. I heard movement again, closer this time, and as I began to open the bike up, the source of the noise began to run faster. The overgrowth petered out as the ditch intersected a crossroad, and I hit the brake, swung the rear of the bike around so I was facing whatever had been following me. I flipped the gun off my shoulder and waited.

The thing in the ditch bounded out after me, wagging its spindly tail tentatively.

At first what I was seeing didn't register—I was expecting a horse-sized centipede or a Throwaway—and I nearly fired before I recognized it was a dog.

"Well, where did you come from?" I asked. "What's your name?"

The dog took a few cautious steps closer and sank to his belly, showing his submission, chin resting on his paws.

"I don't suppose Jasmine sent you to fetch me?"

If she had, the dog wasn't saying. I was still holding the gun, and I returned it to its place on my shoulder. I got off the bike and walked slowly to the dog, talking softly, hand extended and palm exposed, to show I meant no harm. He was skittish, and backed up as much as I advanced. Even in this light, at this distance, I could see he was malnourished, slat-sided, an ear chewed and mangled. His snout was heavily scarred, and it looked like he had just missed losing an eye. There was a terrible, oozing wound at the base of his throat, high up on his chest.

"What did the other guy look like?" Whatever had done this to the dog had been vicious, and if the dog was here to tell the tale, it must have gotten in a couple of good licks himself.

"Well, here's the deal," I said, inching a little closer. The dog eased backward, but not as far this time. "I need to get home; you need a home. You want a ride?"

I got close enough to pat his head, and I could feel his nervousness. His entire body was vibrating like a struck tuning fork. Dogs are sociable creatures, and all those thousands of years of man/dog companionship couldn't be bred out of the species overnight. Nevertheless, it had seen some things that didn't leave him the happy, drooling idiot most dogs are. Right now, it was instinct versus learned reaction, and I wasn't betting on which way this would turn out. I patted his head, stood, and walked slowly back to the bike. The dog crept along at a distance, limping on his right foreleg.

I started to get on the bike, then decided I'd better just walk it if I wanted my little friend to follow. It occurred to me, as chewed up as he was, the dog was still the first normal creature I had seen since I found myself here.

The shelter was empty. Jasmine hadn't returned, which tweaked my anxiety up another notch. If she wasn't here, it was probably because she couldn't come back; therefore, something had happened to her. The dog stood at the threshold, peering down into the dark shelter, whining softly.

"It's okay," I reassured him softly. He had probably picked up my agitation about Jasmine and was uneasy about following me into an enclosed space. I tried not to think about her, focusing on happy thoughts, and the dog calmed down enough to limp the last few steps into the bunker. I talked softly to him, as much to reassure him as to keep myself from listening to that shrill, insistent voice in the back of my head that was neither Paul nor Max, but somehow both, the one that kept telling me Jasmine was hurt, probably dying, and how could I sit here talking to a dog when she needed me.

Instead, I lit the lantern, closed the door, and sat on the cot. After a while, I found a bowl and poured our first guest some bottled water and fed him a packet of dried jerky. Paul Stein had spent his entire life trying to prove we weren't alone in the universe, but I don't believe I had ever felt so alone in my life.

After the dog—I had started calling him Blood, after the telepathic canine in the Harlan Ellison stories about "A Boy and His Dog"—had settled down for the night on a pile of blankets next to my cot, I snuffed the light and laid down, knowing I wouldn't sleep. I was right.

I argued with myself about tomorrow, whether I should continue looking for Jasmine, or whether I should continue my research. My thoughts went 'round and 'round, like leaves caught in a strong wind, racing faster and faster.

In the end, I decided I had been given the chance to undo the damage Paul Stein had inflicted upon the world, and the time in which I could effect that change was small and growing smaller. Once I lost my deductive reasoning, any chance of retaking the Earth, if we ever had one, would die with me.

My dad used to fix our car himself whenever anything went wrong, and one afternoon I sat under the shade tree and watched him work on a 1976 Ford, installing a new water pump. The crescent wrench he was using to loosen one of the locking bolts slipped, and he banged up his knuckles. I watched him squeeze tears of blood from his knuckles, and he told me, "I've never done a job yet that was worth a tin fart that didn't have some blood in it."

I guess I finally understood what he was saying now. The hard jobs always need a little blood to grease the wheels. It was just that in this case, it was Jasmine's blood I had spilled.

About midnight—I looked at my illuminated travel clock, which I had set using the position of the sun to give me a gauge on the time—the dog began to whine in distress.

Blood's panting started slowly at first, then doubled

its rapidity, then doubled that again, reminding me of an old Victorian steam engine, picking up speed as it hit the open rails. To complete that image for me, he let loose a howl, climbing up through the octaves, like a shrill whistle blast.

"Blood?" I asked, concerned. I had thought at first he was suffering a bad dream, but this was the sound of someone suffering the flames of doggie hell.

I fumbled in the blackness, found the table and the book of matches, and lit the lantern. The cold, blue light elbowed the shadows out of the way and I saw Blood lying on his blankets, his sides rising and falling in a ridiculous pace. His hind legs twitched, as if he were chasing rabbits in his dreams, but his eyes were open, hazed with pain, like hoarfrost on a winter windowpane. His gaze met mine. His tongue lay unrolled like a tiny red carpet to some bizarre world premiere in his mouth.

"What is it, buddy?" I asked, kneeling slowly beside him. "You sick?"

That was a pretty good possibility. The dog had been living wild for probably his whole life, eating whatever he could forage. Something had put up a bit of a scrap, judging by the wounds on Blood's throat. I had treated his wounds the best I could, with the limited medical supplies in the first-aid kit, but that was a ghastly injury. He'd be lucky if it didn't get infected, but surprisingly, the wound, despite its ragged appearance, was fairly clean.

All the same, I didn't really think the wounds were the source of Blood's discomfort, only a symptom.

Rabies? I wondered, and automatically slipped back a couple of feet from the dog. But he had drunk a barrelful of water, had a healthy, bordering on downright gluttonous, appetite, neither of which jibed with rabies. I patted his cheek, and he gratefully licked my hand.

His sides and stomach looked distended. As I touched his abdomen lightly, to probe the cause of the swelling, he let fly a long, fluttering, noxious cloud of tainted wind that brought tears to my eyes.

That time, it really was the dog, and no one around for me to point that out to. I cupped one hand over my mouth and nose, and used the other to fan the immediate air around me. The dog gave me a look of dreadful embarrassment, as if to say, I'm so sorry, I don't know what came over me.

"I know, I know," I assured him. "Better an empty house than a bad tenant."

He wagged his tail, thumping it on the concrete floor. I suppose he might have gulped down too much water too fast, or the jerky was fermenting in his intestines, causing this outbreak of bioterrorism, but he seemed a little better. He even rolled to his belly, which I thought didn't look quite as swollen, and rested his chin on the ankle of my crossed legs.

"It's okay," I told him, rubbing his head. I could still feel the high-pitched vibration in his skin and bones, like a power line carrying a scary load of energy. "Just between us, broccoli does the same thing to me."

The night passed in dribs and drabs, with the dog and me resting for a while, then he would begin to puff and pant again, followed by a growl of pain that would start as a throaty, dreamy growl and climb to a heartbreaking crescendo, like a teakettle coming to a frantic boil. Then he would release the ballast and, pain temporarily relieved, would fall into a deep and sonorous sleep, with only the near-corporeal presence of the foul gas lingering like a malignant presence, trying to materialize for the believers.

My own sleep was doubly disturbed and troubled, by Blood and by Jasmine. On a purely intellectual level, I knew my decision was the right one. In truth, it was the only one, but very often, the things that are correct and the things that are right don't line up on the grid.

I finally managed to slip into a light doze, skimming below the surface, awake enough to receive and process auditory input. I heard a cracking sound, followed by a wet, sucking noise, and in my dreams I could see the Throwaways breaking open Jasmine's bones and sucking the marrow from them. The sound, like something huge and gelid and sloppy-slimy, continued, and in my dreams I could smell the foul stench of gangrenous wounds, mixed with the low, mean fecal stench underlying that, and the smell of...*wine?*

Except it wasn't really wine, but something else that had a similar sharp and unpleasant edge to it, something just about the same color, in fact. I blinked, suddenly sharply aware of the silence in the room. It wasn't that Blood had finally passed through his sick distress and was sleeping soundly now; I couldn't even hear the sound of his breathing.

Awake now, I could still smell the onerous stink of... what? I thought Blood had finally sicked up his stomach contents, but this was worse than that reek could ever have been.

"Blood? You all right?" Nothing. Not even the half-hearted thump of his tail on the blanketed concrete. "Blood?"

I reached down to check him and put my hand into something wet and squishy. I grimaced and jerked my hand back, fingers sewn together by threads of warm, sticky goo. I fumbled in the darkness to light the lantern. Almost at once, I wished I hadn't. My hand was covered not with sick, but with dark, fresh blood.

The dog was lying on his back, his belly open from throat to scroat, his little chest bones sticking up at crazy angles. I clapped a hand over my mouth and thought how much worse that smell was, now that I could see the source of it. The flame danced in the trough, and I recoiled in horror, because Blood's heart was still beating, and the flesh was still twitching–

No, no... Get hold of yourself. It's just the flickering light, making the shadows look like they're moving...

I felt the sickness pass, and then Blood opened his eyes, full of pain and confusion, looked at me, and whined.

I moved closer to him, to break his neck and end his terrible suffering, but he had already slipped his leash, so to speak. That's when my brain began to send out alarms, like a home security system: What had caused this? Was there something lurking in the shelter, waiting for its prey? Is that what happened to Jasmine?

I heard a moan and looked around in alarm, until I recognized the sound of that cry was my own voice.

But it didn't look like something had mauled Blood trying to get *in*. His ribs were pushed outward, as if something had...

"Broken out..." I whispered, feeling a chill whipsaw through me, so violently I bit my tongue with my chattering teeth. Dogs don't usually shed their shells like June bugs; something had definitely used Blood for its incubation process. So therefore...

I sat still, not even moving my head, searching the area near where I sat, trying not to move and draw attention to myself. There was a trail of ichor on the floor, leading away from Blood's body, like the trail of a giant slug. The trail continued on into the darkness, out of the glow of the lantern's light. Far from being a safe haven now, the bunker felt hot and claustrophobic, like a closet built to store shadows and the dangers they hide.

I slowly got to my feet, keeping an eye on the shadows that seemed to close in around me, and turned up the flame. I blinked as my eyes adjusted to the increased brightness. The room was better illuminated, but no less threatening. There were still a lot of hiding places my visitor could shelter in.

The wound in the dog's throat suddenly took on sinister importance. Whatever had caused that damage probably wasn't defending itself from becoming kibble; it had laid its eggs in the warm host body of Blood, like a wasp, and the larvae had probably fed on him until it was time to hatch. When other food was in the vicinity.

As I thought that, I heard something oily slithering nearby, but I couldn't locate it. Drops of slobber, mixed with the dog's blood, pattered down on the back of my hand and arm as I reached for the lamp. I turned the flame up brighter, bleaching the color out of everything, and looked slowly up.

The first thing I saw was teeth, and lots of them. The creature was hanging from the ceiling, its baleful eyes like four huge oil drops. Its hinged mouth was open, and it spat its blinding venom like a spitting cobra. I just ducked the spittle, feeling a bit of the spray hit the back of my neck, burning me like rubbing alcohol. Damn it! Did everything in this horrible place spit venom and neurotoxins?

I threw the travel clock at the creature, but it scuttled out of the way with dazzling speed, its barbed tail curled over its back as it ran effortlessly across the ceiling. I couldn't get a good look at it, but it appeared to be a bad gene splice between a wasp and a scorpion.

It ducked behind a stack of supplies, and I grabbed the rifle. I didn't know just how deadly its poison was at such a hatchling state, but it seemed everything from baby chicks and chipmunks on up was a killing machine, just waiting to have a bash at the nearest unsuspecting passerby.

I shoved the stack of boxes aside with the rifle barrel; I didn't want to get my hand within striking distance of that thing. I needn't have worried; it wasn't there. It had climbed the stack of shelves and was nearly at my shoulder before I noticed movement from the corner of my eye. I spun just as it leaped, using my rifle like a baseball bat, catching the scorpion-thing a glancing blow. It struck the cot and bounced, but it was still alive, and it leaped from the cot to the table and came charging across the flat surface at me.

I fired the gun, and the bullet sheared off its tail. It stopped, ran in pain-maddened circles, giving me the moment I needed to grab my knife and drive it straight through the creature's back, pinning it to the table. It snapped and clawed, still very much alive, trying to climb its way up off the blade, and it would have done it, if there hadn't been a hand guard at the hilt. It hissed and screamed and spat, cursing at me in its insectile language.

I folded the gory blankets around Blood's body and carried him upstairs and outside. The sun was still some way from rising, but I could still see well enough to give Blood a decent burial.

The scorpion-thing had finally died by the time I returned. Nevertheless, I left it impaled to the table. I didn't trust anything to stay dead around here.

CHAPTER FOURTEEN

When I woke, I found I couldn't move.

The second thing I noticed, although I couldn't see it, was that my leg was swollen, filling my trouser leg like a sausage casing.

I grunted and tried again to sit up, but I was well on my way to becoming an inanimate object. My head throbbed with every slow, ragged throb of my heart, and I felt nauseous, but I tried to remain calm, tried to keep my stomach quieted, because if I vomited while I couldn't roll over to clear the airways, I could easily choke to death. The scorpion-thing had apparently gotten in a lick I missed. I was frightened, but my heart refused to climb any higher, beating just enough to keep me alive.

I wasn't sure that was a blessing. I was unable to move, unable to defend myself. I was unable to even feed myself.

I was paral—

No. No. No. I wasn't that. I was just temporarily unable to move.

But all the same, if the poison didn't wear off, I'd lie here and starve to death with food and drink no more than two yards away.

Somewhere in the corner where I had thrown it when

I tried to hit the scorpion-thing, I could hear the travel clock still ticking, the only sound in the room. My own breathing was too shallow for even me to hear. The clock calmly carved up the hours into sixty same-sized minutes, the minutes into sixty bite-sized seconds.

I concentrated, focusing all my consciousness into one simple action; this was no different than when I woke to find myself in this body. I had been unable to control it then, and willpower allowed me to shape it to my commands. I was vaguely aware of my right hand, resting on my belly. Even my tactile input was dubious at this point. I imagined lifting my hand, visualized it rising with an unsteady tremble before my eyes...

Focus.

But I had a terrible fear that my hand *wouldn't* respond this time, and that thought was enough to almost make my heart race—

Focus!

Lift it...*See* it...*Feel* my hand where it rested on my stomach, *see* it rising into the periphery of my view. I was going to have to raise it high, because I couldn't move my head *or* my eyes to check its progress.

Focus...

Focus...

I became aware of how terribly I was straining to perform just this one simple act. I could feel diamonds of perspiration sheening my forehead and upper lip, and the veins in my neck stood out in bas-relief. I felt like a man trying to lift an entire mountain range. I gasped, more like a weak sound of surprise, and stopped struggling against the effects of the neurotoxins for the moment. My lungs ached as if I had been running the Boston Marathon, and red and purple fireworks burst and pulsed at the edge of my vision. My heart seemed to take a pause, as if it had to think about what it wanted to do next; finally, it decided the sensible thing to do was resume beating.

Too much, too soon.

The venom was still too powerful.

Sweat burned my eyes and I couldn't wipe it away. I realized with a bad jolt that I couldn't even *blink* it away. My eyelids were locked open. I could only stare at the rough concrete ceiling to the bunker.

This was bad.

All right, I thought, don't panic. *If I couldn't move my hand, let's just see if I can move a finger.* It wasn't much, but it would be a start.

I concentrated again, this time on my little finger. I thought I felt it twitch, just a little, but it was impossible to tell. There was no way to see it, and my neural impulses were all apparently in government work, because they were taking their sweet time getting back to me. I thought I might have wet myself, as my nervous system turned to mush, but I couldn't really tell.

I had traded one cell for another, commuted my death sentence to a life term. As brutal as hanging would have been, at least it would have been over in a few agonizing minutes. If I couldn't shake off my paralysis, I could probably count on a few agonizing *days*.

And there was the word I had been trying very hard to dance around, which was funny, considering I couldn't dance. Not anymore. Because I was paralyzed. I felt a low moan try to escape my chest, but my voice was helpless, my larynx frozen. The best I could manage was a soft hiss, like steam escaping a radiator on a cool winter morning, flat as paper because my lungs were nearly paralyzed, as well.

Paralyzed.

I wanted to sleep, to escape my madhouse inmate inner voice, but I couldn't even close my eyes. I lay there and listened to the clock ticking away my life with infuriating calm.

I literally could not gauge the time I laid there. The door to the bunker was closed so I could see neither the sun nor the stars, and I couldn't see the clock, I could only hear its maddening *tick-tick-tick*.

My eyes were dry and aching, and I thought I would have given just about anything for that sweat now. Anything to lubricate my sandy, gritty eyes. They felt like two ball bearings burning out in their sockets. I struggled to blink, but my eyes felt too big and too dry for my eyelids, even if I could move my eyelids, to close over them.

God! Was every moment in this damned place a brutal, violent, hard-won victory?

I hadn't eaten much the day before, spending most of my time studying Jasmine's blood sample, and I was ravenously hungry. I could smell the discarded tins that held the canned fruit and the MREs, just a couple of feet away from my head, in the little wastebasket. The aroma of those few miniscule scraps, still sitting in the trash, was driving me insane.

I groaned inwardly; if I was this Pavlovian over the smell of food already, what would I be like in, say, two days? Or had it already been two days? Probably not, probably nowhere near that, probably only a few hours, at best, and that was a truly frightening thought.

I thought of all that bottled water, sitting row upon row against the opposite wall, just out of my reach. Terrible mistake, because now I was aware just how dry my mouth was. I tried to swallow, but I was as dry as an Oklahoma dirt road.

I remembered all the times I was sick as a boy, lying in bed in the middle of a fever-addled night, burning up, wanting a glass of water but too weak and light-headed to get up and get it. But all I had to do was call for my mom, and she'd wake and bring me a glass of ginger ale and a cool cloth for my head, and she'd turn my pillow cool-side up. But Max had never known that kind of affection. In Max's world, you lived like a wild animal. You crawled back to your lair to lick your wounds, and you either got better or died.

It was not a world that forgave mistakes, or paralysis.

When I tried not to think of water, I became aware of how much my eyes hurt. I tried to blink, but I could only continue to stare stupidly at the ceiling until it lost all sense of distance and perspective. That flat, dull gray of the concrete was my only view, and it seemed to ripple and flicker as my eyes twitched in their dry sockets. I could shut out one thought, only to have another, equally unpleasant, pop up to take its place.

So dry.

All I could think of was that water sitting just an arm's length away... For me, it may as well have been on the moon; it wouldn't have been any more out of reach.

I thought of all the water I had drunk, in coffee and tea and straight from the garden hose on a hot day when I washed my car. All the water I had left running in the sink as I shaved, or washed dishes; how many gallons of cool, cool liquid had I wasted on my lawn as I sat on my patio and read some new book, listening to the *whit-whit-whit* of the sprinkler, and how much water sluiced down the drain during my daily shower, and how many hundreds of thousands of gallons of bottled water had I simply *passed by* in the supermarket or 7-11? How many drinking fountains had I blindly ignored in the park or at the mall? All the water I refused to drink when I visited Mexico. Had I actually spit it out at one time? Not anymore. I was a changed man, I'd seen the error of my ways, and the spirit of deprivation had done it all in one night. Or two.

I wasn't nearly as hungry as I was thirsty, but thinking of it, smelling the discarded scraps, roused my hunger, but I could no longer salivate. If anything, it made my mouth dryer. It was like having two unruly kids in the car: *I'm hungry, I'm thirsty, I'm hungry, I'm thirsty...*

No.

Think of something else. Think of anything else. It had been a while since I ate or drank, but not that long. It would take a while to really feel the effects of deprivation. I realized that what I was feeling now was nothing, not even a glimmer, compared to what I would feel when the real hunger and thirst came calling.

I tried to lift my finger, and again I couldn't tell if I managed to raise it, or if it was just the trembling of my paralyzed muscles refusing to obey my mental directives.

I remembered watching my dad waste away on a similar bed when I was a younger man. My father had emphysema, and a viral infection turned that into pneumonia. He was in ICU, and his doctor called my mom, stepbrother and me aside to tell us the bad news. We took the news at the nurses' station, and as we stood there, I noticed a bank of monitors, and each one showing a black-and-white image, viewed from a corner near the ceiling, of every room in the Intensive Care Unit. All that horrible human suffering contained in those monitors. How could anyone watch that eight hours a day and not be suicidal?

I found my dad's room and saw him remove the canulet from his nose. My dad had been a vital, healthy man all his life, until the emphysema reached the end stage. He was dying by slow, humiliating turns in the hospital bed, and he wanted only to duck out while he still had some slight control over his own life. Without the canulet to provide the oxygen, it wouldn't have taken that long, but I told the doctor what I saw, and she affixed the canulet back in place, and ordered soft restraints for my father to keep him from trying such a thing again. After all, who was he to decide how and when to end his own life?

I wasn't ready to let my father go, and my selfishness accomplished nothing other than causing him to linger for several more days as the pneumonia and emphysema conspired to make every breath a monumental struggle. I was ashamed of my weakness ever after, and my cheapening of his courageous act. I felt like he must have felt, bedfast, waiting for a miracle cure (which certainly didn't come in my dad's case) or waiting for the inevitable: hallucinations from spiking fevers, followed by seizures, just little ones at first, but growing in ferocity.

So thirsty.

Don't think about that.

My eyes hurt so much, I would have happily traded food and drink for just one good refreshing blink. I wished I could close my eyes. I wanted to shout my growing frustration, and even that was beyond me. The light from the lantern was too bright. I'd laid down on the cot after burying the dog, too exhausted to blow out the lamp, and fell asleep.

I felt as if I was running my own torture chamber, bright light and the drip-drip-drip of the seconds.

One day?

Two?

The smell of the food, sitting in the trash, spoiling, tantalizing and nauseating *(don't think about it)* and I can't sleep to escape it because I can't close my eyes. Just a moment's peace now, that's all I want.

Three days?

I felt my hand tremble, but now I didn't know if it was because my system was finally purging the neurotoxins, or if it was the onset of petit mal.

I watched in dumb horror as the ceiling and bed seemed to slowly trade places, until I felt as if I was floating overhead, looking down on the ceiling. My lips were dry and fused together. I could no longer hear the clock. I suppose it had run down, and I tried to think how long they ran before they needed to be rewound, trying to get some idea of how long I'd been here.

I heard flies buzzing like whispers in a movie theatre, refusing to shut up. One of them landed on my nose, but I couldn't see it. I could still only stare straight ahead, at the ceiling, but I could feel it walking on my nose, my cheek and neck and mouth. I tried to open my lips to gulp it down, but they were too dry.

Day five. I guess.

Sara came to see me. I don't think it will be long now. She offered her hand to me and I actually raised mine to take hers.

The venom was wearing off. I managed to turn my head, trying to find Sara again, but she was gone.

I raised my hand and held it before my eyes, swollen

and irritated, and let it drop with a thud on my chest. It looked kind of thin, but I thought I could probably still find some meat on it. If it gets down to that, if I have to...

A week. Maybe.

I had some seizures; nothing too bad, but they were getting worse, and coming more often, as my heart stumbled and staggered without the electrolytes it needed. Eventually, the big one would come along and my body would arch as my locked-up muscles strained, and I'd ride that bucking pony on out of here.

It was now or never. The venom wasn't purged from my system yet, but I couldn't wait for that to happen or I'd be too weak to move at all. I still didn't have control over my body, but at least movement had returned to my right arm, and right leg. I tried to get my body rocking, trying to roll over. I crooked my right leg and pushed away from the wall, upsetting the bunk and myself. I hit the floor hard, unable to break my fall.

I was making grunting animal sounds as I tried to drag myself across the floor with my right arm, pushing with my right leg. I didn't have the strength to go far, but my first stop wasn't too distant. I reached for the trash can, missed, and reached again, arm as stiff and uncoordinated as any George Romero zombie. I managed to spill its waste on the floor. I hooked the tin trays from the MREs with my hand and pulled them closer, and buried my face in the stale, rotting, fly-blown scraps, trying to open my fever-stitched lips to lick the pans.

Whimpering, I pried my lips open with my good hand and wrestled my tongue, fat and swollen, from my mouth. I lapped up every spoiled scrap of food that still clung to the MRE tins, maggots and all. I gagged, and my stomach cramped as the rotten food hit it, but it was finer and more satisfying than any meal I'd ever eaten in the best four-star restaurant. I upended the empty fruit tins and drank what little syrup remained, cutting my tongue as I tried to lick the very last drop. I was definitely the post-apocalyptic poster boy for gluttony.

Exhausted, I lay on the floor, belly-down with garbage scraps strewn about me, like a starving dog that's upset the neighbor's trash cans. The cool concrete of the floor felt good against my fevered head and body. I shivered from the cold, chilled now, but I didn't care. For the first time in perhaps a week, I was feeling something other than high-octane despair.

Face buried in the crook of my arm, I felt the room spin, and all I could do was try to hang on and hope I landed safely in Oz.

I woke, aware of a presence in the room. I was still lying on the floor, my muscles stiff and cramped from the cold, hard cement and several days' worth of inactivity. The lantern had nearly guttered out, but there was light from the open exit hatch.

I tried to speak, but my mouth was still too dry, tongue too swollen. I turned my head and saw the legs of a Throwaway standing near me. I think it was trying to decide if I was alive or dead, or possibly just fascinated by all the food and water stacked against the walls. It muttered something to itself, a hissing, slithery sound like a snake over sand. I located the rifle and tried to push-drag my stiff body toward it.

In that moment, the Throwaway took a sudden interest in me and what my spastic hand was reaching for. He grabbed the rifle by the barrel and raised it over his head like a bludgeon, taking a couple of tentative swings with it, gauging its weight, I suppose. He aimed the rifle butt at my skull, but I instinctively threw up my right arm—my only functioning arm—to block it. The impact numbed my forearm, and the creature raised the rifle for another blow.

I kicked out with my right leg, catching the In-betweener in the shin and spoiling his aim. Kicking and dragging, I pushed myself under the table as he brought the rifle down for yet another blow. The rifle crashed down on the tabletop, splitting it down the middle, spilling everything to the floor. The knife that impaled the scorpion-thing to the table was imbedded too deeply for me to be able to wrest free, and I didn't waste my time trying. I grabbed one of the syringes that had fallen to the floor, and pulled back on the plunger, filling the tube with air. Even so, I still had scant control over my movements, and it was a monumental effort to grip the syringe and fumble the plunger up with the thumb-ring.

The Throwaway grabbed me by the throat and jerked me to my feet, bringing me within inches of his hideous face. He had several rows of teeth, I saw: the outer ring was for grabbing and rending, while the inner rows were for chewing. He had the nictitating eyes of a lizard, and soft, pebbled scales like a bad skin condition covering his neck and arms. His back and belly, for all I knew, may well have been plated with armored scales.

He unhinged his jaw, and pulled me closer to that Freudian nightmare of a mouth. My right arm was still numb from the blow of the rifle, but I swung my arm from the shoulder, like a block of wood, bringing the syringe up and embedding it in his jugular. He grunted something and threw me away. I crashed against the concrete wall and landed hard on my cot.

I gasped in pain, trying to pull air into my lungs. The

Throwaway charged at me and I brought my right leg up, planting my foot against his chest, just managing to keep his snapping jaws from my throat, but that wasn't going to last long. I had time for a crazy thought: *If these things were In-betweeners, what were the full-blooded N'lani like?*

The syringe still jutted from the creature's neck, and I gripped it with my right hand, driving the plunger down with my palm.

The air bubble I injected into his bloodstream hit his heart like a runaway freight train. His fingers gripping my throat snapped open, and his eyes widened with shock. He step-stumbled back, grasping at the syringe that still jutted from his throat, quavering in time with his pulse. He made a choking, bleating sound and backed into the opposite wall, and his legs folded. He slid down the wall to a sitting position, hands resting palms-up on his thighs, eyes closed and head cocked to the side as if he was enjoying a beautiful passage of music.

I probably didn't look much better, and it occurred to me to wonder if this Throwaway had traveled in a pack. If so, I could probably count on more unwelcome visitors, like trick-or-treaters who keep coming to your door, long after you've run out of candy.

I thought about getting up, closing and locking the door, but just the thought of it exhausted me. My eyes slid closed like two heavy roll-gates.

There was a hand touching my cheek, softly, and I opened my gummy eyes, sticky from fever and long, wasting sickness. I looked into the eyes of an old, weatherworn woman. Her eyes were brown and bright as polished berries, caught in a network of wrinkles. She smiled, revealing uneven teeth. It was, I think, the most wonderful face and the most beautiful smile I'd ever seen.

"Hello, son," she said. "What have you gotten yourself into now?"

CHAPTER FIFTEEN

As I found out later, the morning I left Jasmine to conduct tests on her blood in my home lab, she woke not long after that. Her first concern was not that I was gone, but that she felt as if she were dying. I forgot how bad that first hangover of your life can be, especially if you're one of those people who is seldom sick. Not as if I'd had a lot of my own, but at least I'd had some experiences to compare it to.

Her head felt as if she had a pricker-plant growing behind her eyes, and her stomach was a bitter stew. She tried to stand, and the pain in her head drove her back down to the cot. Greasy sweat rolled down her face and body, and her stomach made animal noises, growling and groaning.

Dimly, she noticed the cotton swabs that were taped to her inner elbows, and pulled them loose. The Band-Aids tugged at her flesh and small arm hairs, making her yelp in pain, and the sound of her own voice made her head throb like a rotten tooth.

Moving slowly, she made her way to the door and opened it. The sun, already risen by this point, was intensely bright on her eyes, and she groaned in misery. "Max, where are you?" she called, now starting to realize I was gone.

She crawled up the short flight of stairs and sicked everything up from the night before. I should have realized not only would the wine be a hard blow to her system, but so would food from my time, packed with preservatives and chemicals that her natural diet never included.

When she felt like she might actually live through the day, she began to wonder just where I had gone without her. Of course, in my defense, it wasn't as if leaving a note for her to discover would have done much good. Sara was always beating me up about that, saying that for a man who liked to keep journals, I wasn't much for writing notes.

Jasmine waited patiently for me for the better part of the day, waiting until the sun started its path westward, and then she began to worry. She touched the necklace I had given her at the Trocadero, the one that meant she now belonged to me, and she decided to go out looking for me. At the time she was making that decision, I was testing myself to see if I could still read.

Armed with only her knife and lawn darts and a day's supply of food and water, Jasmine started off toward the town, the exact opposite direction of where I had gone.

When you destroy an animal's native habitat, that animal has to look elsewhere for shelter. I saw that happen time and time again with the deer and raccoons and possums around my home every time some new corporation decided what the people of Mountain View *really* needed was another mall or apartment complex. When that happened, the bulldozers would flatten another section of forest, and the animals who had been living there would suddenly find themselves homeless. Although they didn't debase themselves by standing near the freeway off-ramps and offer to wash your windshield for a buck, or wear crude, handmade signs around their necks that said "Will Eat You For Food," the forest wildlife very often ended up in someone's backyard, rummaging through their garbage cans, or in the case of the deer, drowning in someone's in-ground swimming pool.

The Throwaways were now homeless animals.

Many had died in their boltholes when the city burned. The Throwaways had taken over the basements and attics and lofts of most of the downtown buildings, like green-skinned yuppies, but by the time they realized their homes were ablaze, the fire had made escape nearly impossible.

The In-betweeners living in the upper stories fared somewhat better. Clutching their infants or, in some cases, their unhatched eggs, the creatures raced across the burning rooftops, leaping from building to building, coming at last to the last building on the block, where they climbed, lizard-like, down the brick facade to the street.

Other egg nests, cut off by the fire, burst from the terrible heat. I hadn't given much thought to the In-betweeners having mates and offspring, and when Jasmine told me about this, I felt sick and unclean. They had been nothing more than the kind of monstrosity you'd expect to see in a low-budget sci-fi film, or perhaps popping up and waving a club at you in a Point-of-View shoot-'em-up video game, but they were living things with children of their own.

How could I *not* have realized this? It was one thing killing the Throwaways who were slavering for my blood, but this was cold-blooded homicide, no better than what the N'lani did to mankind. The N'lani did it because they *could*, and so did I.

The Throwaways were scattered throughout the woods and hills bordering the town, and Jasmine's search for me led her straight into their encampment in Frontier Park. Most of downtown had burned quickly, but the park, away from the worst of the inferno, was still a relative safe haven. At least, until the winds shifted and blew the fire toward the In-betweeners once more.

Many of the creatures that had survived the fire had only done so at a cost; they had been burned badly, and some floated between life and death. Jasmine watched from a distance as the creatures gave one another what ministrations they could, tending to the dying and comforting the survivors.

One of the injured, a hatchling of just a few months, lay untended on a bed of nettles. It was frightened and in pain, away from the others, and Jasmine could no longer bear to simply stand by and watch it suffer. The hatchling had terrible burns over most of its body, scaly flesh blackened and crumbling. It had no hope for living out the night, and Jasmine slipped closer, wrapping herself in the cloak of shadows. The hatchling mewled and spat at her, snapping and biting and clawing, even as she gave the creature her bottle of water to drink, and tried to wash and tend its wounds.

The hatchling trembled once, arching its back so high Jasmine could hear its blackened flesh crackle and pop. And then, slowly, the little body relaxed, went limp, and settled into its death. Jasmine arranged the little body with as much dignity as she could give it, and turned to go.

The hatchling's mother had returned in time to see Jasmine tend the body, and she and Jasmine stood facing one another. The mother had lost an eye in the fire, trying to get her hatchling to safety, but that one good eye was more than capable enough of expressing the mother's anguish and grief. She moved past Jasmine, not raising an alarm to alert the other nearby Throwaways, and went to her child. Grief is a common thread, the mud-vein that runs through any species, the language we all speak, at one time or another. It is only by the random grace of the universe we find anyone who will listen.

Jasmine realized I had not been captured by the In-betweeners, which only made her more curious and more worried about my whereabouts. She alternated between concern for my safety, and certainty that I had left her alone and stranded far from her own home.

She walked quietly, moving as silently as a cloud across the face of a lake, and passed through the ranks of the Throwaway males who were out hunting for us, for what we had done to their nests and their mates and their hatchlings. The night made them dull and sluggish, as it would most any lizard, and before one could sound the alarm, she managed to close the gap between them in three quick strides, and slit its throat.

It hissed, its cry of alarm and anger bubbling out of the gaping wound in its throat. Jasmine moved on, taking great pains to stay downwind of the vengeful creatures. They had carried *that* much of man's genetic disposition with them into this new amalgam of shapes, at least. It was as if, far from embodying the best of both species, the In-betweeners were repositories for the worst traits of each. By night, they prowled more like the lizard they resembled, down on all fours, tongue flicking in and out, head swishing from side to side, as if the dark sorcery of the night unlocked whatever ancient genetic code was buried deep within their hybridized DNA. When Jasmine told me about this, I had to wonder which was the more disturbing image: things that looked like reptiles, walking upright like a man, or half-men scurrying along on their plated bellies like lizards. Neither picture was likely to win my vote for the cover of next year's Mountain View telephone book.

Some of the creatures, drained by the cool night air, lay belly-down on flat rocks that retained the heat from the sun, watching Jasmine with dull, disinterested eyes.

By the time the sun lightened the eastern sky—about the time I finished burying Blood—Jasmine was convinced she must have put some serious distance between herself and the Throwaways. She ate the little food she brought with her as she ran, not wanting to stop until she felt safe. Her water she had given to comfort the dying In-betweener child.

The Throwaways were relentless, following her spoor, despite their slowed metabolism. A few times in the night, she was sure she heard a slithering movement behind her, or to her side, or from just ahead of her, but it may have been nothing more than the wind ruffling the tall snake grass.

But as the ground and air warmed, the In-betweeners regained their vigor, and their upright posture, and their hellish speed quickly negated what little geographic advantage Jasmine had managed. They harried her like hounds chasing a fox, running her until painful, molten stitches ripped up her side and cramps threatened to hobble her, while the raptors would take turns hunting, so they were always fresh, always near enough to deprive her of even a moment's rest.

The creatures climbed the trees, leaping from branch to branch, bole to bole, keeping pace with her from overhead, calling to the other Throwaways in their hissing and grunting language, alerting the rest to Jasmine's whereabouts. Once, she turned and flung a lawn dart at her treetop pursuer, catching him square in the eye, driving the tip of the dart deep into its tiny brain. The creature slowed, but didn't die, as if all systems had just been kicked over to the back-up emergency generator. And that's exactly what had happened; the understudy brain suddenly found itself headlining for the stricken star. But by the time the secondary brain sorted out the sudden influx of information it was receiving, Jasmine had used the momentary confusion to race farther ahead.

The other Throwaways were equally confused without the information from the scout, and fanned out in random, widening arcs, hoping to pick up her scent once again.

It didn't take long for the In-betweeners to catch up with Jasmine, even after that. Earthquakes and other disasters had changed the face of the California landscape, and a great fissure had been torn across the countryside. The crevice ran through San Francisco, through homes and streets and parks, all the way through the hills of Mountain View. The water from the Bay had swept in to fill this new riverbed, and it was this that reined Jasmine up short.

She stood at the top of the cliff, looking down at the rushing waters twenty or thirty feet below. The gap was too great across to jump, and the crevice continued on in either direction as far as she could see.

She stood bent at the waist, head down, hands on her thighs, trying to catch her breath and decide her next course of action, when the Throwaways caught up with her.

They knew she was cornered, and fanned out in a pincer movement, cutting off any hope of retreat. They slowly advanced on her, hissing and spitting their rage and hunger. Jasmine drew her knife and waited for the first one to attack.

She didn't have to wait long; the Throwaways were

not patient, and the first one broke formation and charged her, running low to the ground, screeching a shrill war cry as it came. Jasmine waited until the last moment, then dropped flat on her back, holding her knife point-upward with both hands as she did. She thrust the blade into the Throwaway's chest, the creature's unchecked forward rush serving to eviscerate itself on the knife.

A rain of scalding hot blood pattered down on Jasmine, and the lizard-thing's stomach opened like a hideous window, its purple and gray intestines unspooling in a sudden rush, like a spring-loaded novelty snake in a can. The creature mewled, staggered past her, toward the edge of the cliff. The intestines looped around Jasmine's arm, snaring her like a cowboy's lariat. The creature stumbled on unsteady legs, and went over the precipice.

Jasmine was suddenly dragged along behind the In-betweener, sliding across the ichor-slicked grass toward the edge of the drop. She hacked furiously at the ropy intestines that linked her fate to her attacker's, but she was gone, pulled over the rim and dropping fast.

The creature hit the water and Jasmine followed a moment later, still tethered to him by several yards of guts. The In-betweener went down, down, sinking toward the bottom of the rushing river, dragging Jasmine with him. She had lost her knife in the plunge, and the water buffeted her along, tumbling and throwing her against the rocky river walls and outcropping stones along the bottom of the trench. She spotted the burnished light of the sun laying on the surface of the river and kicked for it, but the weight of the body kept her from reaching it.

The impact of the fall had driven what air she had managed to gulp down from her lungs. Frantic, Jasmine did the only thing she could do: She *chewed* through the intestines still mooring her to the In-betweener. The water around her darkened at once with a thick, oily cloud of blood and bile and waste. The body of the creature lodged in a nest of boulders, while the currents continued to pull and push Jasmine onward. The intestines stretched taut...tauter...and *snapped* with a violent suddenness. She went tumbling out of control, end over end, without the anchor of the hybrid-thing to give her any ballast. She smashed against outcroppings, jagged canyon walls, and the skeletal rooftops of submerged homes that had been swallowed by the new fault line.

Jasmine struggled for the golden coins of sunlight, kicking with all her might, knowing even in that instant she wouldn't make it in time. She kept fighting, because that was what she had spent her whole young life doing, but the light dimmed, and went out.

The current emptied out several miles later into an inland tidal basin, and deposited her on the marshy banks of the pool. She lay there, half in and half out of the water, unable to move, unable to call for help, or even open her eyes. The moon rose and set, and rose and set again.

She was at last discovered, still lying on the marshy banks, by Jon, one of the children who lived in the nearby collective. If he hadn't been shirking his chores and gone sneaking off to play, Jasmine may well have lain there until she perished from exposure. As it was, it was a close-run thing.

At first, Jon didn't notice her, lying among the reeds and cattails. He was too interested in seeing what other treasures the currents had swept to the tidal pool. Once, the tides brought in pieces of a sailing ship, carried along from San Francisco Bay, but mostly the currents only brought a few odds and ends, like water-bloated pieces of furniture, or driftwood, or exotic sea life. Sometimes it carried with it a gassy body, green from decomposition and its extremities plucked clean by the little fishes and crabs. But Jon couldn't recall the tides ever leaving an offering like this one before.

He approached Jasmine cautiously; sometimes the things deposited in the basin were not dead, merely stunned, and a lot of them woke up feeling nasty. Jon stood near her, just out of reach, and broke off a length of reed. He touched it to her cheek, ready to jump back in case this one woke up feeling mean, as well. He still carried the scars on his right forearm from the baby shark he tried to pick up without first checking to see what its mortal status was. And sometimes, he knew, the gas-swollen bodies would fart if you touched them just right. But this one didn't really look like all the others; she was pale from shock and exposure, and her clothes were torn and her flesh bloodied from all the shale outcroppings she was thrown against on her wild, E-ticket ride, and the flesh that wasn't lacerated sported black and purple bruises, like smudges. She was, perhaps, more dead than alive, but so had the baby shark been.

When she didn't react to the reed brushing her cheek, Jon grew a little bolder, running the tip of his branch across her eyes, down her nose and neck, coming at last to the V-shaped tear in the front of her tunic. The fabric was still quite wet, and Jon could see the prominent "woman things" through the thin cloth.

He looked nervously around, making sure no one else was near, and slipped the stiff reed under the tunic's sodden edge and lifted, just a little. "Holy Joe!" he cried, although he wasn't really sure what he was seeing. He just knew the older kids were always excited about these things, and it seemed he should be, as well.

He continued to stare, becoming dimly aware that he was being studied, in turn. Jon gasped in alarm, dropping the reed, because Jasmine had turned her head and was staring at him through bruised, lidded eyes. "Holy Joe!" he cried again, his heart making a wild, crazy lurch. He stepped back several paces, ready to run, if need be, but the boy needn't have worried. Jasmine didn't have the strength left to be much of a threat to him or anyone. Her eyes were unfocused and unfixed, not really taking in what she was seeing. She blinked in slow motion, and drifted back to sleep.

And now Jon was faced with a problem: did he go tell someone about this woman, helpless, probably dying, that he found at the tide pool when he was supposed to be doing his chores? Surely someone else would come along and discover her...*surely?*

All the same, he moved closer to her once more, and pulled her the rest of the way out of the pool. He saw her legs were also ragged and bruised, and she had lost her sandals during her violent, water-swept journey.

Jon noticed the darts still tucked into her belt, and, watching Jasmine for any sign of reaction, worried one free to inspect it. He touched his fingertip to the point, and hissed with a sound like a knife being dragged over a whetstone as a bead of blood formed there. He absently put his finger in his mouth and sucked at the wound. He didn't know what to do, and thinking was not one of Jon's strong points. At last, he decided to leave her there and say nothing.

Tucking the dart under his own belt, the boy ran back toward the fields, where his chores awaited him, and tried not to think any more about the woman.

I can't tell you what Jon thought as the day wore on and the sun skimmed toward the horizon. I only know what Jasmine later told me. Jon was not a thinking boy, but he was a good boy, and as the night enfolded the small collective in its shadowy embrace, he began to worry more about the woman he left at the tidal pool. But then he probably told himself, *She's dead by now. Anything I say is only going to get me in deeper trouble.*

The night wind prowled among the small hovels, moving between them, rattling windows, testing doors, snuffling around the chimneys and skating under the thatched eaves, like something alive looking for a way in. It was a search that was bordering on frenzied. There was no need to fill these children with a bedtime-fear of boogeymen or other bugaboos, because there *were* monsters that prowled the night, and no monster-prayer would banish them back to your dark closet or beneath your bed. If they wanted to eat on you, they could, and your mother couldn't stop them. They were monsters; they did as they pleased. That was just the way things were.

Jon threw back his covers and went to wake his grandmother.

At first she tried to tell the boy it was all a bad dream, that's all, a bad dream, nothing to be afraid of, you go back to bed now, and when he saw she wouldn't believe him, he went to his mattress and lifted the edge and removed the dart he had hidden there earlier. He presented it to his grandmother, who turned it over and over in her liver-spotted hands. She said she thought she'd seen one of these a long, long time ago, then woke Jon's father.

Bat-winged shadows chased after one another in the starry sky, shrieking their shrill and tuneless song. They flew in wide, slow circles, intrigued by the flickering torchlight procession that made its way from the hovels, across the field and fallow land to the swampy bank of the tidal pool. After a while, the chittering, flying things wheeled and flew away, looking for nighttime insects, or perhaps a field mouse or a shrew. Their two-headed silhouettes printed themselves across the gibbous face of the moon like strange Chinese calligraphy, forming a word, a sentence, a paragraph, and then they were gone.

Jon led them to the spot where he had found Jasmine, but she was gone. His father eyed the boy critically, ready to cuff him one, when Jon's grandmother saw the muddy footprints. She held her torch of horsetail weeds near the muddy, uneven ground, and saw not only Jon's footprints, but the bare footprints of a woman. The trail led back into the reeds, and barely ten yards from the edge of the basin, Jasmine. Jon knelt close to study her face by the light of the guttering torches. Her eyes opened, and she said without emotion, "You're the little turd who looked at my tits."

The next time she woke, Jasmine found herself lying in bed in the small hut belonging to Jon's grandmother and father. Jon's grandmother had prepared an herbal poultice and had smeared the ghastly smelling paste over Jasmine's more serious cuts.

Her return to consciousness was not like waking from a heavy sleep, but more like rising from the swift and violent waters that had nearly claimed her. Jasmine's fever had already begun to climb back down as the infection in her wounds was drained by the herbal medicines, but she was still as weak and wobbly as a newborn colt. She tried to move, and a sharp, white bolt of pain stabbed through Jasmine's back. She had pulled several big muscles in her fall from the cliff, and bruised herself down to the bone on the underwater rocks she had careened from.

"Wh-where?"

"Don't you worry about that, pretty girl," the old woman told her. "You just rest and heal. You have my deepest sorries that Jon didn't tell us about you sooner. But, stars willing, you'll be fine again."

When she asked how long she had been here, Jon's grandmother told Jasmine "A day."

The old woman turned from the cauldron hung over the small hearth fire and handed Jasmine a bowl of weak soup. It was an herbal brew, she said, to help her to rest and regain her strength. Jasmine's hands shook as she took the stone bowl, spilling some of the hot broth on the covers, but she managed to take a few sips of it.

"I have to get back," Jasmine said, her voice thick and slurry from exhaustion, and the herbs that were already coursing through her system. "I have to find him. He'll wonder where I am."

"Who will, dear?" the old woman asked, taking the bowl from her fingers, even as they relaxed and uncurled. Another moment and she would have dropped it. "Who will wonder? Where are you from?"

She ran her leathery hand over Jasmine's creased brow, and the hand was softer and cooler than the girl had guessed it might be. The worry between her eyes melted away beneath that gentle touch, the way a sculptor's hand soothes away a mistake in soft clay. Had she died and gone over? If it weren't for the pain in her back and joints, like ground glass, she would have thought so. And even the pain was beginning to fade now, making it harder to be sure she hadn't died.

"Who will miss you, little one?" the old woman asked again, softly.

Jasmine had to concentrate to manage the next bit; the soporific was getting her off like a rocket. "M-Max," she said, turning her head to the side and mumbling into the straw-filled pillow. "Max."

When she woke the second time, she was in only marginally less pain than she had been, but she was more herself, more *there* than she had been for several days. She took notice of the little house in which she rested; the central room was small and described a hemisphere, with small, latticework windows all around that semicircle. A large stone hearth dominated most of the curved wall, and near that a large wooden table. A small fire burned, and a black metal kettle simmered above the flames, sending out tantalizing plumes of smoke.

An entryway to the other rooms of the little dwelling was located to Jasmine's right. A great, rough wooden pillar stood in the very center of the house, and Jasmine said it looked like the trunk of a big tree. I wondered if perhaps that's just what it was, if the hovels were a collective of tree houses, set up off the ground to make attacks by marauding, rival tribes or other night-walking creatures more difficult.

She kicked her bedcovers back and tried to sit up, driving a jagged scream of pain through her back. Jasmine quickly laid back down, gasping from the pain.

"Steady, there. I wouldn't try to do too much just yet," Jon's father advised her. "You were in pretty bad shape when Jon found you."

She looked at him in the dim evening light and blinked. "Max!" she said.

He studied her, making her uncomfortable, and making her look at him again. She realized he was not I, after all. "How do you know Max?" he asked.

Her hand went to the necklace around her neck, but it was gone, swept away by the wild, rushing water. "I belong to him," she answered simply. She continued to study his face, so much like mine and still so different. "Who are you?" she asked. "Why do you look like Max?"

"And why shouldn't I look like my little brother?"

Well, you know how it goes. It's always awkward when the girl who belongs to you meets your family before you do.

The next morning, with Jasmine lying in the bed of a wooden cart pulled by a dray horse, she led Max's brother, nephew, and mother to the bomb shelter, using the smoldering ruins of Mountain View as her true north.

A couple of Throwaways were near the shelter, and Jasmine noticed with alarm that the door to the bunker stood open. The creatures charged the horse, causing it to rear in fright, nearly upsetting the little cart and its passengers in the bargain. Jon tried to protect his grandmother and Jasmine, putting himself between the women and the Throwaways. By now, the lizard-things had buried their sucker-maws into the neck of the horse and were gorging themselves on its blood. The horse bucked, reared, smashed the skull of one of its attackers, but the hideous thing continued to feed, its jaws continued to draw blood.

In an effort to keep the cart from going over, Dolan uncoupled the horse from the wagon, and the horse, freed of its burden, galloped and kicked and leaped in ever-higher mad pirouettes, trying futilely to shake loose the In-betweeners.

"That's Max's horse," Jasmine told them, pointing to the Soft Tail.

"It's like no horse I've ever seen," Jon said in obvious awe.

"Your uncle," Dolan reminded the boy, "never was one to do anything by half."

Near the edge of the old orchard, the horse stumbled,

went down, tried to get back up. It let loose a shrill, seemingly endless cry of fear and pain, and then was quiet. Even at that distance, Jasmine said they could still hear the sound of the creatures feasting and the suckling of blood.

By the time they had entered the bomb shelter, I had managed to dispose of the third Throwaway (I was later grateful that they arrived when they did; if their presence hadn't distracted the other two creatures, my fate would have been no happier than that of the old gray mare) and sat, spent and helpless, on the cot.

Max's mother noticed the scorpion-thing, still pinned to the wreckage of the table, right away, and sent Jon and Dolan out to search for the herbs she would need to prepare a curative for the poison still lingering in my system. Jasmine sat beside me on the cot, holding me tightly, or as tightly as her own injuries would permit. I tried to hug her back, but my arms may as well have belonged to someone else—and I suppose, to be technical about it, they did—for all that they listened to my mental commands.

"I was so worried," I told her, struggling to form the words. "I thought—"

"I know," she said, kissing me, our words overlapping. "I thought—"

We laughed a little, just happy to be with one another again. Jasmine at last leaned in and whispered, "Your mother seems very nice."

CHAPTER SIXTEEN

Have you ever gone to a family reunion, and everyone's pleasant and happy to see you, but there's something just slightly...*off?*

After my father's death, I lost touch with his side of the family. I got busy with college, then marriage and career, and before I knew it, years had passed. So when the invitation came for the Stein family reunion, Sara convinced me I should go, reacquaint myself with that side of my history. The gathering was being held on a Sunday afternoon in the park, and I didn't recognize a single soul there. But that was no big surprise; it had been years since I'd seen anyone, after all. Everyone was glad we could make it, and they all made a big fuss over Maryvonne, who was perhaps nine months old at the time. But the more we talked about family and the old days, the more I realized we had come to the wrong reunion. We'd spent most of the afternoon talking with these people, eaten hamburgers and ears of corn and three-bean salad and macaroni salad and seven different types of dessert, and there was no good way to bring up our little faux pas without looking like complete idiots. I told Sara my suspicions and she said Maryvonne was feeling a bit choleric and we'd probably better get her home, but we'll see you all next year, okay?

The real Stein reunion was being held in another part of the park, and we quickly found them and caught up on family news, who's getting married, who's gotten buried. As we were sitting there at one of the picnic benches, one of our poseur relatives walked past on an after-lunch constitutional and saw us. She didn't even try to hide her surprise at finding us here, and I have no doubts she raced right back to the other group and promptly told them about the professional family-reunion gatecrashers, or at the very least I'm sure we were described as anything from insane to assholes.

For years after that, whenever we were in a crowd in the parks or in an outdoor concert, Sara would ask me if this was another family reunion. I really didn't mind telling people the story, because it made me smile to think there were all these strangers out there who told the same story, but only Sara and I knew the punchline.

Somewhere out there, in an empty house, in a dusty closet, in a family album that no one has looked at in far too long and that was only my family for a day, there are pictures of Sara, Maryvonne and myself. They were nice to us, but we were in the wrong family album. We simply didn't belong there.

That was how I felt with Max's mother, his brother, Dolan, and Dolan's son, Jon. They were nice enough, but they weren't really my family.

My mother (it felt odd to call her that, and it was about to get even odder) brewed the herbs into a potion that would help counteract the scorpion-thing's venom, and Dolan sat next to me on a stool beside the bed.

"How have you been, Max?" he asked. "Last I heard, you were in jail."

"I was," I agreed, "but I got out early for good behavior. I found God while I was in prison, but I didn't ask Him what He was in for."

Dolan rolled his eyes and shook his head. "Don't be an ass," he warned, and added, in a voice low enough that our mother couldn't hear, "Haven't you worried mom enough with your stunts? You're welcome to stay with us until you're well enough to travel, but we don't need the trouble you make finding its way to our door...understand?"

I nodded. The poet was right when he said, Home is the place where they have to take you in...but he forgot to mention that they don't have to let you stay there a moment longer than strictly necessary.

My mother brought the bowl of steaming herbal brew to me, and I managed to sip a few mouthfuls. It tasted bitter, and I could feel it burning like a coal in my belly, its fiery tendrils spreading out through my entire body. I realized it was my nervous system beginning to wake up, my muscles unlocking, after several days of near rigor mortis.

I began to sweat heavily, baking from the inside out, and an oily perspiration formed on my flesh. It smelled foul, and it was as thick as paste, and I realized it was the neurotoxins being purged from my system. My mother dabbed at my forehead and cheeks and neck with a cloth, wiping away the foul-smelling, neutralized poison. It was the smell of long sickness, and suffering, and desperation. It was a terrible thing. It was the smell of what my life had become. She folded the cloth and threw it aside.

"How do you feel now?" Jasmine asked.

I moved my head, a little cautiously, but there was no pain, no locking of joints. Reassured, I worked my arm and shoulder a bit, and found it moved like a well-oiled piston. "I feel great," I said, and I did.

"Are you hungry?" my mother asked. "You must be starving after all that."

After everything I had just gone through, that struck me as an incredibly mundane thing to ask. This was a world where spiders the size of Volkswagens prowled the streets; a world where lizard-men liquified the meat and muscle of men and animals and drank us like a Goddamn smoothie; this was a world where sad-eyed dogs carried scorpion-things hidden inside them like Russian nesting dolls, and my mother was acting as if it was the most normal thing in the world. But then, however much my world may have changed, her world had not: she was still my mother, and this was what mothers in any time did. They looked after their children.

Dolan had gone to fetch another horse to pull the dray, since Jasmine and I were not yet in any condition to walk the several miles back home, and he told Jon to stay here and keep an eye out for trouble. But the look he gave me just before he left told me what he really meant by that: He didn't want me to say anything that might upset our mother. He didn't want the kind of trouble I made finding its way to their door.

That wasn't hard to understand. He was only doing what I would have done in a similar situation, and I think he sensed something different about me. He didn't know what it was yet, but he knew I wasn't Max. Not the Max he grew up with. I was the guy who had wandered into the wrong family reunion again and Dolan sensed it.

Jon wrenched the knife still pinning the desiccated scorpion to the broken table plank free, and shook the blade several times until the shriveled body—even in death it looked malignant—slipped off and dropped to the floor. I expected it to leap to its feet and start chasing after Jon, but it had the good decency to remain dead. Jon noticed among the breakage of the table another object, and laid the knife aside to pick up what he had discovered.

"What's this?" he asked, holding up the microscope for me to see. His questioning hands twiddled and twirled the magnification knobs. "What does it do?"

"It's a microscope," I told him. "You use it to magnif–you use it to make small things look bigger."

"Can I make myself bigger with this?"

"Being big isn't everything you think it is," I said.

My mother looked at the microscope, her mouth open and her brow creased. At last she said, "You can look at it, but be careful with it." It was a delicate piece of work, and not even this world's most gifted craftsmen could ever duplicate it. Yet, at one time, they were common enough.

"Mom? What was that about? Have you seen a microscope before?"

She counterfeited a smile and shrugged. "Maybe. I thought it looked familiar. Maybe I saw one when I was younger."

"You were born before the N'lani–the Masters–came?"

"Yes. I was just a little girl. I was there the day they arrived. People said my father helped them."

I felt a chill climbing my spine like a ladder, despite the baking heat of the herbal brew still swimming in my system. "What–what was your father's name?"

"I can't remember," she said, but her eyes said she didn't *want* to remember. She had locked that door because she had seen something traumatic that she didn't want to risk stumbling across again by accident.

"When you were a little girl," I said, speaking softly, "the boy next door to you was named Langdon Donahue. He wanted to marry you, even then, but you only had eyes for Buster Ellis. Your dad used to call you 'Vonnie,' but that wasn't your real name."

The door to her past was not going to be opened by force, but I thought perhaps it could be coaxed open, if

I just jiggled the knob patiently. Not just that door, but a whole series of doors, one behind the next, like the doors of a Philadelphia shotgun-house.

"Your real name is Maryvonne, do you remember that? Your mother's name was Sara and your father's name was Paul. He wasn't a traitor. Something terrible happened to him that day, but he would never have done anything to hurt you or your mom."

Vonnie stood still, and emitted a little gasp—the sound, perhaps, of an air-tight door opening, just slightly. Maybe it would be wide enough to let a few memories slip out.

"Max?" Jasmine asked, beginning to sound marginally alarmed. Not by me, so much, as by the pained look on Vonnie's face as she struggled with all her might to brace her back against that door and dig her heels in. That was a door that had no business being opened, ever again.

We don't need the kind of trouble you make finding its way to our door...understand?

I thought I did, finally. It had taken me long enough, but give me this much: what had happened to me was hardly one of those ho-hum, not this again kind of experiences. Paul Stein's consciousness had been reborn in the body of his grandson. But how did I prepare Vonnie for something like this?

"What are you doing? How do you know these things?" Jasmine asked again.

I ignored her and said softly, "Your father loved you more than any other father ever loved his daughter."

"Then why did he leave me? Why didn't he come back?" It was the voice of an old woman, but she was expressing the pain of that lost and abandoned little girl whose childhood ended on that sweltering September morning.

"I'm sure he tried," I told her. "I'm sure he's still trying. He just hasn't found the right way back to you yet."

Jasmine and I rode in the back of the dray, nestled in the dry, sweet-smelling straw, while Jon held on at the corner of the wagon, ducking the low-hanging branches. Dolan and Vonnie sat on the buckboard, and I could feel her eyes upon me, burning through me, as if she could see Paul Stein hiding inside her son.

And what did I really hope to accomplish? I wasn't sure, but I suppose I was desperate to reconnect with my history, to be the father that my little girl lost almost fifty years ago, even though my daughter was now older than I was when I...when whatever happened, happened. I wanted something that made sense in this senseless world. I just wanted my life back. I wanted to go to the right part of the park and sit at the right family reunion.

The horse clopped along over the heat-cracked and broken road. In the distance, I could hear the *whirrrr* of an insect, but it was no sound I had ever heard before. But then, I'm sure it was a sound made by an insect whose like I'd never seen before. Even the least thing about this world conspired to remind me I was not a part of it and never could be.

"How are you feeling, Max?" Dolan asked.

Homesick, I thought, but I didn't think Dolan would understand. I made a dismissive grunt. "I think I'll live," I said.

"Good to hear."

Jasmine nestled a little closer, snuggling her cheek on my right shoulder, and I put my right arm around her and kissed her lightly on the tip of her nose. I don't suppose Dolan really meant it when he said it was good to hear I'd live, but on this day, with the smell of straw in my nostrils and the warm weight of a beautiful woman against my chest, it *was* good to hear I'd live. No, this wasn't my world, but it could be, I thought, if I abandoned my battle with the N'lani. After all, I had it on good authority that no one fights the Masters. Hell, any little kid knew that.

"It's gonna be great to have you with us, Uncle Max," Jon said. "Jasmine can help Grammy and Mom, and you can help Dad and me on the farm."

"Your Uncle Max won't be staying that long, Jon," Dolan said, turning his head to look back over his shoulder. "Isn't that right, Max?"

"Sure," I said, not sounding disappointed in the least. "What kind of life is that? Who'd want it?"

Despite what Dolan said, Jasmine and I did stay at the collective longer than any of us might have imagined. It felt wonderful to be reconnected with my family, even if it was something of a lie. Despite Dolan's initial reservations about me, I proved to be a good worker, laboring with him and the others in the fields, clearing stones from the ground, pulling trunks, walking along behind the horse, guiding the plow in straight, neat, sensible rows. There are no straight lines in nature; only man feels the arrogant need to impose such order upon his surroundings.

My earlier guess about the hovels being built among the trees was correct; perhaps a half-dozen or more little roundhouses, like Hobbits' shires, stood ten or twelve feet above the ground, built around the trunks of redwoods, and those little homes interconnected by a cunning series of wooden walkways and gangplanks. It was a remarkable achievement, and it made me wonder why the N'lani chemicals in the water hadn't seemed to have as great an effect on these people as those who lived in the city.

At first I began to wonder if the collective's water source was free of the contaminant, but I prepared a few slides to study under my microscope, much to Jon's utter delight and amazement, and saw the chemicals were present. I was at a loss to explain it. How could they possibly be immune to the liquid Alzheimer's?

"Jon, are you a big boy?" I asked him as he peered into the microscope.

"I'm not a boy," he said, bristling slightly; "I'm almost a man. My father says so. Even Grammy says so."

I smiled at him. "I think they're right," I said. I stood up, left the little wooden table in front of the hearth and found my bag stuffed away under Jasmine's and my bed. I opened the box of medical syringes and took two out, keeping them hidden away from Jon. I needn't have worried; he was too busy looking at the miracle of microscopic organisms. "Would you like to see what goes on inside your body, Jon?"

He turned away from the eyepiece; he was the All-American Boy, even if America no longer existed anymore. "Like how?"

I showed him the syringes. "With these. We can take a little blood from our arms and study it under the microscope."

Well, what boy ever turned down the opportunity to look at blood, even if it was his own? Jon agreed that would be fun. "It hurts a little bit," I warned him, "but it's nothing bad. I'll go first and show you."

I smeared alcohol on the inside of my left elbow, made a hard, tight fist, and found a good vein. I jabbed the syringe in, drew a sample of blood, and extracted the needle. Jon, who had never had an inoculation in his life, watched it all with rapt fascination. I laid the syringe aside and dabbed the spot with alcohol again.

"See?" I said. "Think you can handle that?"

"Aw, that's nothin'," the boy informed me. "Once, I cut my leg on a sharp stone in the field. Grammy had to stitch it up with twine and she made me wear a poultry over it."

"Poultice," I corrected. The image of the boy running around the farm with a hen stuck to his leg struck me as wildly comical, and I had to bite the inside of my cheek to keep from laughing.

I swabbed Jon's arm with the alcohol, and told him to make a big muscle for me. I kept him distracted, talking about how tough he was, so he wouldn't notice the little sting of the needle. I was afraid he'd jump and break the needle, but Jon was the big boy he said he was, and gritted his teeth and ignored it. I drew his blood and swabbed his pinprick injury. "Let's not tell your dad about this, what do you say, Jon?"

Jon agreed to that one readily enough. I had the impression Dolan didn't let the boy have a lot of fun. Granted, it was a dangerous world, as I'd seen over and again, and a moment's distraction could get you killed, but Dolan seemed almost compulsively set against Jon being a boy. Maybe he remembered the way I turned out, and wanted to make sure the black sheep gene didn't repeat itself in this new generation.

While he held the cotton ball in place, I prepared two slides, Jon's blood and mine, and put his under the microscope first. I looked, but the N'lani chemical wasn't present in Jon's system. I prepared another slide, with another drop of the boy's blood, in case the first slide was contaminated somehow, but the results were the same: there were no signs of the chemical.

I let him take a look, while I stood back and tugged at my lower lip. The chemical was in their water, but not in Jon's bloodstream. I was pretty sure, if I were to take samples from any of the other people in the collective,

I'd find the same thing: no traces of the liquid Alzheimer's.

"This is what my blood looks like?" he asked, unwilling to look away from the eyepiece. I adjusted the magnification to give him a better view. After a while, he got tired of looking at his blood sample and said, "Let's look at yours now." Apparently, the white corpuscles are always whiter on the other slide.

I changed slides and looked at my sample; the chemical was present in my blood, but to a lesser degree than it had been just a few weeks earlier.

How was that possible?

The crops were in at last and the little collective was ready to celebrate another hard-won year. Their fete was unofficially known as the Feast of the Harvest Moon, and was held on the eve of the first full moon following the reaping, and the women were busy preparing the food and drink they would serve in the festival area in the clearing between the trees in which the huts were built. Very old plastic triangular flags were strung between the trees, like rows of red bats hanging upside down. I imagined someone had taken them from a former used car lot, or perhaps Jon had found them washed up one day in the tidal basin.

Long, low trestle tables were readied; they were planed planks of redwood, each end set into a notched tree stump. At the end of the celebration, after all the dances had been danced, and the plays reenacting Nancy Drew mysteries as best as Vonnie could recall the books she used to read as a child, games played and the tests of strength ended, a straw man would be thrown upon a bonfire, a pile of brittle sticks and dried husks stacked high to form a teepee, as thanks for another good harvest. I suppose, if it had been a bad harvest, a straw man would have been thrown upon the fire as a plea for a better year next year.

I had already seen enough of straw effigies when Strawberry-Nose and his dim-witted friend were testing the gallows, but this was done without the cruel, mindless glee that had been heaped upon my stunt double.

It was during the harvesting I began to understand how it was possible the people of the collective showed little or no signs of Alzheimer's: I remembered reading once that 60 percent of the plants in Tahiti are there only because their seeds were carried to the island long ago by winds and seasonal migratory birds. The plants we harvested were like none that had grown on earth before; of that I was certain. I didn't think they were mutations caused by the sudden shift in warming or nuclear residue, but plants whose seeds had blown here through the portals, carried by solar winds blowing across the gulf of light years from the N'lani home world, or borne on the wings of impossible birds.

Those same plants, now part of the diet, probably produced a counter-agent to the liquid Alzheimer's, or perhaps the herbal remedies everyone here partook in had an extra curative property no one suspected. I had taken it upon my shoulders to be the savior of this world, the hero in my own story, and nature had already taken care of it for me. It was a reminder of Paul's hubris, and a reminder that the world got on fine without my help.

The weeks Jasmine and I spent on the collective were slow and peaceful, and at night we would fall into bed, exhausted from a good day's work and ready for sleep, or almost ready. Paul Stein had begun to reassert his place here, setting aside all thoughts of raising a militia and chasing the N'lani off our world and back to theirs. I felt connected again, even though there were times I tried to act like Vonnie's father rather than her son. Even Dolan, who had been insistent that Jasmine and I leave as soon as we were able, seemed to be reconsidering his position, and in fact seemed happy to have rediscovered his brother.

We often ate our lunches together during the harvest time, sitting on the big, flat rock at the bottom of the field, getting to know each other again. Dolan wasn't such a bad guy; he just didn't know how to show it.

"You've done good work, Max," he said, tearing into his lunch. As he spoke, speckles of wet food punctuated his words. "I guess..." At last he said, "I think maybe I was wrong about you. Whatever's done is in the past. If you want to stay here with us, I know mom would like to have you."

"What about you?" I asked. "Do you want me to stay?"

"I said so, didn't I?" he asked, his restless eyes scanning the horizon for the plagues all farmers have been vigilant about: twisters, locusts, fire, Throwaways. There didn't seem to be much likelihood of the first two, but the second two were anybody's guess.

"Sorry," I said with a crooked smile. "Guess I wasn't paying attention."

All that day before the Feast, the children worked to make the straw man, taking a pair of old clothes that, the year before, had belonged to one of the farmers who had died. That was part of the tradition as well, I learned; whenever someone died before the new harvest could be brought in, their old clothes were stuffed with straw, then burned, as a symbolic return to the earth, a closing of the circle of life that never ends.

I had been working on restoring the tractor I found at the A-frame house, riding the motorcycle out to the old orchard after working in the fields with Dolan all day. I suppose it was my idea of a peace offering to him, a way of making the lives of everyone on the commune a little easier. I didn't tell Dolan about it, in case I couldn't actually get it up and running again, but after a couple of rough starts, I thought I had the tractor running about as well as could be expected, and I felt I was ready to show Dolan.

In the end, it was Dolan's effort to reestablish a link with me that saved our lives.

After several minutes of chiding and cajoling, I managed to convince Dolan to come with me, I had something I wanted to show him. He argued that we had to get ready for the Harvest Moon Feast, but I finally got him to agree to come along, it'd only take a few minutes, and we'll be back in plenty of time. Anyway, it wasn't like anything was going to happen while we were gone, was it?

But Dolan flatly refused to ride with me on the Soft Tail, so we took the horse and dray, but that was all right. It gave us time to talk, the way brothers do. I nearly asked him if he remembered the pillow forts we used to build, but caught myself. That was the problem with living a double-life. Sooner or later, you'd trip yourself up.

I watched the electric poles glide slowly past us, and pointed them out to Dolan. "Do you know what they are?" I asked. "What they used to do?"

My brother shrugged and said he never really gave it much thought. "They're a part of the before-time," he said. "Mom was there for it, but she doesn't talk much about it."

"They used to carry electricity," I explained. "A long time ago, the people who lived here before us, the people from our mother's time, used that electricity to light their homes and heat them when they were cold, and cool them when they were hot."

Dolan looked aslant at me and said nothing. "Sounds like devil's work t'me," he ventured at length.

"No, it was just the opposite. It helped make their lives easier."

"Make 'em soft, did it?"

"Yeah, probably," I admitted. "A bit."

He snorted with satisfaction. "That's why they aren't here now. They were too soft."

"But if God gives you a brain, and you can use that brain to make your life easier, shouldn't you? What if someone could find a way to get the power flowing again?"

He considered that for a while, and answered, "Just because a person *can* do something doesn't mean that person *should* do it. Maybe it was a test. God tested 'em by givin' 'em the brains to... *do* these things you're talkin' about...and they failed that test. God gave 'em brains, but he didn't give 'em wisdom. You ever think about that?"

More than he knew. Sometimes it was just a matter of saying *Yes* to the wrong impulse. The problem was, recognizing which impulse was the wrong one, and maybe Dolan had done just that.

After Dolan's Luddite-like reaction to my suggestion someone could get the Mountain View power grid running again, I thought I had a pretty good idea how well he'd take to the tractor, but he surprised me. He understood at once that the tractor would mean more efficient planting time, and would allow the collective to plant a larger and more diverse number of crops in the same amount of time, or haul stones and tree stumps from the turned earth in a few minutes instead of several hours, sometimes days. The only thing about Dolan I could count on with any consistency was that Dolan was a source of constant surprise.

"You did a good thing, Max," he told me, and, after an awkward moment, gave me a quick and clumsy hug.

"C'mon," he said. "We'd better be getting back to the Feast before they eat all the food. And, Kera has a part in *Nancy Drew and the Mystery of the Ticking Clock*."

I cocked my head toward the tractor. "Race you?"

My brother, the great stone-face, actually laughed. "Shut up and get on the wagon," he said.

The first thing that struck us was the unnatural silence.

Even from a kilometer or more away, we were surprised by how *quiet* the Harvest Fair was. The games and competitions should have been under way by now, and there should have been cheers and laughter and music on the air, but the air was as still and unbroken as quarry water. The sun had nearly set, streaking the western sky with gouts of red, and the moon was hanging over the star-stippled eastern horizon, the color of a bad infection. Even the evening song of the cicada was absent, as if the world was holding its breath.

Dolan said, "Hang on," and spurred the horse into a gallop before I could grab hold of the buckboard.

We spotted the first body lying in the weed-choked swale, but we didn't bother to stop. His head had been torn from his shoulders and thrown into the opposite ditch. Its eyes were open, the pupils rolled up into the back of its skull, and the mouth hung wide, as if it were in the middle of a mighty scream when head and body ended their alliance suddenly and violently. Whatever did the job was a tough bastard.

As we grew nearer, we could hear the sound of a voice, droning on in a flat, skidding monotone, but we could make no sense of the words. "Split up," I whispered to Dolan, and grabbed my rifle from the back of the cart where it was propped against the seat. I was already off the wagon and skirting the collective, moving through the tall grasses and weeds before Dolan could bring the horse to a halt.

From a distance, I could see candles burning in the common between the trees, and cook fires crackling beneath the black iron cauldrons, and the evening breeze carried the scent of something so sweet it was nearly cloying to my nostrils, but I could see no people. And I could still hear that infuriating, flat, monotonous voice, echoing and reverberating.

I made my way across the clearing, not bothering to seek cover; I had a bad feeling I was already too late, and that the danger was gone. All that would be left was the bloody aftermath. My breath came in short, heady snorts, fear compressing my heart like a fist squeezing a tin can. I was coolly certain what I would find, and I was right—it was just that I couldn't begin to guess the level of violence directed at the colony.

I still couldn't make out the words the voice was saying, but now that I was closer, I could hear it was mechanical, and repeated itself. That gave me a very bad feeling, because until now, I thought I was the only one who knew about such things.

I pressed my back against the nearest tree, peeking around the trunk into the great clearing beneath the elevated huts, clicking the safety off and pumping a shell into the chamber as quietly as I could. I was sure I was alone, but... well, it was a world where crooked trees cast crooked shadows. I stepped around the bole, into the clearing, gun raised and ready, but there was no immediate danger, and I didn't think there would be.

We don't need the trouble you make finding its way

to our door. Dolan was right. We definitely didn't need this kind of trouble.

Whatever was cooking in that cauldron was so rich and sweet-smelling that I nearly vomited, and the smell of it seemed to be trapped here among the tree trunks, caught like an echo in a canyon. The contents of the pot were boiling furiously, a thick, oily steam rising from it like a spectral manifestation.

There was wreckage scattered everywhere; I looked up and saw the tree houses had been gutted, their outer walls knocked down. No, not just knocked down, but *ripped* open, the contents of the huts strewn and bashed about. The network of rope bridges between the homes was broken at several points, and one of the women was hanging upside down, her ankle tangled in the severed rope. Her arms dangled limply over her head, her fingertips just inches from the ground. Her hair fell around her face and hid her features. She looked nothing like Jasmine, but my heart stumbled and staggered in its rhythm because I *knew* it was her. I parted her hair with my fingers, like parting a curtain, and looked at her face. Her eyes were stunned and unfocused, or perhaps they were merely focused on something only she could see. A single ruby drop of blood glistened on her lip.

I let her hair fall back into place, hiding her features once more. The droning voice continued, but by now it was nothing more than background noise, like the television nattering on in the other room.

That *smell...*

I had to know what that sickeningly sweet smell was, and I peered over the edge of the pot. "Oh, shit!" I cried, and clapped my hand over my mouth. There was a body stuffed into the pot—really more of a 55-gallon drum pressed into service as a cauldron—its flesh red as a fire truck and sloughing from the bone in thick, putty-like streamers. Wild clumps of its hair floated like a garnish on the bubbling face of the slurry, and its eyes locked on mine with an unholy magnetism. I felt myself being drawn into a staring contest I couldn't hope to win, but I couldn't look away.

I cursed and pushed the heavy cooking pot over with the sole of my foot, its contents dousing the fire with a loud *hissssss!* Thick clouds of steam coiled upward, away and away, past the Hobbit-huts and through the lattice-work of interlocking branches. I didn't want that nearly corporeal steam to touch me, and it sickened me to think I had been inhaling the fumes of a boiling corpse, as if its death had settled as microscopic particles in my lungs.

There were bodies scattered everywhere across the clearing, like the leaves of autumn. The smell of blood, like a junction box burning out, was everywhere, and flies the size of a debutante's brooch were buzzing about, lapping their blood like free product samples.

And still that voice repeated itself with the infuriating patience of the damned. I became aware of it again as the blood drums pounding in my ears slowly died down, and I realized, with a jolt, it said my name. *Max...*

I turned toward the voice, and raised my gun. "Max!" It was Dolan, running toward me from between the trees across the clearing. I lowered the gun. "I found Jasmine!"

"Is she—?"

"She's hurt, lost a lot of blood, but she'll live, I think."

I didn't even realize I had been holding my breath until I heard it leave my lungs in a bellowing *whoosh!*

"What about Jon?" Dolan asked, stopping beside me, surveying the inconceivable carnage. His eyes were wide, his mouth hanging open, the expression of a man who's fallen off a cliff and hasn't hit the bottom yet.

I shook my head. "No sign of him. No sign of mom, either," I added.

"Maybe they got away," he said, softly. I thought he sounded as if he were trying to convince himself. "They probably got away."

"It's possible," I said, but I think we both know it wasn't. "Did Jasmine say anything? Did she say who did this?"

"No, she's still too groggy to talk."

"And you just left her?" I snapped. "Alone?"

"What was I supposed to do, Max?" Dolan growled back, jabbing his finger into my chest. "Stay with your woman, or look for my son? Tell me, Max, if you were me, which would you do?"

"All right," I said. "You're right."

"I packed her wound, put her in the back of the cart. I did everything I could before I came looking for you," he added.

Dolan stopped, listened to the mechanical voice I had been hearing since we first got near enough the colony. "What is that?"

I didn't know, but I had the feeling it had been left for me. Suddenly, I didn't want to find the source of the voice. I had a very bad feeling about it. Not just a bad feeling, but the dean of all bad feelings. I didn't want to hear what that voice had to tell me. I knew it had to be on a par with the late-night voices that had spoken so tirelessly to Gary Yokum.

"It's coming from over here," Dolan said, his voice a husky whisper.

"Don't worry," I told him. "It can't hear us. It's a recording."

"What–"

"It's...a voice that can't hear us, but we can hear it."

"How can–"

"Nothing."

We followed the sound of the voice, eerily distorted

by the natural acoustics of the amphitheater formed by the ring of trees, so that the voice was first here, then here, then here, everywhere at once, and nowhere. We separated, he moving in an eastern ellipse, I describing the western arc, both of us converging at last on the source of the voice.

I thought I had already seen the worst of the ruined lives in this colony, but what we saw then showed me how incredibly limited my capacity for cruel imaginings was. Seen the worst? Hell, we were just getting started.

It was our mother—my daughter, my Vonnie, the only one left alive who remembered, however spotty that memory may have been, the name Paul Stein—staked to the trunk of one of the trees. A huge steel pike had been driven through her chest, deep into the thick wood, and strain as I might, I couldn't loosen her stake. If I hadn't seen a small patch of white fabric on the shoulder of her tunic, on which her lolling head rested, I would have thought her outfit was a gay scarlet. But it was all her blood.

There was some kind of hellish contraption of techno-organic design, like a half-mask, covering the right hemisphere of her face. I tried to remove it, and saw there was a prong, like an interface cable, driven deep into her right eye, all the way to her brain. When I tugged at the Talking Mask, the ruined gelid mess of her eye *puckered* like a pair of lover's lips, refusing to let go of the probe.

The voice was a recording, but it was using her larynx to form the words. The bastards had turned my only child into a While You Were Out message. There was a whine of some sort issuing from her slack mouth (a thread of bloody saliva ran from the corner of her mouth and stitched her lips to her shoulder), and I absently identified it as a carrier wave. It was ambient noise, and from this noise the words were formed. The oscillating howl of the carrier wave filled the spaces between words, like mortar between bricks.

"Turn yourself in to us, Max. You will never know a moment's rest, the friends and families and alliances you make today, we will tear apart tomorrow," the message repeated. *"End your resistance. Let us rehabilitate you. What was done here tonight will be done again and again until you surrender."*

Dolan stood with his own mouth open in an unconscious imitation of Vonnie. He was in the grip of more emotions than he could name or master, and it was only because of that psychic overload that he didn't break and run. "Max, what..." he muttered.

"You will become a pariah, an outcast, shunned by everyone, because they will know death follows you. No rest, no home, no family. Soon, they will all turn against you, hunting you, trying to kill you before we kill them for harboring you. You won't be able to trust anyone you once cared about. We have the child. Their fate becomes his unless you surrender."

The message began to repeat itself and I didn't know how to shut it off without ripping the Talking Mask from Vonnie's face, tearing her flesh and eye with it. She's been hurt enough by life. I couldn't do her any more harm in death. I motioned for Dolan to help me, and together we tried to slide Vonnie's body off the pike, since even together we couldn't wrestle it from the tree. As the body neared the end of the pole, a set of metal flanges sprang out of the end of the handle, like a four-barbed fishhook, preventing us from freeing the body. I suspected that was standard N'lani battlefield issue, to make sure their victims, even if they survived impaling somehow, couldn't be rescued.

"What do we do now, Max?" Dolan asked; he sounded terribly lost. I suppose he probably was. After all, Dolan had spent most of his life tilling the earth. This was all out of his realm of experience. He was handling it better than most would have, but it wasn't going to take much before he pulled into his shell like a turtle and just waited for all of this to be over, and he could resume his old, everyday life. I don't think it had quite sunk in yet he was never going back to that existence. He had lost his wife, and his son had been taken by the N'lani to ensure my surrender. As soon as that fact struck home, how long would it be before Dolan insisted I do the right thing and give myself up to the Masters? And if I refused? Well, I had to sleep sooner or later, didn't I? I wouldn't be able to trust anyone, perhaps not even my own brother. He had trusted me, and what had it gotten him? I had brought the trouble I made to his door. The trouble had come C.O.D., interest due, and everyone around me had to pay the cost.

"We can't leave her like this," he said.

"Burn it," I told him. "Burn it all."

"You can't mean that," he said. "Max, these people–"

"Are dead. They're going to become food for birds and animals and God knows what else. You really want that?" I snapped.

He was quiet a long while, and I thought he was going to argue for their dignity, but once again, he surprised me. He retrieved one of the flickering torches and looked at me. I nodded, and Dolan touched the flame to the tree in several places, watching a small ember glow between the strips of bark, smolder, catch, and little vines of fire began to climb the trunk. He walked around the ruined colony, putting things to the torch.

"...have the child. Their fate becomes his unless you surrender..." Vonnie said again with exasperating patience. And then, she lifted her head from where it lolled on her shoulder, turned her face slowly to mine, her one good eye filled with pain and horror, and said, "Daddy...?"

Dolan was standing near me, and I looked to see if he heard it, too, but the look on his face told me he hadn't. I turned back to Vonnie, and her cheek and chin were once more resting on her shoulder, if they had ever been off of it.

There was a dull cough of an explosion overhead, as the glass of one of the windows blew out. After a moment, another dull blast, and another, this last one nearer, diamonds of fire-opaqued glass falling like pixie dust. The heat made the carrier wave break up, until it warbled up through the octaves into a mad wail of feedback. It sounded like Vonnie was screaming.

"Let's get out of here," Dolan said, clapping his hand on my shoulder. At last he had to pull me to get me moving.

"Let's go kill some goddamn lizards," I said.

CHAPTER SEVENTEEN

Whatever else you could say about Dolan, you wouldn't be wrong in saying he was a master of understatement. When he said Jasmine had lost some blood, I expected a few cuts, but she had just missed having her jugular severed, and she was as white as the victim of a vampire attack. The ground around her was dark with her blood, leaving a vague, Jasmine-shaped outline in the dirt where her body had rested. He had carried her from where she had fallen and put her in the back of the dray, where he had taken care of her wound as best he could, packing it with the poultices Vonnie had taught him. The bleeding had stopped, but she was going to need stitches. What was it Jon had said when I had asked him if he was a big boy? *Grammy had to sew it up with some twine.*

I didn't have any twine, but I thought I could find some fishing line back at the bomb shelter, or at least in the A-frame home, and a syringe needle to stitch her up. Her blue eyes fluttered open, but she didn't seem to see me. If I had to guess, I'd have to say she was probably starting to see dead relatives and that long, long tunnel of light.

"You just hang in there, sweetheart," I whispered, clutching her hand in both of mine. It felt as frail and weightless as a bird, as if her bones were hollow, and it was disturbingly cold. I had felt that same kind of cold before, that night in the hospital when my father died and I held his hand as he went. It's a cold that comes from within, not like any other. Once you've felt it, you never forget it, although you try.

I sat in the back of the dray with Jasmine, keeping her warm by huddling close to her, talking to her, trying to keep her from listening to the voices of glory.

"How's she doing?" Dolan asked, glancing back over his shoulder at us.

"You saved her life back there, Dolan," I said. "I want to thank you for that."

He turned away, and I couldn't hear what he said, but it sounded like, "Don't thank me yet."

Dolan carried Jasmine down the steps into the bunker and arranged her on a cot while I found some monofilament in the toolshed in the field behind the A-frame house. I used one of the discarded syringe needles, sterilized over the open kerosene lantern flame, to stitch Jasmine's shoulder wound. I cleansed the jagged cut with alcohol, inspected it to make sure there were no arterial nicks or foreign matter in it, and instructed Dolan to hold her down on the cot while I pushed the needle through the meat and muscle of her shoulder. Her eyes, floating like blue moons in contrary orbits, suddenly grew sharp and focused, and she let out a cry of pain and alarm.

"Hold her still, damn it!" I shouted, jerking the line taut, pulling the seam of her flesh together.

I had no way to anesthetize her, short of getting her drunk or bashing her over the head with the bottle; either method seemed about as bad as the surgery itself, so we just had to press on, ignoring her cries of pain, and her tears. How did the Hippocratic Oath go? *First, do no harm.*

I sewed tight little stitches, like a series of Xs along her wound, the way a lovesick young girl might sign a letter to her fella. Jasmine must have hated me then; it must have seemed excessively cruel, the length of time I was taking to do the job, but I wanted to make sure the suture, half-assed at best, didn't come open again.

After a while, her cries of distress became dull, accepting grunts of resignation, and at last I knotted the end of the line and cut it. Her skin was clammy to the touch, and she was skating over the thin ice just above the deep, black water of shock. I pulled the blankets up close around her and sat patting her hand. "You don't have to forgive me for this," I told her. "You just have to live... deal?"

Her eyes opened and focused on me for a moment. Jasmine licked her dry, cracked lips and murmured, "I'll see what I can do."

I sat with her until I felt confident she fell into a light, easy sleep, then went out of the bunker to find Dolan. I didn't have to go far, because he was sitting on the back of the cart, studying a shaft of straw he held between his thick fingers. He glanced up at my approach.

"Thank you for your help," I said, pulling myself up to sit on the flatboard beside him.

"I'll make a poultice for her after a while," he said. "It'll help the healing."

I nodded my thanks again, and said, "We'll get Jon back. Whatever it takes, I promise we'll get Jon."

He turned his head to study me for a long time, as if I was some exotic form of alien life. I suppose in a way that's just what I was to him now. "You know what it will take to get Jon back. Are you prepared to do that?"

I looked down at my own hands, although they were empty. "No," I said softly. "Not just yet."

Dolan made a hissing sound, like a snake coiled in hiding at the side of the road. "When will you be prepared, Max? When will you ever be ready to do the one right thing? As long as it doesn't hurt you?"

"What if they'd wanted you to turn mom over to them?" I asked. "Would you do that?" He made a sour face as if the whole idea was preposterous, but I pressed on. "When do we stop rolling over for them, pissing on ourselves like submissive dogs?"

"You can't fight 'em, Max."

"Same song, different lyrics," I said. 'No one fights the Masters.' That song seemed to be Number One with a bullet in these parts. "And let's be honest, Dolan. *Brutally* honest, yeah? What makes you think they'd give you Jon even if you did give me to them? What makes you think Jon's even still– "

Dolan was fast–his right fist came up out of nowhere in a nasty corkscrewing motion, catching me on the jaw and snapping my head to the side. I flailed to catch myself, but I went over the edge of the wagon and landed on the ground with a thud. Dolan was standing over me at once, hands balled into fists at his sides, trembling visibly as he struggled with himself not to strike me again.

"Dead or alive, Max, I think they'd settle for you either way," he said. "Me, I don't much care, either. They left us alone until you came back. All those people would still be alive if it hadn't been for you. So do you think I really care whether you live or die?"

I pulled myself up using the wagon wheel, keeping an eye on Dolan as I did. I'd thought of him as soft, but I was starting to see how wrong I was. He just chose his battles a little more realistically than I did.

"Maybe they would be alive," I said, smearing the blood from my mashed lips with the back of my hand. "And maybe Jon would still be here. But it's happened now. You can't stay uninvolved. Don't you want to avenge your family? Your friends? That's the way these creatures work. Even if you give me to them, do you think you'll ever be safe again? Or Jon?"

I was prepared to bring in the whole Weapons of Mass Destruction spiel if it came to that, but I didn't think Dolan would get the reference. He cursed and banged his fist on the bed of the wagon and stood glowering at me.

"Let's try this one my way," I said, still not sure whether I was getting through to him. I still had all my teeth, so I supposed, on one level at least, he was listening. "If we see we can't do it, then I'll turn myself over to them. You have my word."

He was quiet, and I could almost hear the gears grinding in his head as he tried to decide the right thing to do. At last he said, "All right, Max. We'll try it your way, because you tried to put that whole life behind you. I know that. But I'll tell you this: I'm glad I don't have to carry the weight of your soul around."

The next few days, as we waited for Jasmine to recover, Dolan spent most of his time away from me, sifting through the charred ruins of the colony, burying the few bodies the fire didn't claim.

Nevertheless, he always saw to it that Jasmine's poultice was changed and a fresh one applied before he would disappear for the day. He was a man of principle, even if he would have liked to leave me on the doorstep of the N'lani city, like an orphaned baby in a basket. Not that it was hard to understand—if the situations had been reversed, and there'd been a chance to save Maryvonne, I'd have felt the same way.

On the third day, Jasmine's fever spiked high, and Dolan went in search of some herbs Vonnie had once taught him to use on Jon when he had a bad fever.

"I could just let her die, Max," he told me as he mounted the buckboard. "I could take my time finding the medicine, or I could tell you I couldn't find it and you'd never know different, and by the time I get back, her brain would be baked in her head like bread in an oven. Or maybe I'll tell you I'll find the medicines if you turn yourself over to the Masters first. Do you care for *her* enough to do that, Max? Because I know you don't care enough for me or Jon."

I felt my lungs calcify; I couldn't seem to get any breath, like trying to breathe through a straw. "Dolan, this isn't the time–"

"I know you, Max. You have trouble trusting anyone, and as the day rides by, and there's no sign of me, you'll start to wonder if I'm coming back. You'll wonder if I'm going to let your woman die. As long as you've been my brother, you'll still wonder that."

"I already gave you my word–"

He took the reins in his big hands, his face turned away from mine. "I know what you said. But I've been thinkin'...how can I trust a man who can't trust anyone else? See my fix, Max?"

"If you let her die, Dolan, I *will* kill you," I said, and I knew it wasn't just a threat, but a fact. "We can both trust that." I could actually see myself doing it, taking the deer rifle and gut-shooting him, dragging his death out as long as possible. I don't suppose Cain and Abel had anything on Dolan and me. The world could end, but as long as there were families, there would always be dysfunction.

"You just proved my point, Max," he said, giving the reins a little snap to get the horse moving. "But I'm not like you. I want you to think about that while I'm gone."

I watched him go, the wooden wagon wheels kicking up a thick cloud of dust that hung in the still, hot air long after he was gone from sight. I turned and went down into the shelter to sit with Jasmine.

I tried to lower her fever with cool cloths on her forehead and alcohol baths, but it was just busy work and I knew it. I wasn't accomplishing any good. If she was going to be saved, it was going to be because Dolan was a bigger man than I was. But although I didn't want to think it as the day rode by, I started to worry he wasn't going to return, that he was going to prove to be the disappointment to me that I was to him.

But I'm not like you. I want you to think about that while I'm gone.

Maybe, but in my experience, the acorn—or in this case, the ape—never falls far from the tree.

Jasmine's eyes, gummy with fever, seemed to fix on me for a moment. "Jude?" she croaked. "Jude, why don't you say something?"

"It's not Jude. It's Max," I said tightly.

After all this, she still called his name when she was hurt. And did she call his name in her mind and in her heart when we made love? I told myself it was only the fever, that she was in a freefall between the past and the present, that one looked about the same as the next to her right now, but I just couldn't seem to make myself believe it.

Now she saw me, and for a moment she knew me, and she took my hand in hers. I'm ashamed to say I didn't want to hold her hand. "Max," she said, thickly. I held a bottle of water to her lips and let her sip it. She nodded, and I set the bottle on the floor.

"Max, where's Jon?" she asked. Jasmine started to sit up, but the pain in her shoulder, coupled with her blood loss and fever, drove her back down onto the cot.

"Take it easy," I told her. "You've been hurt pretty bad. Can you remember what happened?"

She looked at me as if it were a foolish question. "Of course I can remember," she said. "Why wouldn't I?"

Oh, I dunno... Because for a minute there, you couldn't remember my name, so I guess I just assumed your memory might be a little out of whack, I thought. But what I said was, "No reason."

She winced at the pain in her shoulder, and asked for another sip of water. I gave it to her, and then she told me what had happened:

All day long, the huts of the colony had smelled of such things as cooking potatoes and gourds, and pies and breads baking in the ovens. Vonnie had spent half the day standing at the little window that faced out onto the interconnecting walkways between the huts, each hut set slightly higher up the boles of the trees than the one before it, giving the colony a stepladder effect. Neighbors paused on the walkway outside Vonnie's window, asking her about a certain recipe, asking her to taste this, does this taste right to you?

The children were impatient for the Harvest Feast and the games of seeking, like an Easter egg hunt, I suppose, and, of course, the bonfire. They stole little bites from the cooking pots and ovens, unable to wait until the Feast to taste the dishes that created such intoxicating aromas. Their mothers, tired of telling them to leave that alone, that's for the Feast, not the likes of you, finally sent their children outside, where they ran up and down and back and forth on the rope-and-wood bridges between the huts.

As evening fell and the sky lowered toward dusk, the women began to take their dishes down to the sheltered common area in the bowl formed by the ring of trees. There, they placed their food on the great trestle tables, and kept a wary eye on the children. The Feast was coming, coming soon, but it couldn't arrive soon enough to satisfy the kiddies.

The men-folk had their own little tradition; they would go down to the tidal pool and get drunk on fermented root-brew—probably the closest thing to wine or beer this place had to offer.

Jasmine had spent the day with Vonnie and Kera, Dolan's wife, in the kitchen, leaving Jon to amuse himself. But no one had seen him for several hours, and Jasmine volunteered to go find him. She climbed down the rope-bridge to the ground and went searching for the boy.

It was also part of the annual tradition for the men to take their oldest son down to the tidal pool and initiate them into the ways of the bitter-root brew. Jon, being a big boy and Dolan's oldest son, wanted to take part in the tradition with his father, but his father was nowhere to be found. By that time, we were on our way to the A-frame house to view the tractor. The men at the basin said they hadn't seen Jon, but offered Jasmine a drink. She tasted it, remembered her previous run-in with the fermented grape, and handed it back.

It was that which saved her life. A few minutes after she had gone searching for Jon in the opposite direction, near the Bad Weed that bordered the colony, the N'lani shock troops surfaced from the tidal pool.

These men were farmers, not fighters, and they were drunk on their asses to start with. Even if they hadn't been, they never stood a chance, although a few managed to escape and run back to the colony to warn the women and children. The N'lani were huge and lumbering things, but they were relentless, and that made up for their lack of land speed.

I could imagine the slaughter, try as I might *not* to. The farmers would have carried knives, long-blades, and they would have tried to fight back, but the scaly skin of the N'lani was too tough for such meager weapons. The N'lani had steel pikes and swords, like a samurai's *dotanuki,* able to slice through bone. Dolan told me of the ghastly wounds these men suffered when he found them several days later, searching the ruins of the colony. Bodies of the biggest men cleaved in half, straight down the center, from the crown of their head to their crotch, lying on the ground in two separate pieces, like cartoon cats in the most violent animated shorts. Heads were chopped off the shoulders of others, the force of the cut sending the head flying like a foul ball in a sandlot baseball game, to get lost in the weeds or in the tidal basin.

Other bodies, Dolan told me, were crushed, their rib-cages pressed through their spines, or giant fist-holes had been punched through their stomachs and out their backs. Whatever else you could say about them, the N'lani were creatures that enjoyed their work. And, their work done, the creatures swarmed toward the colony.

By this time, Jasmine had located Jon in one of the fields, where he was practicing his sling, aiming small rocks and clods of dry earth at the stalks that had been picked clean. He was old enough this year to enter some of the big boy games of skill, and he wanted to win. Jasmine showed him a couple of pointers on how to improve his range and accuracy with the sling, which he greedily absorbed. He did as he was instructed, and almost instantly improved his aim.

The sounds of screams and destruction filtered to the

bottom of the field, vague and distant, but unmistakable. Jasmine told Jon to hide someplace safe, and ran for the colony.

What she saw when she got there froze her blood: the N'lani were among the little tree huts, scaling the trees like the lizards they resembled. Barred doors were not a problem to them; they simply tore down the outer walls, shredding the wood with their long, taloned fingers. The N'lani quickly killed the women. If there's any mercy in this tale, it's this: the women died quickly.

Everyone except Vonnie, that is, whom they somehow knew to be Max's mother. She had been singled out for the humiliation of being turned into an organic outgoing message machine.

Jasmine had been watching all this from the Bad Weeds, which were as thick as blackout curtains, trying to form a strategy to rescue a few of the colony women or children without getting herself killed in the bargain. But Jon took any chance of that out of her hands when he saw the N'lani holding Vonnie to the tree, and the other lizard raise his steel pike for the impalement. She was still alive, kicking and fighting to the end. I had hoped nailing her to the tree had come after the fact, but I knew now that simply wasn't so. She had been very much alive, and very much aware of what was about to happen. And *why*.

The creatures kept demanding Max, in that slithery, slimy voice: *Give us the one we want and we'll go away.*

Jon broke past Jasmine, who thought she had left him down in the field, and charged into the clearing, screaming at the creatures to leave his grammy alone. "Jon! Get out of here, boy!" Vonnie warned him. The N'lani turned and watched with flat bemusement as Jon slung rocks at them, each one scoring a solid, if ineffectual, hit.

There was nothing to do now but go down fighting, doing her best to protect the boy, and Jasmine sprang from the Bad Weeds, letting loose a shrill, piercing battle cry. The lizard-man held Jon off the ground, the back of his tunic pinched between thumb and forefinger, as if humans were something disdainful, and touching them was to be avoided at all costs.

Jasmine drew her knife as she ran, but the N'lani holding the pike was alarmingly fast. He wheeled and threw the spear at her, tearing a huge divot out of her shoulder. The impact staggered her backwards, so that she fell into the shelter of the Bad Weeds. If the N'lani had known she had survived the attack, I have no doubt they would have finished the job.

As she drifted toward unconsciousness, Jasmine struggled to raise her head. She could feel her own blood pulsing away with every heavy throb of her heart. The world funneled down into a small window of vision for her, but through that window she saw the N'lani drive the fatal pike into Vonnie's chest, and the second creature lock the Talking Mask into place on her still-twitching corpse. Almost at once, the carrier wave began its hideous whine, making it sound as if Vonnie were screaming in agony and terror. Perhaps she was.

Jon quit struggling for a moment, shocked into submission by the cold cruelty he had just witnessed. The N'lani holding the boy said something to the other, and they laughed, a sound like dead autumn leaves rattling. Jasmine grunted and fell back into a spreading pool of her own blood, where she lay until Dolan found her.

Her story told, Jasmine drifted away from me again, carried by fever and weakness to those dark borderlands all of us visit sooner or later, but from which few of us ever return.

Speaking of returns, I was beginning to wonder if Dolan was ever going to. He had made a point of planting it in my mind that Jasmine's life was in his hands now, and, should he fail to return with the medicine root she needed, her brain would boil in its own juices. I could too easily imagine him sitting in the dray, around a bend and out of sight, watching the moon rise, knowing I would be frantic with worry. But he was wrong about that: Had Jasmine not called me Jude, perhaps I would have been more concerned.

I looked at her as you may a stranger you see napping by the poolside. She looks familiar, but you realize you never knew this woman. Not really.

I belong to Jude.

I looked up at the sound of the bunker door opening, automatically reaching for the .38 handgun I had found tucked away among the supplies of the shelter.

It was Dolan, back from his mission.

He stopped when he saw I had the gun leveled at him. I had been trying to teach him how to use the handgun, and what he lacked in aim, he more than made up for in respect for the damage the weapon could do.

"That's a fine how-do-you-do," he said. His eyes flicked nervously to where Jasmine lay, and I understood at once his trepidation. Before he had left, I had threatened to kill him if she died. I thumbed the safety back on and laid the gun on the table.

"She's still alive," I told him.

"You don't sound very happy about it," he said, stepping across the threshold and closing the door.

"It's...complicated."

Dolan found a bowl and placed the medicinal roots in it, and began grinding them up into a paste. "What *isn't,* where you're concerned?" He took a bottle of water and mixed it into the mushed root, and handed it to me. "It needs to be heated," he said.

I fired the little kerosene stove and dumped the contents of the bowl into a metal pan and let it come to a boil. "Whatever happens to her now," I said, "thank you."

He threw in another handful of mashed herbs and watched the stew come to a frothing boil. "I told you I wasn't like you," he said softly, the cold light of the lantern and the cooking stove twinkling in his eyes.

"The fact that you could even make the threat in the first place tells me you're a lot more like me than you'd like to believe, brother-mine," I said, and fixed him with a smug smile. I'm sure, by the cold light of the lantern, it looked more like a devil's leer, and maybe that's just what it was. There was no point in only one of us being unhappy. Share the wealth, I always say. Piss on 'em, and share every drop of the wealth.

Sometime during the long and speechless night, Jasmine's fever broke. She tottered on unsteady legs across the little room to my cot and lay down with me. I rolled over, turning my face to the wall. After a while, she found the strength to return to her own bed.

Now lie in it.

With her fever broken and the infection cleared, Jasmine regained her strength quickly. By the end of the week, we were as ready to travel as we were going to be. Call it precognition or call it deep-rooted pessimism, or whatever you want to call it, but no matter how things turned out in the city in the desert, I knew I wasn't going to be coming back from this one.

CHAPTER EIGHTEEN

I rode alone, letting Jasmine ride in the dray with Dolan, resting in the back, among the supplies, rebuilding her strength. At least, that's what I told myself. I tried not to think about her at all, trying to concentrate on some kind of battle plan once we reached the city. It was frustrating for me, to be forced to travel at a slow enough speed for Dolan to keep me in sight. Sometimes I'd open the bike up, and roar off down the road, leaving them in my dust, but then I'd have to pull over to the side and wait until the horse and dray were once again able to catch up with me.

There were gas stations along the road into the desert, each one of them promising that this was LAST CHANCE GAS! Without electricity to power the pumps, all the gasoline was still trapped in the underground tanks. With Dolan's help, I was able to lift the heavy cover off the chute the big fuel tankers used to refill the tanks. We dropped the metal plate and I uncoiled the long siphon hose I always carried in the bike's utility bags.

I squeezed the hand-pump and waited until I could see the gasoline start to make its loop-de-loop through the tubing and into the nearly dry tank of my Soft Tail. As soon as my tank was filled, I swung my leg over my bike and pulled away, before Jasmine had the chance to say anything to me.

We camped that night on the California/Nevada border, the stars shining brightly above us, like Christmas tree lights. Earlier, I had bagged a couple of jackalopes while I waited for Jasmine and Dolan to catch up, and had them roasting over an open fire by the time the dray horse clopped into view.

"Table for two?" I asked, bowing at the waist and extending my right arm toward the little camp I'd set. "Reservation for the Dolan party?"

Dolan unhitched the wagon and tethered the horse to a bit of deadwood and rubbed him down. Jasmine took the blankets from the back of the cart and spread them out on the hardpan. She looked at me questioningly, a look that, despite my best effort to remain immune, nevertheless broke my heart. "Put your blanket next to mine," I told her. She smiled, a little shyly, but did as she was told.

Jasmine knelt on the blanket, leaning over the small fire to sniff the aroma of the hares. Grease ran from their roasting bodies and hissed on the burning sticks. "What are they?" she asked. "They look like..."

"Look like what?"

She shrugged, and crinkled her nose. Then she delivered the coup d'état and tipped her head to one side, her long golden hair spilling over her shoulder, gleaming in the firelight. The tight, tiny Xs in her shoulder caught the light as well, and reflected back little rainbows, and at the end of each rainbow was Jasmine. God, I'd missed that. "They look like rats," she observed, trying not to hurt my feelings.

I laughed. I supposed they did, at that. While Dolan was tending the horse, Jasmine turned toward me, still kneeling, hands on her thighs, palms upward, head bowed. "I'm sorry I couldn't help your mother, Max," she said. "I know you're mad at me for that, and for losing Jon, and I don't blame you. I don't blame you if you hate me."

"Is that what you think this is about?" I asked, incredulous.

"Isn't it? Have I done something else?" This time she raised her face, this time her eyes met mine as she searched for an answer. I nearly looked away, but even if Paul Stein didn't understand such things about dominance and submission, Max did, and he knew to look away from Jasmine would be to submit, to put myself in the one-down position. Max wouldn't allow that, no matter what, and so I returned her gaze, until she once more looked away.

All the while I did it, I cursed myself. Jasmine had blamed herself for what had happened to Vonnie and Jon and probably the whole colony, and all I could think about was how pissed I was that she called me by Jude's name. It hurt, sure, but pain is only weakness leaving your body.

"Yes," I lied. "I was upset, but I know you tried. I know you did your best."

She nodded. That much was true. I know she did her best. Dolan finished rubbing the horse, blanketing it for the night, and putting its feedbag on, and joined us at the campfire. He looked at the desert rabbit, brown and crisp, on the spit, much the way Jasmine had.

"I don't mean to question the menu," he said, his upper lip peeled back in an unconscious imitation of Elvis. That was okay; we were getting close to Reno, and there probably hadn't been a good Elvis impersonator in these parts for fifty years. "But..."

"You two are having rabbit," I said, "and I'm eating crow."

The desert comes alive at night.

I lay with Jasmine coiled tightly against me, like a spring about to release its stored kinetic energy, the fire burning low, as if it were getting sleepy. A knot in the wood exploded, sending a skirl of orange fireflies chasing after one another into the night sky, a slow, dancing spiral. The picked bones of the hare were buried out in the desert, the dirt tamped down so as not to tempt any nocturnal predator. There were enough of those in the old days; now, God only knew what things walked the rumor-choked desert floor.

A shadow, perhaps that of a hawk, spread its great wings across the face of the waning moon. I watched as it dropped out of the sky, wings swept back, head flattened, and dived on something that let out a high, womanly shriek. The hawk arced away, back into the sky, trailing something from its beak.

Somewhere in the darkness, a coyote howled. Somewhere, farther away in the darkness, a coyote howled back.

When we returned from burying the bones of our dinner, I insisted on laying a circle of rope on the ground around the perimeter of our little camp. For some reason, desert scorpions—the run-of-the-mill kind, not the bastardized things that had some kind of co-op time-share plan inside the guts of a sad-eyed dog—won't cross over a rope. The ones that hid inside a dog...well, I didn't imagine there was much we could do about them if they raced across the alkali flats, their bodies black and malignant, like tumors.

I watched a shower of falling stars scratching their chalky tails across the dark skies, and I made a wish upon each of them. It was only one wish, made over and over. I'd tell you what I wished, but then, it might not come true.

There were more cars sitting in the roadway as we grew closer to Reno, as if people were on their way to gamble and party until the end of things when they suddenly forgot how to drive. I wondered idly what had happened to the bodies; did the people simply sit in their cars, waiting for the cloud of befuddlement to pass, only to realize too late it wasn't going to lift, or did they get out of their vehicles and start walking, toward the city or across the baking desert?

I thought of the hawk-thing I saw last night, gliding on the breeze across the pocked face of the moon, and the horrified shriek of whatever it had caught. It was a bad end, but there were no doubt worse fates than that riding the winds and searching for their prey.

The desert road shimmered in the stark sunlight, as rippling heat snakes slithered skyward. Sunlight glittered off the mirrors and windows of the abandoned vehicles, making me wince as I crested the slight hill and started my descent. In the distance, quartz rocks glittered on the flat alkali plains like diamonds from an overturned jeweler's case. Jasmine rode with me now, arms around my waist as we weaved in and out between the cars.

Overhead, although we couldn't see the real city yet because of the blurry heat that smeared the horizon, we saw an inverted mirage of Neverland, hanging above us like a fairytale curse. Jasmine gasped and gripped me tighter, her eyes fixed on the mirage. "It's all right," I told her. "It's not really there."

"But I can see it."

"It's a mirage," I explained. "The real city is over the horizon."

I don't suppose she really knew what a mirage was—having lived her life in the abandoned subway tunnels of Los Angeles doesn't really prepare one for desert hallucinations—but she understood the calm tone of my voice, and if I wasn't worried, she wasn't worried. Still, I could feel her craning her neck to look at the upside-down projection of our destination.

I tried not to look; there was something subliminally disturbing and disquieting about its architecture, something that bypassed reason and went straight to the quivering lump of jelly sometimes jokingly called your lizard-brain. The architecture looked *wrong*, somehow, its dimensions and proportions just slightly off. Maybe not enough to notice with the naked eye, but down deep, in the subconscious. What could live in such a place? And how could it not be driven insane?

I looked away—*tore* myself away—at the last moment. If I hadn't, Jasmine and I would have driven blissfully unaware straight into the small band of nomads on the lane ahead of us. I had a strange moment of disassociation when I saw them, not sure if they were just one more mirage, or the wandering, earthbound spirits of those unfortunates who died along the road.

The people scattered, even as I hit the brakes and went into a sideways skid, headed straight for the back of an abandoned Cadillac. It was all I could do to keep the bike upright, and for a heady moment, I wasn't sure I would. I was getting ready for the bone-shattering impact and the bitter taste of my own blood—because there was no way, not a chance, I wasn't going to slam into that glistening hunk of Detroit—but then the tires gripped the tarmac with a scream like babies being tortured, and the bike was upright once more. I maneuvered the 'cycle past the starboard side of the Caddy. I could actually *feel* the scalding heat of the metal as we passed the car; if the Caddy had been wearing another coat of paint, we wouldn't have made it.

I got the bike under control and whipped it around to face the way we had just come. There *were* people on the road, carrying what few meager possessions they owned upon their back.

"Jude!" Jasmine said. I felt a moment's anger, because I thought she was once again calling me by his name. But then I found his face in the little knot of people, now swarming back together on the road, like iron filings being drawn by a magnet. It *was* Jude.

"I think you have something that belongs to me," Jude said, looking at me through slitted eyes. His shoulders were hunched, and his hands were twisted into murderous hooks at his side. Jude was not subtle, and it wasn't hard to guess what he was about to do.

I drew the rifle from the saddlebag and fired a warning shot at his feet. The shell kicked up a little puff of tarmac and dust, but it did the trick. It stopped Jude in his tracks. His little tribe, much smaller than the last time I had seen it, backed away, leaving Jude to face me alone.

"Not anymore," I said. "She belongs to me now."

I felt Jasmine shifting uncomfortably on the seat behind me, as if she were debating with whether to step off the bike and go to Jude, or remain with me. A little pressure to the trigger would settle the issue, once and for all. Things would have been better, all around, if I'd just done it.

"Is that true?" he looked past me and asked Jasmine, his chest heaving with a barely contained rage.

Her cheek was resting against my shoulder, like a frightened child hiding behind a grown-up. I felt her nod. Jude still seemed undecided, ready to risk his ferocity against my speed with the gun, and for a moment, I wasn't so sure I'd come out on top in that competition.

But the moment passed its center of balance, when it could go either direction, and then Jude seemed to deflate. He had talked himself out of it... *this* time.

"Keep the bitch," he said. "If you can." He started to turn away, dismissing me as if I no longer existed.

"Where are you headed?" I asked. "You're a long way from your home."

He stopped, looked back at me. "We no longer have a home, thanks to you," he said. "The Masters came looking for you. They destroyed the tunnels. Caved them all in. A few of us got out. Some of us fought back, but they killed most of my people, men and women, and they took our children."

Behind me, I thought I felt Jasmine's body tense, as rigid and stiff as carved marble when she heard the news. I didn't understand the significance of it, just then, but I would before long. Would I ever.

"They said it was for helping you," Jude continued. "They said they would return our children to us if we told them where to find you. They said no one will ever be safe again until you came to them." He stepped a little closer, his head extended on his thick stump of a neck. "Do the right thing," he told me through gritted teeth. "Give yourself to them. At least *die* like a man."

"You won't be around to see it," I promised him. I looked for saner faces in the crowd, and found one I thought I recognized from the lockup. "Why are you headed for Neverland?" I asked him. It occurred to me the N'lani had to have attacked Jude's tribe days, possibly weeks, before they raided Dolan's colony. Still, how had they known I had been with Jude's tribe? How did they know I had headed north from there?

"We've come to fight them," he answered. "They've taken our children. We've come to get them back."

"Have you, now?"

Jude turned to his people, arms upraised, like a referee declaring the kick was good. "There will be no need to fight if we simply give them what they want!" he shouted to be heard over the rising babble of excited voices. "I think dead's just as good as alive to the Masters!"

They started to advance, and for a second I felt as if I were back in the downtown streets of Mountain View, surrounded once more by Throwaways, or living in the lawless days of the Wild West, facing down a lynch mob. Either way, it was picking up all the mindless momentum of an avalanche racing toward me. One of the men nearest me ran forward, his knife raised above his head, ready to deliver a downward stroke that would probably all but decapitate me. His eyes were wide and unblinking, his yellowed teeth bared, his tongue sticking out past his desert-dry lips.

I brought the gun around, pumped a new shell into the chamber and fired. The bullet struck him dead center, and he made a surprised sound as his back opened up. His intestines tumbled out and hit the road with a wet smack. That stopped the forward momentum of the little avalanche.

"The Masters can't be trusted," Jasmine said, rising to stand on the seat behind me. "They won't return our children just because you crawl to them. If we want our children back, we'll have to take them." And this next bit I knew she addressed to Jude, although I couldn't see her turn her head his direction, as she was standing behind me, her hands balancing herself on my shoulders. "And if not, then at least die like men."

Jude's jaw muscles worked as he chewed on something hard and bitter; I imagine it tasted a lot like irony. Had she ever really loved this steaming little puke-chunk of a human being?

I watched a blurry figure appear on the far horizon, at the top of the rise back the way Jasmine and I had come, and knew it was Dolan and his old dray, catching up with us. I directed the little group's attention in his direction. "The Masters have my brother's boy," I said. "We're on our way to get him back. I never meant for any of this to happen. I didn't intend to involve any of you in my fight, but it's happened, and there's no turning back. Before you saw us today, you were willing to fight for your children. Now you're just willing to give me to the Masters and *hope* they return your children? If you want your children back, you'll join us. If not, the world is better off without the children that cowards like you have brought into it."

Well, it wasn't the kind of keynote speech you'd want to deliver to the PTA, but soccer moms and workaholic dads were all ancient history now. Political correctness was a thing of the past, and it only took an invading force of lizard-things to wipe it out. You could find the good in anything if you just looked hard enough.

"So...who's with us? Anyone?"

For a moment, I thought no one would step up to the plate, as if Jude's hold over these people was that strong, but familial bonds proved to be just a little stronger, and a small, sickly man with a growth on his neck like a goiter shuffled forward.

"The Masters killed my family," he said, and doubled over withed a phlegmatic cough. He was bent forward, his hand braced on the shoulder of one of the other men, as he coughed. Something dark and shiny came up and hit the tarmac. I had a feeling the growth I took for a goiter was a little more fatal than that. When he'd caught his breath again, he raised his head, his lips and chin smeared with blood as dark as ink. "The kids are all I got left of 'em."

That broke the deadlock, and the rest of the tribe, a person or two at a time, shuffled forward to join me. Jude looked at these people, at Jasmine, with barely contained rage.

"They have our child, too," he told Jasmine. "Doesn't that mean anything to you?"

Jasmine stepped down from the seat, lithe as any jungle cat and just as quietly. Of course, she could have been banging on a marching drum and I wouldn't have heard it, because my mind was busy replaying those four words Jude had spoken: *They have our child.*

"Yes," she told Jude. "More than ever, it means I *have* to do this."

She stood closer to Jude now, maybe closer than we ever were, and glanced back at me over her shoulder. I looked away, but not before I saw her take his hand in hers and give it a squeeze. But when Jude tried to take her in his arms, she stepped back. Not far, certainly not a distance that couldn't be bridged, nor a bridge that couldn't be repaired, and I wished I'd shot the son-of-a-bitch when I had the chance.

I looked up, at the inverted city hanging above us all. "Let's do this thing," I said.

CHAPTER NINETEEN

Neverland was still a day's hike, but we could see the glow of its countless lights in the eastern sky, as garish and bright as Las Vegas, still far to our south, ever was. The original Vegas was just a dream in the desert, a mirage built on a bedrock of bone and sanctified by spilled blood. In her heyday, when Vegas still had her looks and her charm, she could pull men in to their doom, like some high-rolling Circe, transforming those who fell under her spell not into barnyard swine, but fools who broke the back of their ship on the shoals of financial ruin. All those fifteen thousand-plus miles of neon tubing are dark now, and the thirty million annual tourists can no longer hear the siren song, but nevertheless, whether here or to the south, here we come, more gullible sailors rushing to their destruction.

Except, somehow I doubted that we'd get a complimentary All-You-Can-Eat meal for our trouble, and a Giraldi mint on our pillow. I couldn't shake the sense of fatalism that had dogged me since we set out, like there was something I was missing. I told myself it was emotional fallout from losing Vonnie again. It was finding out just how deep that bond between Jasmine and Jude really ran. It was having my simple, quiet life within the colony turned upside down, like the Neverland mirage in the sky.

I had spent the rest of the day discussing war plans with Jude and his people, but I didn't know how much of it really sank in. They had the attention span of the MTV generation with a sugar-buzz, but they all seemed to remember I was in charge, even Jude.

While we were making palaver, I kept stealing glances to see how Jude and Jasmine interacted, or didn't, but I simply couldn't tell. All I could remember was whose name it was she called when she was fevered, and whose child she had carried. More to the point, I remembered whose name she had *not* spoken in her delirium, and I wondered why we're drawn to the things that will destroy us, the things that turn Paradise into Perdition.

"Max?" Jasmine said, brushing her hair back from her cheek, exposing the little love scar I had sewn on her shoulder. "Is something wrong? You're staring at me."

I saw the smirk on Jude's face and wanted to smash it off of there, but I needed his cooperation to keep his tribe involved in the attack. This was not the time for such distractions or divisions, so I let it slide, but we both knew a reckoning would come as soon as this was over.

That was my mistake, thinking it would wait until then.

Jasmine surprised me—and Jude as well. When it was time to turn in, she unrolled her blanket away from both of us and laid down without a word to either of us. She had rightly assessed the situation, knowing that no matter which of us she laid with, the other would carry that rage of rejection inside, never knowing when it might go off like a land mine at just the slightest touch or word. The situation we were entering would not excuse mistakes.

One by one, like lights going out, the little group of refugees bedded down for the night. I was restless, and went walking until I left the soft orange glow of the campfire behind me. I sat on a boulder and looked neither at the camp nor at the lights of Neverland, but toward the south, away from everyone and everything.

I heard someone approaching, and turned to see who it was, although I recognized the sound of the footsteps as belonging to Dolan. I was right. He came near my boulder, but didn't ask to sit. Like me, he looked away from the city and the camp. He looked away from me.

"Not much to see out here," he finally ventured.

"You should sit where I'm sitting. The view is better."

He laughed, more like a deep hiccup, but didn't take me up on my offer. "I don't trust him, Max," he said at length.

"Who?" But we both knew.

"That one. That Jude. I don't trust him." Dolan sat down on the rock behind me, his back to mine. "He watches you when you think you aren't looking, have you noticed that?"

"Yeah." I thought about it a second and asked, "When did you notice it?

I could feel him shrug his big shoulders. "When he thought I wasn't watching him, when do you think?"

I laughed, and finally asked what I could no longer stand not to. "What about Jasmine? How does she act around Jude? Does she look at him when I don't know it?"

"No," he said. "She only has eyes for you, Max." He was quiet for a moment, and when I thought he wasn't going to say anything else, he added, "That's what I mean: You have trouble trusting anyone. Why is that?"

Because people are cretins, I thought. "Dolan, there's one thing I want you to promise to do for me, will you do that?"

He hesitated; I guess he had his own trust issues, but at last he said, "What's that?"

"You're right, I don't trust Jude, so if something happens to me in the city, something that doesn't seem, I dunno, right... Something that looks like Jude might have been a part of, I want you to promise me you'll use your gun and blow his head off. Will you do that?"

"That's hard, Max."

"Yeah, well, last time I looked, it was a hard world. Will you do it?"

He said he would, and I'd just have to trust that he'd keep his word. We talked a little longer, remembering our lives as boys, and mom and dad, and after a while, Dolan excused himself and went back to the camp. I realized what we were doing was saying good-bye, putting things right between us, or as right as they were likely to get, and getting ready for the worst, even if we hadn't known it at the time.

When I returned to the camp, everyone was asleep and the fire had burned down low, but there was still enough light to see Jude had moved his blanket so that he lay beside Jasmine, his face to hers, his left hand on her right hip. I went and found my bed. I lay back on my blanket, arms folded beneath my head for a pillow, and watched the clockspring of stars high overhead, the light of dead and forgotten days, racing to catch up with us.

We were on the road and moving again as soon as it was light. I fought the urge to ride ahead and do a little recon of the city, to get the lay of the land, and also just to get away from everyone and everything. I longed to open the bike up and bullet down the highway, and remember how good it was to be alive. How can you not feel good on the open road, with the countryside flashing past you like a backdrop in a play?

Neverland loomed before us, and I once again had that feeling of nausea, the sense that right angles were not quite ninety degrees, that lines were not plumb, that windows and doors were not totally rectangular, but leaned a bit more toward the trapezoidal. Again, it was nothing you could really see with the naked eye, but you could feel it, somewhere down deep inside you, the way Paul Stein had felt the ambient energies of the portal as it powered up that September morning. I looked over at Jasmine and saw that she felt it, too. She returned my look, and tried to add a smile to it, but it felt counterfeit, and I couldn't tell if it was because she was squirming on the inside, same as I was, or because she thought I was a fool.

I cut the speed of my bike as we approached the city, expecting to be challenged, by either a N'lani guard or a Throwaway, or even one of the techno-organic dragonfly things, but it was almost criminally easy getting in, as easy as walking into a 7-11. As I cruised down the deserted main street, the spires of the city towering over me like cliff faces, I slowly understood why the architecture seemed slightly off.

The buildings were a hybrid of steel and glass and some manner of organic material. The city wasn't built, it was *grown,* like a fungus or a cancer. The design of the city was imprinted on the cells, and they grew up around the template of girders, like flesh covering bone. Great, pulsing veins flowed through the outer walls of the buildings, and it was through these veins that the light of the city, a phosphorescent blood, traveled, absorbing the sunlight during the day, glowing more visibly at night.

I got off my bike and laid my palm against the wall of the nearest building; it was warm and fibrous to the touch, but pebbled, like a lizard's skin. Which made me wonder, did the buildings *molt* like lizards, as well? Did the spires slough off layers of dead epidermis each season? I grimaced and drew my hand back, wiped it on the front of my tunic.

"What's the matter?" Jasmine asked.

"The building..." I began, and then pulled up lame. How the hell could I begin to explain it when I didn't even understand it.

"Is this another of those things?" she asked, her nose crinkling a bit. "Like bodies and blood?"

Jude was standing nearby, a half-smirk on his face. I wondered just how much pillowtalk they had shared, and how much of that talk was about me.

The streets were not laid out in a grid, but rather, seemed to wander as aimless as tourists between the buildings with no clear destination in mind. I wondered again about what lived here, and about its mental health. Already my head was aching, and I was glad I hadn't eaten breakfast. I closed my eyes a moment, let the sensation pass, and slowly opened them once more. Better...for now.

There was a buzzing in the back of my head, almost sub-aural, and as I listened, the buzzing resolved itself into countless voices, music, sounds. I looked around the streets, but they were deserted. If I was having another of those "episodes" that landed me in the ol' psycho-silo back in college, I had picked an incredibly inconvenient time to go nuts. But the more I listened, the more I became convinced the voices were not coming from my own mind, but still from somewhere within, as if I were picking up low-wattage telepathic transmissions. I turned in a slow circle, as if I was a radio receiver trying to find the best position to pick up the broadcast, but it neither improved nor worsened. It was *there*.

I shook my head, as if that would clear it, and tried to ignore the voices; countless thousands of them, and I was hearing each one of them. I was beginning to wonder if the city had driven me mad already, or if the city itself was insane.

"Yeah, something like that," I finally answered her. "Don't you feel it? Any of you?"

"Feel what?" Jude asked, that half-smirk becoming a full-blown sneer by now. No matter what else happened in this city, I was going to wipe that smug, conceited look off his face.

"Dolan? Jasmine? How about you?"

They both nodded. "I thought it was just me," Dolan said. "But yeah, I feel..." He didn't have the words to describe it, but that was all right; neither did I. "What is it?"

"I don't know," I admitted. I thought I understood that, whatever subliminal sense of malaise the city projected, it only seemed to affect those that had purged the N'lani chemicals from their systems. "If it starts to get to you," I told them, "get out. We don't know what the effects will be, so don't risk it."

Jude started to protest, as if we were being cowards and looking for an excuse to cut and run, but the grim look on Dolan's face made him reconsider. I leaned in closer to my brother and said, "Remember your promise to me."

"Remember your promise to *me,*" Dolan said. "If this doesn't work..." I nodded. I knew the rest of that litany. I would turn myself over to the N'lani...assuming we could even find one.

I decided not to take the bike, just in case that sense of vertigo struck me again while I was driving, so I left it leaning against the wall. We moved deeper into the city, splitting up into little groups, with Jude, Dolan and Jasmine acting as team leaders for parties of three or four. We agreed to meet outside Neverland after a quick recon, and I watched them hurry off in different directions. I preferred to explore alone, since I was no longer sure on just whom it was safe to turn my back, but as I started my search, I noticed all the buildings looked about the same, as if they were not only grown, but cloned. There were no signs, nothing to indicate sites of any importance. I couldn't very well search every building until I found the kids; I was going to have to find someone from whom to beat some answers.

Unless...

I wondered about that low-level buzz I was picking up, and placed my hand on the surface of the nearest building. That was when I first noticed it, after my initial contact with the building epidermis. I focused on the image of children, and opened my mind to receive. The building answered almost violently, flooding my mind with slam-cut images and voices. I cried out and fell back, breaking contact with the rippling surface. That was pretty much the equivalent of being told "You can't get there from here." Obviously, the Vulcan mind-meld was obviously not the way to go here.

As I sat up, I saw an aperture iris open in the building, dripping and drooling like the toothless mouth of an idiot. I got to my feet and moved closer, keeping a safe distance just in case the building was hungry. I looked in, through the slit in the wall, deadly certain the walls would slam shut as soon as I poked my head in. Now that I was closer, there was a fetid odor trapped within the construction, but at least there seemed to be enough fresh air.

I stepped quickly through, not giving the maw the chance to iris shut. The light inside the building was a phosphorescent green, like algae. There was a set of stairs that spiraled up through the building like a giant twist of DNA. I followed it to the second level. The stairs were soft and spongy as fatty tumors, covering a frame of bone. At last they opened out onto a long, featureless corridor, and I moved down the hall, randomly pressing my hand to the fleshy wallpaper.

At last another aperture appeared, and I looked in. It was someone's apartment; or, more accurately, it was like a monk's cell, barren except for the most basic of necessities. There was someone in here, resting on an inclined chair, and I stepped closer. It was a woman, and she was staring straight ahead. Her eyes were moving, as if she were reading a line of moving text, or watching something. From the ceiling and walls, several thick, surgically implanted cables issued and entered the back of her skull. More tubes grew up out of the floor and burrowed under the flesh of her inner arms and thighs. I touched one of these tubes and felt something wet and warm pulsing through it, like blood.

"Hello? Miss? Can you hear me?" I stood right in front of her, but her flicking eyes didn't seem to register me at all. I may as well not have been there. For her, I don't think I was.

The atmosphere in here was thicker, somehow, heavier, and the room was stifling and close. It was difficult to catch a good breath, and even the gravity in here seemed greater somehow, as if I were some deep-sea diver working at tremendous, crushing depths.

I looked at the wires that hung from the ceiling and gently touched them; at once, I could hear the voices again, whispering prurient things, salacious things, and I could feel the woman's mind and body responding to those words and images. I pulled my hand away, breaking the contact, but I still felt as if those voices were breathing in my head, like a deviant midnight phone call.

What in God's name was this place?

I shouted in her ear, but she didn't respond. I grabbed her hand in mine and lifted it from where it lay on the arm of the chair, and let go. The arm hung there where I had left it. I sighed and placed her hand back on the armrest. But when I touched her flesh, I noticed an interesting thing: it was pebbled to the touch. Not as reptilian as, say, the skin of an In-betweener, but not human, either. Not anymore.

I backed from the room, watching the woman, and touched my palm behind me to the wall. The aperture opened quietly and I backed out of the room into the long corridor. I sprinted up the spongy staircase to another floor, and found another row of the same strange kind of cells, each holding men or women, but all of them jacked into some weird cyber-porn channel. I wondered vaguely if that charge would show up on their bills when they checked out of this living hotel. They were all healthy, from what I could tell, but they were little more than vacuous shells, waiting for something to come along and fill them.

I had to know just what was in the tubes that flowed into their veins and arteries, so I took my knife and, grabbing a handful of the slimy tubing, severed each one. A foul gout of blood and nutrient and other fluids sprayed out, spurting in rhythmic pumps like a heartbeat. I dropped the tubes and wiped my face on the front of my tunic. The liquids continued to pump, and the tubes writhed and twisted and coiled and uncoiled on the floor like a basket of snakes. I still didn't know exactly what the fluids did, but I suspected they kept the shells alive with nutrients, and I wondered if the blood was some manner of DNA cocktail. It might account for the *becoming* state the bodies were in, somewhere between human and...not human.

There was no point in climbing any higher in this tumorous Mustang Ranch, so I descended and found the ground floor, where I palmed the wall and watched as an opening appeared. I stepped through and out onto the street. Almost at once, I could breathe freely again, and while the city still baked under the grueling desert sun, it was cooler out here, and gravity seemed lessened. I felt as if I could simply leap and soar over the tops of the tallest of these obscene buildings.

Was the entire city nothing but a warehouse for these zombie-things? Certainly seemed so, but what function could they serve? And did I really want to know that? I found my bike, where I had left it leaning against the wall of a building, and grimaced in disgust as I saw the wall had begun to grow around the bike, as if it were trying to absorb the mass of the bike to add to its own. Or perhaps, given time enough, the building would clone a techno-organic bike.

I gripped the bike by the handlebars and wrestled it free. The pseudopods retreated like scolded puppies, disappearing back into the building facade. I swung my leg over the bike and was just about to kick-start it when

Jasmine came pelting down the intersecting avenue toward me, waving her arms frantically, calling my name.

"Max! I've found them!"

Some small but entirely sensible voice inside warned me to ignore her and just ride out, hit the open road and ride until the bike fell apart beneath me, but the heart is a stupid beast, not caring who its master is, and mine was no better.

"Found who? The children?"

She stood next to me now, her face flushed from the run. "The children," she puffed. "We need your help getting them out."

She climbed onto the back of the bike and I started it, driving the way she had just run from. "Are they all right?" I asked, the slipstream whipping my words back at her.

"Yes, I think so, but we just need your help."

"Where are they?"

Jasmine stuck her arm out, over my right shoulder and past my face, pointing to the intersecting avenue ahead. "That way," she said. Again, the sensible voice tried to warn me, but it was lost among all the others I was picking up like a broken transistor. I leaned the bike into the turn, and came to a dead-end, surrounded on three sides by the hideous buildings.

She jumped off the bike, not giving me a chance to really think this one through. I started to put the stand down when I heard the by now familiar sound of pseudoflesh lensing open behind me. I turned and saw the N'lani stepping from the apertures, cutting off my retreat. I looked at Jasmine, who lowered her face and would not meet my eyes with hers.

"You cheap, lying..." I pulled the gun from its holster

over my shoulder and leveled it at her. " I pulled the trigger.

At the same time, one of the N'lani struck the rifle with his *dotanuki*, just missing my hand and shearing through the gun at the stock.

"I'm sorry, Max," Jasmine whispered. She still hadn't raised her head, didn't know how close she had come to losing it in a red splash of bone and devious brain. "I'm so sorry..."

I threw the stock aside and revved the bike, wheeling it in a tight little circle, pointing toward the opening of the cul-de-sac. The N'lani blocked my path, but it wasn't as if I had much choice now. I held the brake and stepped hard on the gas. The back tire kicked up a cloud of burning rubber, and then I let go of the brake. The tires bit the pavement with a sound like a witch's scream and the bike surged forward like a missile, which is exactly what it was. I leaped from the seat at the last moment, just before the bike slammed into the nearest N'lani roadblock. The force of the impact drove the lizard-thing back and opened a hole in their ranks.

I was through it in a flash, before the creatures had a chance to recover. I thought I was going to make it, and then I felt a terrible, crippling pain in my thigh. One of the invaders had pierced my leg with his pike. I tried to keep running, but my leg muscles had gone on strike. I cursed and went down, and in seconds, the N'lani were on me, gripping and tearing at me with their long, hooked talons.

I grabbed my knife and drove it deep into the soft underjaw of one of the creatures, driving the blade up through his jaw and pinning his tongue to the roof of his mouth. I tried to pull the knife loose, but the other lizard-things wouldn't give me the chance. One of the monsters produced a nasty looking device and touched it to my right temple. I heard a high-pitched whine, as if something were powering up for a terrible discharge, but I never did feel the shock of electricity that sent me spiraling down into unbroken darkness. I felt all the muscles in my body clench up and seize from the jolt, and the muscles in my back bowed so tightly I thought my spine would snap, and then my muscles turned to water.

Just before I blacked out, I promised myself I'd kill every damn one of these soulless things, starting with Jasmine.

CHAPTER TWENTY

I could feel and hear, but I couldn't see or move, and I didn't like what I felt. I could tell I was in an inclined chair, no doubt like the bibulous chairs I had seen back in the living cells, and I could feel the tubes that were burrowed under the flesh of my forearms and thighs. I couldn't tell if I'd been subjected to the cyberjacks into the back of my skull, but my situation wouldn't have been much worse if I had.

Suddenly, my vision was awash with colors I'd never seen before; not bright and brilliant, but like the sick light I glimpsed when I looked into the opening portal and first saw the N'lani and their homeworld beyond them. I could feel my eyes scanning back and forth, like the eyes of those who had been interfaced, and I knew my situation was as bad as it could be. I was online.

Death would have been an improvement.

In the world that was going on outside my head, I could hear the N'lani talking in their slithery tongue, and although I couldn't tell what they were saying, it didn't take much imagination to guess who was the subject of their conversation. I tried to lift my arm, tried to imagine myself reaching to the base of my skull and tearing loose those coaxial cables that were downloading God knew what into my brain, but I couldn't. The concept of self, as individual, had ceased to exist for me. I could no longer recall what I looked like, and I knew I would soon forget there had ever been a life before this one. I was just one more cog in the great, rumbling wheel of the N'lani empire that had rolled across my planet. I was becoming part of the city, and if you are hearing this, or perhaps reading this, then you are part of this story, all part of the conspiracy to keep you dull and complacent while forces greater than you can guess go about their deeds.

A slow, lazy alarm of terror began to sound somewhere in my head, probably in the same vicinity where I had heard that small, sensible voice, but it no longer seemed to have any bearing on me. It was like hearing someone else's car alarm go off. It wasn't your car that was being molested, so what did it matter to you?

I tried to picture Sara and Vonnie, but I couldn't. It was as if a big computerized dialogue box had suddenly appeared before my eyes—or *behind* my eyes, since that was really where I was seeing the unworldly colors—bearing the script, ACCESS DENIED! I think I groaned, but I wasn't sure. It might have been the guttural lizard-speak going on around me, instead.

I realized with diminishing surprise that the N'lani words were beginning to make sense to me. The download of information into my brain's hard drive was starting to take hold.

"..ssslrkbicameral mind...distresssssss..."

If I could still register such a thing as disgust, the serpentine *feel* of their words crawling over my brain, like ants over a discarded piece of fruit, or like nails being dragged over the chalkboard of my mind, would no doubt have triggered that response.

I could *taste* the otherworldly light on my tongue, the way the N'lani must, and I could feel the entire living city all around me. Except that wasn't quite right...I felt the people who were jacked into the cyberworld, which was broadcast by the city. It was a world of debauchery and bacchanalian delights—music no one had heard before, sights no one had ever seen, dreams no one had imagined, lands no foot had ever trod upon. It was a virtual paradise, emphasis on the first word. Nothing was real, but every want and need was anticipated and carried out several steps over the *extreme* line. It was the N'lani equivalent of preparing veal, except they weren't readying the humans for consumption, but procreation. Even with emotional Novocain, that one came as a surprise.

My orientation film, for want of a better description, showed me the N'lani homeworld, where life began in a fashion similar to Earth's. Only instead of the dinosaurs perishing in a hit-and-run with a meteor, or a volcanic eruption that clouded the skies and brought about the ice age, dinosaurs continued their dominance over the planet. Mammals appeared, but these harsh environs bred harsher mammals, and they challenged the dinosaurs for the turf, like two rival gangs. The dinosaurs continued to evolve, both in physical ferocity and intelligence, in order to survive the threat posed by the mammals, who also continued to evolve apace with their enemies. After a hard-fought battle extending over many generations, the N'lani were the last race standing.

Like the dinosaur, the N'lani had two brains, but unlike the dinosaur, both brains were fully developed, and the lizard-men quickly mastered science and wormhole technology. They already had the war part down.

Unfortunately for them, the universe is like a doddering old man that repeats his same stories, and their homeworld was no exception. Their planet, for whatever reason, was dying, and they were about to go the way of, well, the dinosaur, unless they found a new world to which they could migrate.

But even after their conquest of Earth, the N'lani found our atmosphere inhospitable to them, and after our nuclear strikes against the invaders had accelerated global warming, the planet was becoming equally hostile to humankind. The solution was to breed a third race, a hybrid of N'lani and human, that could flourish in this ruined atmosphere. The Throwaways were the first failed attempt.

Neverland was where the breeders lived, kept in a docile, nearly mindless state, living in their cyber worlds, while nutrient feeds kept their bodies strong and healthy, and N'lani DNA was introduced to theirs, accounting for the pebbling effect of the humans' skin. The outside world—anything beyond the walls of the living city—was left to live or die by its own devices. They were inconsequential—as long as they left the N'lani alone, and the liquid Alzheimer's kept them scattered and disorganized, the N'lani tolerated their existence.

But I was a curiosity to the N'lani, because they realized I had a bicameral mind, and they wanted to understand that. The download of information stopped, and my vision went black once more. With the input suddenly halted, my emotions began to wake up, like anesthetic wearing off, and I felt sick and panicky. I became immensely aware of the probic vent implanted in my skull, and the tubes snaking their way under my flesh. But the blackness began to lighten to the pearly grayness of early morning, and shapes in the room took on definition.

I almost preferred the blindness, for I was inches from the visage of the N'lani commander, P'th'ithis. His breath was foul, like a gangrenous wound, and almost scaldingly hot on my flesh.

His voice was something like granite slabs grating over

one another, and his words were like their shavings: "Mmmmmanling," he growled, "what ssssecrets do you hide, hmmmm?"

P'th'ithis cupped my face in his big, webbed hand, his talons raking my flesh and drawing little runnels of blood. The tip of his claw rested against the cornea of my right eye, and I wanted to blink, but knew if I did he would simply add pressure to pop my eye and leave it hanging on my cheek like some gelid grape. It was one thing for Max to be stoic against the adversities of his human captors, but there was no way the N'lani commander wasn't going to get the information he sought. All three of us understood that, and I also thought if I interested P'th'ithis enough, he would keep me alive. Alive, I still had a chance to escape before I became one more cyber-junkie drone. It was hardly going to equal Sheherezad's *1001 Arabian Nights* for delaying tactics, but I'd take what I could get for now.

So I talked, and I told him about the N'lani portal in the early days of the 21st century, and the accident, and waking up in this body, in this time, and although it was impossible, I think P'th'ithis's eyes widened. Then his mouth broke into a scimitar-lined smile. "We've sssss-poken," he said. "We're old friendsss, you and I."

That alarm bell that had been ringing so slowly and lazily was wide-awake now, because I thought what he was saying just might be true. I thought of those nights in Phoenix, those nights I couldn't recall, those blocks of missing time, and this slithery, hypnotic voice, mesmeric the way a cobra casts a spell with its weaving and bobbing head, and a lot of things suddenly made sense.

"Alllll the way back to your tadpole dayssss," the N'lani commander continued, his voice sibilant and strangely restful, soothing. "Your fassscination with ssspace...where do you sssupposse that came from?"

"No..." I said, or mouthed the word, at least. My mouth was too dry to actually speak, because if what P'th'ithis said was true, my life had been nothing but a bullet that this creature had forged, and shaped, and, when the moment came, fired in the only direction it could be fired. None of the things I had accomplished in life were truly my own. Even the life I had lived hadn't belonged to me because the path my life took was not my choice. I had met and loved Sara, but that had only happened because that was the only course I could take.

Had I picked up transmissions from the N'lani homeworld on my crystal radio when I was a child? The nervous breakdown I had suffered, the drive to contact alien life, my sudden understanding of the schematics embedded in that radio transmission we received at Phoenix...were they all part of my program? My subconscious commands?

P'th'ithis understood the look on my face, for he licked his dry, scaly lips with his long, serpentine tongue and said, "There were otherrssss around your world. All of them arriving at the ssssame conclussssion sssimultaneousssly. Did you really think that was coinsssssidenssss?"

"Russia...England, Japan...All of them..."

"Jusssst like you," the commander said. "All friendssss of the N'lani."

I had another epiphany, one I really could have done without. "Gary Yokum," I said. "The man before me at Phoenix..."

The lenses of his eyes nictitated, and P'th'ithis nodded, as if his big, scaled head was too heavy for his neck to support; his head *was* big, badly proportioned with his body.

Gary had killed himself because he couldn't stand to listen to the voices any longer. He had not said yes to the wrong impulse at all. It had been the only possible answer, the same response I had tried to give just before I had my breakdown in college. His answer had just been a little more definite than mine, that was all.

P'th'ithis laughed, a sound like the dry heaves, and caressed my cheek once more with his taloned hand—*paw*. He had an aura of antiquity about him, and I wondered what the N'lani lifespan was. P'th'ithis was old enough to have guided Paul Stein's life, and had probably guided many more lives before mine, to set all these events in place. I suspected nanosurgeries had found the cellular deathwish and shut it off at a genetic level.

"It will be a pleasssurrrre mmmaking yourrr rrreacquintansss," the lizard-king told me, then turned with surprising grace and lumbered from the room. He walked with his head thrust forward, chest perpendicular with the floor, tail held up, serving as a counterbalance; it flicked every now and then as he moved. "We'll talk about the old timesss, and then I'll pick yourrr brrrain," he added, and chortled. That was probably the height of N'lani humor, but it wasn't very amusing to me. He was no doubt interested in the bicameral mind in hopes of advancing the N'lani's hybridization of races.

Ironically, the world the N'lani had chosen to inhabit had been well-suited to them, for the most part, until we fought back with the nukes and screwed with the atmosphere. I thought it explained why the N'lani struck so hard and fast with their shock troops; they knew our weapons were no threat to them, but what the weapons could do to the atmosphere *was*. Or perhaps the portals themselves, with their black hole energies, threw Earth's orbit out of balance, brought it too close to the sun. Whatever the reason, now they were faced with two dying worlds, and probably not enough time, even for their long-lived race, to find a third alternative. The hybridization of races was essential if the N'lani were to continue. I didn't like to think it, but it was equally essential if humankind was to continue.

Even if I could stop the mingling of races, *should* I? Either way, it seemed to me the human race was destined to go the way of the dodo.

I tried to lift my arms, to pull the tubing from my flesh and the back of my skull, but that part of me was still short-circuited. I was still jacked into Neverland, even though I was no longer receiving downloads. The question was, could I exert any kind of influence over my surroundings, or did that bitstream only flow in one direction?

I willed the tubing to leave my arms, pictured it happening, but that was as far as it got. This was worse than the paralyzing venom of the scorpion-thing, because at least with that, I knew I'd die after a few days, but these damned machines kept me alive and healthy, and unlike the other inhabitants of Neverland, P'th'ithis was going to keep me aware. At least this time I could close my eyes, and the darkness that followed was one of my creation. It wasn't much, but at least it was mine.

I heard the wall lensing open, and I opened my eyes, expecting to see P'th'ithis returning, but what I saw was the last thing I would have expected. It was Jasmine, entering the room as quietly as a cat. She looked to make sure we were alone, but waited until the aperture closed once more before she spoke.

"Max, I'm sorry," she said. "I know you hate me for what I did, but it was the only way to find the children."

"Did you come to ask forgiveness? Because if you did, I can only wish you good luck with that whole livin'-that-long-thing."

This time she wouldn't look away. She said, "I followed

them when they brought you here. I've come to get you out."

I had a feeling there was more she wasn't telling me. It was too convenient that we just happened to encounter Jude's tribe on the way to Neverland. I suspected Jasmine had sold me out to the N'lani a long time ago, and that Jude's people were in on the slaughter of the farm collective. I didn't believe the creatures could survive for long away from the specialized atmosphere in Neverland, not long enough to search all of California for me. Jude had probably alerted the authorities I was with his tribe, for whatever reward was being offered, but before the authorities could respond, I had absconded to northern California with Jasmine. Maybe I was being paranoid, but it was the only thing that would explain how the N'lani had found me.

Still, whatever her reasons, Jasmine had come back for me.

She stepped closer, studying the network of wires and tubes with me at its center. She tried to pull the tubes from my arms, but they wouldn't budge.

"You'll have to cut them," I told her. "Where are the others?"

She knelt before me and removed her knife from her belt and hacked through a snaking mass of tubing. There was a spurt of blood and other fluids, and I felt an accompanying pain, as if the tubes were an extension of my own veins and arteries. I suppose, given the nature of this place, that's exactly what they were. She saw the look on my face and hesitated before chopping the second set of cables.

"Do it," I told her. "It's only pain."

She nodded, her face still showing concern, but did as she was told. I felt the pain, but it was roughly several inches outside of my own body. I was covered with a thick, oily sheet of sick-sweat, but we couldn't stop now.

"The others got the children out of the city," she said.

"So, it's just us?"

"I couldn't leave without you." Jasmine saw how much pain I was in and looked dubiously at the cables that fed into my inner thighs.

"Give it to me," I said, taking the knife from her. I grabbed the thick tubing and severed it in one upward slash, and before I could talk myself out of it, cut the last set to my thighs, and the one to my navel. The pain was staggering, and I had to lean back in the chair and press the thumb of my right hand into the soft webbing of my left hand to keep from graying out.

Only one thing left to do now, and I just prayed these cables weren't embedded in my brain or else I'd quickly go from having two minds to no mind at all. I reached around behind my head, my forearms still trailing the leaking tubes, and gripped the cables jacked. I closed my eyes, and before I could change my mind—while I still had one—pulled with all my might...

CHAPTER TWENTY-ONE

"Max?"

He looked up from where he sat hunched forward in the chair. "I'm all right," he told her. "We have to get out of here before P'th'ithis returns."

His fingers strayed to the port still in the back of his skull. On all sides of its flat, rectangular metal shape, he could feel the exposed edges of bone. He ran his fingertip over the bone, his skull, surprised by how smooth the edges were. The N'lani had done a good job. They had definitely done a job on him, all his life long.

Jasmine helped Max to his feet. He still trailed tubes from his arms and legs, but he didn't think he could stand to cut them any shorter just yet. The initial surgery had been enough to bear, and he thought how he could have used some of that ether he had so casually thrown about back at the L.A. jailhouse about now. He pressed his palm to the wall and watched the door open. They stepped through.

She led him down the spiraling staircase, to the ground floor, and through the aperture. They were out, but that was a long way from being free. Max didn't think they would ever be that. Not while the N'lani were still a presence on his planet.

"I'm not going," he said, pulling away from Jasmine

as she tried to walk him toward the avenue out of Neverland.

"Max, what are you saying?"

"I can't leave yet. There's a portal here in the city. But this one goes both ways."

She shook her head, her nose crinkled, and despite everything, Max found he still had the capacity to love her. "I don't understand."

"You don't have to," he said. "I started this, I'll finish it. You go live your life."

Jasmine took his hand and held it tightly. "I can't without you."

"That would really be too bad, if it were true," Max said, and kissed her. By now, he thought, Dolan would have realized he wasn't coming back, and was honoring his memory by keeping his promise about Jude. Max didn't have faith in many things, but he thought he could be certain about that. He and his brother weren't so different, in the end.

His hand lingered on the holy architecture of her face. And then Max turned and hurried from her sight, and from her life.

The streets were deserted, but Max knew how quickly that could change. At any moment, he expected a horde of N'lani to pour forth from suddenly irised openings in the sides of the fleshy buildings, like spiders bursting from an egg sac, but he was not challenged. Nevertheless, he had no doubts that P'th'ithis by now had discovered his escape, and would be searching for him. Perhaps they already were–if so, they were no doubt searching the boulevards out of Neverland, not these winding streets that seemed to narrow and spiral inward upon themselves.

Even if his brief interface with the city hadn't shown

Max where the gate was, its familiar, ambient energies would have made it impossible to mistake. As he got nearer the portal's location, he could feel the fluid behind his eyes start to bubble and squirm, and the hollow of his chest amplified the odd vibrations.

He felt as if he had come full circle, the story of this journey beginning with one portal and ending with yet another.

Max suddenly realized a curious thing: Why was he having these thoughts? The last thing he could recall was being tortured by the brutal guards at the jailhouse—then everything had gone black. He was certain he had died—not even someone with his resilience could have withstood the constant punishment his body had received. And yet here he stood, in a place he could not recognize, hunted by the Masters and their puppets. His first reaction should have been to kill the woman who'd betrayed him, then search for weapons. But there was a voice calling to him from the depths of his mind, directing his flight from the Masters' laboratories, urging him on toward the metal ring—the portal—that dominated his thoughts. A voice that told him it was time to strike a blow against the creatures that had destroyed his world before they had a chance to strike him down instead.

But no one fights the Masters, he thought automatically, although he'd done nothing *but* oppose them for as long as he could remember.

Maybe it's time someone did, the voice replied. *Fight them, and put an end to this insanity.*

Max snarled as his feet unexpectedly swept him around the next corner, propelling him down the street, away from the sounds of pursuit. Perhaps, he reflected darkly, the Masters were not the *only* ones with puppets to control...

The closer he got to the center of Neverland, where he instinctively knew the portal to be, the more indistinct the shape of the buildings. They looked like giant candles that had been allowed to burn, the wax pooled at their bases. The energies leaking from the portal were playing hob with the genetic architecture, disrupting its program—at least, that was the voice's explanation.

A light, jumpy and fretful, grew brighter the nearer Max drew, the same sick light he—or rather the voice that identified itself as "Paul"—had come to associate with the portal. He stepped into the opening and found himself in the heart of Neverland. He had to shield his eyes from the light, becoming only dimly aware that the light was brightest behind his eyes.

The portal was huge, "Paul" commented, ten times the size of the petty thing he had been a part of in Fort Bragg. Now he understood just how truly advanced the N'lani were, how much more superior their science, their intellect, had been than man's. It was no surprise they had conquered Earth—conquest was at the heart of each N'lani gene. The only real surprise was that man had resisted as long as he had.

Max didn't know what it all meant. He wasn't impressed by the invaders; he just wondered when he'd get the chance to kill them.

He walked around the portal; from the side, it looked like a giant quarter standing on edge. When he reached the back of the portal, he discovered he could look through it, back the way he had come. He went back to the entrance of the gate; from this side, the view was misty and shimmery with lazily dancing energies. There was no way to guess exactly where the portal would deposit him, or if he would survive the jaunt. For all "Paul" knew, only the thick hides of the N'lani could withstand whatever pressures and forces were at play behind that misty curtain. Max's too-mortal shell might easily burst like a deep-sea dwelling fish brought to the surface.

Still, at this point, it was only a matter of degrees; they both knew he wouldn't leave Neverland alive. Max stood at the long, gradual incline to the gate, steeling himself for the jaunt, knowing at the same time there was really nothing he could do to prepare himself, because he simply didn't know what to expect. There was no point delaying. He walked briskly up the gradation and, before he could think of any reason not to, stepped over the threshold, into the aurora borealis of energy.

It felt like stepping into a wall of thick treacle. The curtain of energy actually resisted his entrance, and he had to lean forward, put his shoulder into it, as he fought for every step. Walls of stroboscopic light formed around him, first short bursts, then longer ones, and then resolved themselves into amorphous globs that stretched into fiery blossoms. Now that he was in the tunnel, Max was speeded along like a cork on a whitewater river. Whorls of light resolved and raced together ahead of him to form a superstructure to support the walls of the hyperspace tunnel. Beyond the trestles of light, he could see distant galaxies, stars being born and dying, black holes forming, the fiery cores of new planets taking shape.

His breathing came in snorts, and his eyes refused to blink. "Paul" had to fight Max's urge to reach a questioning hand out and touch the walls of the tunnel. God alone knew what effect that might have on the integrity of the structure. It might suddenly wink out of existence and leave them adrift in airless space, he explained, or it could as easily dissipate Max's atoms to every far corner of existence, expanding ever outward like the universe itself.

"Paul" knew all the theories of hyperspace, that space and time were both dramatically distorted near a source of massive gravity, such as a black hole, for instance. Under these conditions, space could be folded back upon itself, and time, due to the temporal inertia, only flowed in one direction. But this quantum energy was powerful enough to warp time as well, and push the hyperspace traveler out of phase, if only for a few seconds. Now he understood that was how his discarnate consciousness was able to survive long enough to enter the body of his descendant.

Max grunted. "I wish *I* understood how to shut you up, voice."

"Manling!"

Max turned his head, saw P'th'ithis charging down the tunnel toward him. The lizard-thing's head was lowered, tail snapping side to side, as he thundered forward like a bull, running on the balls of his feet. Curiously, as hard as he was running, P'th'ithis never actually gained any ground, but remained as distant from Max as when he had first entered the portal behind him.

But Max had a feeling all that would change the moment they reached the other end of the portal. The commander of the Masters would be on him at once, rending him with tooth and talon.

A moment not long in coming—for seconds later, Max stepped through the receiving portal on the N'lani homeworld.

The air on the Masters' world was thin as gruel, the gravity crushing. Max fell to his knees the moment he arrived. He couldn't catch his breath; what little oxygen he could gasp was instantly squeezed from his lungs by the hostile gravity. It was indescribably cold, the air too thin to hold any heat. The N'lani world, "Paul" explained, was near its end stages.

Around him, filling the vast cavern in which he found himself, Max saw all the other portals that opened to Earth, Like windows to other worlds. "Paul" recognized Beijing and Tiananmen Square; through another gate, another skyline, this time London. Here was Hokaido in the Japanese islands, and here was Red Square in Russia. And there was Fort Bragg, where the story began. There was no life, no movement to be seen through any of these gates. He supposed it was there, just gone to ground, like Jude's people in Los Angeles.

Max strained to raise his hand, missed, managed to raise it the second time and grab the portal console. His muscles spasmed from the effort, and his veins bulged like blue cords as Max pulled himself, inch by inch, to a semi-erect position. His heart pounded like a kettle-drum, and he could feel the pressure of his blood thudding in his temples and behind his eyes. It was all he could do to hold his head up, and he heard his tendons creak like steel cables stressed to snapping.

As soon as he let go of the console, which had been supporting most of his increased weight, both of Max's femurs snapped with a sound like a shotgun discharging. He screamed and grabbed the console to keep from going down, where he knew he would be helpless when P'th'ithis arrived.

He tried to raise his head to look at the portal, but it was beyond him. He could imagine his neck snapping under the weight, just like his femurs. He felt something wet and hot on his thighs, and for a moment wondered if the gravity had simply squeezed his bladder empty. But he managed to look down–looking down was not much of an effort; it was looking at anything above floor level that was a challenge—at his thighs and saw splintered pieces of bone jutting through his pants legs. He was bleeding, but not badly because the high gravity was keeping his blood pooled in his extremities.

He was beginning to gray out. There wasn't enough oxygen for him, and his brain was starved for both oxygen and blood. Max began pounding on the console, trying to break something vital to its function, but his fists were like blocks of lead. He couldn't raise them high enough to do any damage.

And then P'th'ithis was through, bearing down on him like a freight train. The lizard-king plowed into him and sent him sprawling. Max could feel his legs snap again, could see the side of his hip where his pelvis should have been. He tasted blood in the back of his mouth; something important somewhere inside him had been shredded by the Master's raking talons.

"You've come a long way to die, mmmmanling," the lizard-king snarled, but Max barely heard him. P'th'ithis grabbed the human in his powerful claws and raised him until their faces were almost touching. Max could see, from the corner of his eye, the weapon that hung at P'th'ithis's side. It was just inches away, but it may as well have been on the other side of one of the portals.

He tried to speak, but the air was too thin. His lips were turning blue, and his body was trembling almost convulsively.

"Tell mmmme how you did it," P'th'ithis demanded. "How did you ssssend your mmmind through the yearssss?"

The human managed a weak, blood-flecked smile and muttered something even the lizard-king's delicate hearing couldn't make out. He brought Max closer.

"What did you ssssay?" P'th'ithis asked, his head cocked to hear Max's dying confession. "Tell mmmmme."

Max forced the corners of his mouth to turn upward, in a misshapen grimace meant to resemble a smile. "I said...ssssucker."

Their bellies touching, Max had just enough reach to grab P'th'ithis's sidearm. He didn't try to lift it from the holster; it would have been too heavy for him anyway. Instead, he found the trigger and squeezed it. A sizzling burst of energy snapped out of the muzzle, vaporizing the lizard-king's leg. He howled and pitched sideways, suddenly unbalanced. As they went down, Max kept squeezing the trigger, firing blindly; in his mind, "Paul" was hoping one of his mad shots would do some serious damage to the portal's power source.

P'th'ithis's stump had been cauterized by the same blast of energy that had vaporized the leg. The lizard-king crawled closer, mouth open as if he would simply swallow Max alive. The loss of a limb, coupled with the terrible cold of the dying homeworld, was all that slowed P'th'ithis enough to give Max an opportunity to defend himself.

In the fall, Max had somehow managed to keep hold of the gun, and he lay on his back, gun in his left hand, as the Master slithered nearer. He fired, the shot tearing P'th'ithis's head off. And still the lizard-king crawled on; his second brain commanded the body now, jumping into the breach like a good lieutenant for his fallen captain. But the body crawled slower now, blind and dumb. It would find Max in a moment, but "Paul" thought that was all he would need.

With the gun still resting on the floor, Max managed to turn it so the muzzle faced the portal. "Mammals rule...asshole," he managed to mutter, and pulled the trigger.

The energy bolt struck the power well, cracked the containment walls. The true source of power, the black hole, was not in the well, but its time- and space-warping energies were funneled through there, and the results were much the same. The shielding erupted, dissolved as the black hole energies spread out, swirling slowly around the room like a caged tornado. Max watched with a distant, dying fascination as the black hole energies swallowed everything near it. One moment, the object was there, and the next, it had vanished as the acretion disc widened.

P'th'ithis's blind, groping claws found Max and began to rend his flesh with a mad savagery. Max tried to turn the gun to either kill the headless body or himself, but it was too heavy now. Gravity in the room was increasing. Max watched as the black tendrils of energy brushed the lizard-king, and pulled him apart, atom by atom, and swallowed them.

Me next, Max thought. He was right.

He was only wrong if he thought that's where the black hole would end. The portals, powered by the same energies, spewed black, snaking tendrils over the Earth. The London portal, built on the banks of the Thames near the Millennium Eye, shepherded the energy through, and everything it touched disappeared into its mindless, consuming darkness. The Thames emptied like water swirling down a powerful drain, and the 400-foot-tall Millennium Eye flew apart and swirled into the blackness.

In Red Square, Lenin's Mausoleum, the last tangible evidence of the Great Bear's former clout, vanished first. The colorful windows of St. Basil's Cathedral shattered and fell like rainbow confetti, and then the great stones of the church itself went spiraling down the bottomless gullet of the black hole.

All over the planet, the black tendrils slithered from the open portals, seeking one another, drawn together until they closed around the blue-green globe like a black fist.

Almost simultaneously, both Earth and the N'lani homeworld ceased to exist.

Paul Stein seemed to return to himself with a sudden jolt, like a dream of falling, and was surprised to find himself holding a folding chair by the hind legs, smashing the portal he had spent years of his life helping to build.

In the blazing brilliance at the heart of the portal, he could see a misty figure, as big as an Asgardian Storm Giant, begin to form, and another, and another. Beyond those figures, the light of an alien world, a distant galaxy.

He had a moment to wonder if what he had just experienced had been a wild hallucination triggered by the energies of the portal, playing with the neurons in his brain and making them explode in a Xenophobic sense of déjà vu. It was exactly the way he felt when he had his nervous breakdown in college.

But it had all seemed so *real.*

He heard himself shout, "Get Vonnie out of here!" and watched as his own hand gave Sara a push toward the edge of the platform.

But he didn't have long to wonder about it, and whether he had the right to doom two worlds, because the cowling of the portal buckled under his beating, and then–

CHAPTER ONE

When I woke to my cold and moonless room, I felt a mild alloy of confusion and frustration because I couldn't remember where I was or how I'd gotten here. The more I struggled to remember, the more things I realized I didn't know—not the least of which was my name, or the fact I was scheduled to die in three days.

The only thing I could remember was some out-of-context bit of doggerel: *Why do we desire the things that will destroy us, and turn this paradise into Perdition...?*